DETONATE

BY LUNA MASON

THE BENEATH THE MASK SERIES
Distance
Detonate
Devoted
Detained

THE BENEATH THE SECRETS SERIES
Chaos
Caged
Crave
Claim

OTHER TITLES
Roman Petrov, The Petrov Family Anthology (novella)

DETONATE

BENEATH THE MASK

KENSINGTON
PUBLISHING CORP.

kensingtonbooks.com

KENSINGTON BOOKS are published by:
Kensington Publishing Corp.
900 Third Avenue
New York, NY 10022

kensingtonbooks.com

First Kensington Trade Paperback Printing: June 2025

ISBN 978-1-4967-5747-0 (trade paperback)

10 9 8 7 6 5 4 3 2 1

Printed in the United States of America

Electronic edition: ISBN 978-1-4967-5751-7 (ebook)

Interior design by Leah Marsh

Content warnings: explicit language, alcohol use, anxiety, death, murder, graphic violence (including kidnapping, murder, and arson), drug references, physical and sexual assault on FMC (not by MMC), pregnancy (mentions pregnancy complications), cheating (not the MCs). This book is explicit and has explicit sexual content, which include praise, choking, spanking, exhibitionism, anal, and spitting.

The authorized representative in the EU for product safety and compliance
is eucomply OU, Parnu mnt 139b-14, Apt 123
Tallinn, Berlin 11317, hello@eucompliancepartner.com

This book is dedicated to all my readers who deserve to be treated like a princess, but don't want the prince to sweep them off their feet.

Who want the villain to tell them to grab the headboard and take it all like a good girl.

Villains fuck better.

Grayson is ready for you now . . .

AUTHOR'S NOTE

Detonate is a dark, standalone mafia romance. It does contain content and situations that could be triggering for some readers.

This book is explicit and has explicit sexual content.

It is intended to be for readers 18+.

For a full list of triggers please visit the author's website, lunamasonauthor.com.

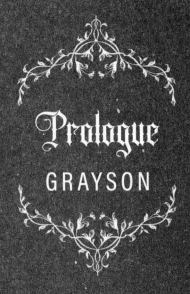

Prologue

GRAYSON

August 2015

Ten years, I've breathed, survived, and lived the war.
    It's all I know.
    Hunt, shoot, kill.
    I walk toward the derelict building. Intel confirms the two terrorist fuckers we're hunting are in here. I tighten my fingers around my M4 Carbine as I trudge in the scorching heat of Afghanistan.
    Casper, my lifelong best friend, follows on my left.
    We joined the Marines and climbed the ranks together. Hell, if it wasn't for us constantly getting in fights when we were teenagers, our parents would never have shipped us off to the military. I have him to thank for that. Where else could I have embraced my overwhelming need to find an outlet for my anger? Legally, anyway.
    The wooden door hangs off its hinges. Two of our guys,

Chase and Paul, are coming in fast from the opposite side of the building.

These terrorists are responsible for the Kabul airport bombings, which killed hundreds of innocent people. They have been off the grid for the past three years since the attack.

Kicking open the door, I aim my gun forward as I take in my surroundings.

To my left is a crumbling set of stairs, and to my right is what remains of this shithole. Pieces of foam flatten under my feet from the shredded remains of a sofa in the room. There's paper scattered everywhere, busted books, and debris from destroyed household appliances.

How the fuck has anyone been living here for so long?

"We have heat markers live upstairs," intel confirms in my earpiece.

"Copy," I respond, pointing up at the stairs to Casper. I edge up the stairs and lean around the corner to scope out the area. The overwhelming stench of a bathroom nearly makes me gag. There's only one closed door. That must be where they are.

With a signal to my friend, I smash it open.

In the right corner of the room, a frail-looking woman cradles a small child to her chest. Their screams ring in my ears.

Something isn't right. What is this—a decoy?

Shit.

I pace around the room, checking for any hidden spots, but nothing.

Shit.

"Out! Now!" I bellow to Casper, who stands guard by the doorframe.

Where the fuck are Chase and Paul?

Casper sprints down the stairs, and I follow behind. As

soon as the realization hits me, I shout, "Casper, Stop. Don't go out th—"

The gunfire drowns out my words. I duck under the hole in the wall. More gunshots echo, and a bullet whizzes past my head and strikes the crumbling stone behind me.

Movement in white catches my eye across the room. I crouch and make my way over to the far end of the room, past the ruined sofa, and wait. One of them is bound to come out soon. The M4 has a visual of a man in a white robe carrying a firearm.

I pull the trigger, and the fucker collapses on the ground.

Chase and Paul peer round the corner. They motion for me to go back as more gunshots ring out.

Casper . . . I need to find Casper.

I crawl toward the entrance, keeping the gun ready to fire.

The sunlight blinds me when I step outside. It's a desert. I haven't had fun like this in a while, and I love a good hunt.

My world crashes around me when I spot my friend lying in the sand with a pool of blood spilling out from his stomach. His hands compress over the wound, and he struggles to lift his head up.

I run to him and drop to my knees.

"Fuck, Casper." I grab the trauma kit from my vest.

Paul and Chase surround me.

Paul stays on guard while we help Casper.

"We have three confirmed kills. No movement spotted," Paul reports.

I rip open Casper's jacket in search of the source of the blood. My hands tremble as my best friend struggles to breathe his last.

"Grayson, don't," Casper whispers through ragged breaths.

I take off his black balaclava to help him breathe.

"Casper, we've got you."

He shakes his head, his brown eyes piercing into me, tears spilling over, almost pleading with me to stop.

"Grayson, I-I'm so f-fucking sorry. I h-hope . . . hope you'll f-forgive me. I l-love you, brother."

Sorry? Fucking sorry for what?

"Don't be sorry. You aren't dying on me." My voice cracks at the end.

He starts coughing and blood splatters out of his mouth.

I rest him on my lap.

"I'm s-sorry," he tries again.

"Sorry for what? Everything's going to be okay."

"For fucking Amelia."

A wave of anger rolls my leg away from his head, letting it thud to the ground. His confession stabs into me as I'm faced with the raw reality.

All those nights where my best friend and wife were co-incidentally too busy to be with me. But Casper doesn't even have the decency to give me the time to hate him.

"No, no, no, no!"

My entire world starts to spin.

I scoot back, away from him, the dust scratching the inside of my nostrils as I sit there, watching the only friend I have take his last breath. His final words still ring in my ear.

My best friend. Who's been fucking my wife for God knows how long.

"GET THE FUCK out of my way, Amelia!" I shout at my whore of a wife.

She keeps flapping around after me, in hysterics, grabbing

onto my sleeves, begging me not to leave her. It's taking all the strength I have not to send the woman flying across the room.

I pack every item of clothing I own.

"Grayson, please. Don't leave me, I promise I'll never do it again. You don't have to worry. Casper is dead anyway."

I rip the drawer's handle out and throw it against the opposite wall.

What a fucking fool I *am!* This woman is vile. Revolting. How did I fail to see that before? Casper was my best friend, the brother I never had, and they fucking ruined everything.

I prowl toward her with clenched fists. She backs into the wall with a fearful expression.

"This is the last time you will ever see me, and don't you ever say his name again. You don't fucking deserve it. Now get the fuck out of my sight. You disgust me."

She sinks onto the floor in a crying fit.

Pathetic.

I head to the airport, ready to start my new life, leaving the darkness where it belongs. I've said my goodbyes to my best friend. It was the only thing keeping me here.

In New York, I'm gonna set up a motherfucking boxing gym. Hopefully, there will be enough fighting to release some of this anger.

My new rule: *No women for more than one night.*

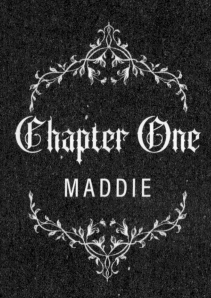

Chapter One

MADDIE

January 2022

My eyes flutter closed and my fingers trail to the hem of my panties. The only way I get off now is imagining Grayson and all the deliciously wicked things he can do with his mouth.

My fingers slide up and down my slit as I take myself back to the day Grayson saved my best friend.

We pull up outside Sienna's ex-fiancé's apartment, the asshole that kidnapped her. Keller had carried Sienna into the car and they were on their way to the hospital. Nico, her moody Italian bodyguard, informed me that her condition was bad.

The rain pelts against the car window as I stare at the entrance to Jamie's apartment. Men swarm the building from all angles.

Grayson stalks out of the building, his face expressionless. He runs a hand across his face, smearing the blood that drips from his hair. His white shirt is stained crimson.

Relief washes over me when I realize he is okay. Despite the past few months of constantly bickering with him, I never wanted him to get hurt, but I never want to stop giving him shit either. It's amusing to rile him up.

Why the hell do I care so much about him?

All these months, his existence has irritated me. But right this second, the only thing that matters is his well-being.

Luca shouts at him from behind, and Grayson turns, revealing the silver gun in his hand.

I grab the handle of the car door and pull, but it doesn't open. The urge to run to him takes over. I need his comfort. I need to know if Sienna is okay. I need to know what happened. This is all my fault.

"Nico, open the door!" I shout.

"It's not safe, Maddie, I shouldn't have even brought you here. Boss will kill me."

"Open the fucking door, otherwise I'll kill you myself," I snap.

The click of the locks fills the car as I swing open the door. In my haste, I only threw on a white shirt and jeans. The rain hammers against my skin, soaking me completely. I run over to Grayson, and he freezes when he spots me. Blood and rain drip off his face, his sandy hair dark from being drenched. Even now, he's gorgeous. His tall, powerful frame instantly makes me feel safe. I know nothing will happen if he's here.

I launch myself into his arms and nuzzle my face into him.

"Sunshine, what are you doing here? It's not safe," he whispers. Tingles spread throughout my body as his warm breath hits my throat.

"I needed to make sure Sienna was okay, that you were okay.

This is all my fault. I should never have left her. I didn't know what was happening," I croak out.

His fingers stroke my hair, soothing me.

"Shhh. She will be okay. I promise, I'm fine. This is not your fault."

Our noses brush. Desire courses through me for this sexy, tattooed, protective giant. The one I've secretly, desperately craved.

His gaze flickers to my lips, then to my eyes.

To hell with it. I want this man.

I slam my lips to his, and his body goes rigid. Embarrassment washes over me as I pull away, turning my head away from him.

"Fuck it." With that, he grabs the back of my head and devours my lips. A metallic tinge of blood mingles into our kiss. His hand pulls the back of my head even closer into him. His tongue dances with mine.

It's the kind of kiss that makes my pussy throb and my toes curl.

The kind that steals all my breath away.

"Grayson, we need to go. Now!" someone barks behind us.

He breaks the kiss, shakes his head, and brings his forehead to mine.

"You need to go, Maddie." He sighs.

"Fuck," he mutters as he turns his back and storms away, leaving me in the rain with swollen lips. Without even so much as a glance back, he gets into a black Mercedes and drives away.

I muffle my moans, biting down on my forearm, as my climax builds. I'm still not used to living on my own and not having to hide my orgasms. In my head, the kiss doesn't stop there; he takes me home and fucks me into next week.

And this is my problem. I can't stop picturing *Grayson* fucking me.

Even though Gregory the accountant kissed me earlier.

I'd been expecting that toe-curling, life-altering kiss that Grayson and I shared last year.

As soon as Gregory's lips touched mine, my brain shot right back to that day. The day that seems to have cursed my dating life since, leaving me incredibly sexually frustrated. No one can get me going anymore. Every damn time, all I see is Grayson's piercing blue eyes and his face smeared in blood. Hence, my date tonight with Gregory in a bid to move on.

Now that he's gone, loneliness and frustration consume me for another night.

———————

SIENNA'S HAPPINESS IS so contagious. But damn, I am sick and tired of being a third wheel.

I sigh into my glass of white wine while leaning over the breakfast bar in their extravagant midnight-blue kitchen. Keller wraps Sienna in a tight embrace. They assume I can't hear the dirty shit he's whispering into her ear. Their four-month-old daughter—Darcy—is nuzzled into Keller's side, a precious little bundle of light.

"Come on, guys. Some of us single, lonely people over here don't need to witness this!" I say, faking a pout.

"Oh, Maddie, what about Gregory?" Sienna asks, leaning back into Keller's arms.

"We're just keeping it casual and seeing where it goes." I know where it's going. Fucking nowhere, but I don't want to lose him just yet. He's nice, we get along well, but as friends.

"And Grayson?" Keller chimes in, trying to cover it with a cough. Sienna elbows her tattooed husband in the stomach. "What?" he questions Sienna, raising his eyebrow.

The mention of his name is enough to fill me with frustration.

Grayson Ward, the complete opposite of everything I need. Mr. Playboy, who gets on about every one of my last nerves. He has done that since the moment I met him last year at Keller's night club, the End Zone. We've just wound each other up. That is, until the kiss that I shall never talk about ever again. He's avoided me since then.

"Maddie?"

Sienna calling my name breaks me out of my Grayson spell.

"What?"

"I asked if you'd heard from Grayson recently?" Sienna says with a soft smile.

"Nope. Why would I?" I shoot Sienna a glare, hoping she shuts up.

"Just wondering. Keller said he's been acting weird since the whole kidnapping thing."

"The whole kidnapping thing . . ." I laugh nervously. "You mean, the day you nearly died thanks to your crazy ex-fiancé?" A day that still haunts me. If I hadn't left her alone, it might never have happened.

"Oh, Maddie. Look, we've never been happier, we are all safe and okay. Please stop blaming yourself. I'm just glad he never hurt you." She rushes over and wraps me up tight.

She is the strongest woman I know. They're a match made in heaven, true twin flames. Proof that love conquers all. She even accepted that her now-husband and his brother were running the mafia and took it all in stride. That shit is wild.

"Anyway, why would Grayson's mood have anything to do with me?" I ask, desperate to change the conversation. I wish

I hadn't told Sienna about the kiss with he-who-shall-not-be-named.

It's been four months since I last saw him, the day I met baby Darcy. The same day he spat his beer out and stormed out without even giving me a second glance after Sienna asked about my date with Gregory. I don't understand him.

"Don't you two have to go get ready? The taxi is going to be here in an hour," Keller announces, breaking the awkward silence that fills the room.

I nod and guzzle the contents of my glass. The smooth bubbles sliding down my throat are giving me the buzz that I need. It's Sienna's first official girls' night out since she gave birth, and I'm sure as hell going to give her a night to remember.

"Yes!" she squeals, grabbing my hand and pulling me away from the counter. "I really need you to give me a makeover. I look like such a mom," she pleads with puppy eyes, running her hands through her fuzzy hair.

I laugh as she drags me down the hall. "That would be because you are one, Si. A damn good one."

A small smile stretches her lips as she wraps me up in a tight embrace.

I return the hug and sigh into her shoulder. I miss having her around every day.

"Thank you, Maddie. I don't know what I'd do without you."

"I told you before, you'll always have me. Love you, bestie."

"I love you too."

We make our way to the master bedroom. This girl has a dream house. It's just too cute that Keller bought this place for her, for them to turn into a family home. It's gorgeous and can fit all those ten kids they're aiming for.

While she hops into the shower, I quickly change into my gold sequin dress that I brought with me. It hugs my figure in all the right places. Then, on her dressing table, I spread out my supplies.

By the time I'm done, she is out of the shower. I swipe on a deep red lipstick to finish my look. I look fuckable, to be honest.

"Wow, Maddie, you look stunning!"

"Aww, thanks, Si. Now go dry your hair so I can get you glammed up." I grab my phone and then settle on her bed, sinking into the mattress. Shit, this must be the comfiest bed I've ever laid on. Now all I want to do is lie here and scroll aimlessly through Instagram.

"Have you seen your parents lately?" Sienna asks.

I can't resist the eye roll at the mention of my mom.

"Eurgh, no. Not for a while, thank God."

"Oh God, Mads. Is she still on her *you must get married before* your *childbearing days are over* warpath?"

"Oh, of course. She's desperate for me to find a date to bring to our family Valentine's meal. I swear she does this every year to remind me that I'm single. I mean, nothing I ever do is good enough. Unlike Eddie, my *perfect*-ass brother with his *perfect* wife and *perfect* job."

"I hate that she's like this with you, Maddie." She sits on the edge of the bed next to me. "I have no doubt you will find the perfect man. Don't let her force you into anything."

I wish I didn't feel this need to please her. I'm even avoiding my dad now, although I miss him. I just can't handle my mom's uncomfortable judgment about everything in my life. Even my weight, for God's sake.

"Yeah, maybe." It's so embarrassing. "I just want someone to make me feel safe, to love me, you know? I don't seem to click with anyone. No matter how many dates I go on."

"Well, maybe you're looking in the wrong places." She nods, tapping my hand before getting off the bed and heading back into the bathroom.

What does that mean?

A knock at the front door booms through the house. Sienna flips on the hair dryer, so I get off the bed.

The knocks get incessantly louder as I pad toward the staircase. Jesus, someone's eager. If they wake Darcy while Keller's putting her down for a nap, he will kill them.

"Hang on, I'm coming."

I can't wait to rip this asshole a new one.

Chapter Two

GRAYSON

The constant buzzing in my pocket distracts me from dousing the warehouse in gasoline. I glance over to the three men who are tied up and gagged. Their blood mixes with the tears streaming down their faces.

Yes, I'm a fucking monster. Get over it.

I stop pouring for a second as the fumes burn my nostrils. The pure adrenaline rush, knowing you're about to burn a whole building to the ground, is enthralling.

I pull out my phone from my back pocket, and Keller's name flashes on the screen. He's the one I'll always answer the call for, no matter what.

"Frankie, I gotta take this. Keep on pouring," I shout over to Frankie, holding out the can of gasoline to him. He's busy moving the drugs into the car. He didn't want to get any mess on his new fucking navy suit. Luca's newest recruit. Apparently, he was a bodyguard for the Capri family in Italy. He needed to come back to New York for some family shit.

Frankie walks over, rolling up his sleeves.

"Let's set these fuckers alight." His deep Italian accent is like music to my ears. His gray eyes flash with a darkness that mirrors mine as he turns and starts throwing the liquid around the room.

I chuckle and answer Keller's call.

"Mr. Killer himself." I can't help but mock his famous boxing name. "Keller 'the Killer' Russo" being chanted by thousands of fans to an actual killer, a mafia hitman. Well, not anymore, since he's Mr. Family Man now, and I've never seen him happier.

When he stepped out of the darkness, it paved a way for me to enter. Luca, the *boss*, gave me an outlet for all this pent-up rage. The carefully constructed life I portray, the boxing trainer to the stars, the playboy, the billionaire—it is all a mask to the real me. The darkness that consumes me.

I'm trained to kill.

It's what I'm good at.

Now I get to keep up the cool, professional facade that I created when I turned my back on my life in Chicago and moved to New York. That day, I saved Sienna when I killed the five men holding her without blinking an eye. Luca witnessed the rage in me and recognized my potential. He now uses it to his advantage. And, well . . . mine too.

Since that day, I haven't looked back.

"Grayson, what are you up to?" Keller asks.

"You don't wanna know, Keller, you might get jealous."

"Oh, I don't think so." He chuckles, then adds, "Do you wanna come over for a beer? Sienna's going out with Maddie tonight, and Darcy is just off to bed."

Maddie . . . Fuck. My cock twitches just at her mention.

I can't help the visions that flood my brain of her when

she ran toward me outside Jamie's apartment. She launched herself into my arms and wrapped me in a tight embrace, her ass resting perfectly in my hands. I was so stunned that the woman I thought couldn't stand my entire existence jumped into my arms. Then when she slammed her lips down onto mine, everything changed.

She was the first woman I'd kissed in seven fucking years.

And fuck, it was the hottest kiss I'd ever had, and ever will have.

I haven't been able to get it out of my brain, no matter how many cold showers I take.

So, I did what I always do after I've been with a woman. I ghosted her.

Except, this little ray of sunshine doesn't seem to be going away. She's here to stay. Smothering me in her rays while I thrive in the darkness. I don't crave the light. But I can't get her out of my mind.

We aren't compatible. I just can't shake this burning desire to consume her. Whenever she's near me, all I want to do is bend her over and fuck her until she shuts up.

I can't help it.

She's intoxicating. Out of bounds.

"Sure, I'll be there soon. Make sure those beers are cold."

"Yeah, yeah," he says and hangs up.

I retrieve the lighter from the inside of my suit jacket, then take one last glance at the warehouse. The place is falling apart anyway. I'm helping them out. Well, minus the three bodies.

The Falcones might think they've one-upped us by taking our shipment, but they don't realize how easy it was for us to take it back and kill their men. Stupid fuckers.

Smiling at the men, I flick the Zippo, and the flame dances before my eyes. I toss it onto the floor next to them, and the angry flames start to cover their bodies. That's my cue to leave.

Frankie follows closely behind me, chuckling.

I slide into the driver's side of my white Audi RS 6.

Frankie jumps into the passenger seat and quips, "Fuck, what a shitty way to die."

"I can think of worse. We'll do that next time."

The engine roars to life as I drive toward the shimmering lights of Manhattan.

<hr />

I PULL UP into Keller's goddamn fancy mansion, and even the gravel driveway is extravagant. I kill the engine next to his fucking massive fountain and shake my head with a chuckle. He did go out all out to give his woman everything.

I knock on the wooden door and shove my hands into my pockets. A wave of nerves hits me from nowhere. I don't like it. Not one bit.

A couple of minutes pass, and he doesn't answer. I knock louder.

I know *she's* in there, I can feel it.

My body almost vibrates with excitement; my heart flutters in my chest. The effect this woman has on me is unnerving.

"Hang on, I'm coming!" Her voice makes my breath hitch.

I know she will be fuming at me, more standoffish than normal. She doesn't know about my no-kissing rule, or my past. Even after I killed Sienna's captors and was smeared in their blood, she didn't falter. She isn't scared of me, of who I am.

She doesn't realize the angrier she gets, the more turned on

I get. There's just something about watching her try so damn hard to resist me that makes my cock twitch.

The door flies open, and her eyes land on me, her feelings evident as she scrunches her nose up and squints.

Oh, she's angry all right.

I devour her with my eyes. The woman is smoking hot. She has on a short tight glittery dress that stops below the V of her thighs, barely covering that pussy I've been dreaming about for the last year. I trail my gaze further, landing on her tits that fill the dress perfectly, giving me a delicious view of her cleavage.

When I finally reach her face, she crosses her arms over her breasts, still scowling at me. That little silver sun necklace rests on her collarbone. Even looking like she wants to murder me with her bare hands, she is beautiful. Her emerald eyes hit me straight in the heart. Those plump lips are begging to be wrapped around my cock.

Fuck, I need to get laid. I cannot be thinking about her like this. Not that it ever seems to help.

"Fuck, sunshine, you look incredible," I rasp.

She simply raises her eyebrow at me. "Gee, thanks." The blush spreads across her chest. Apparently, I get under her skin as much as she has clawed herself into mine.

"Are you just gonna stand there, or are you gonna let me in?" I ask, smirking.

Her dainty fingers wrap around the door as she pulls it toward her, opening the gap. I stride past, my right arm gently brushing her side, sending bolts of electricity through my body. I hiss in a breath at the contact as she gently closes the door and turns to face me.

"Nice shoes. I think they'd easily take someone's eye out if you need." I wink at her. Part of me honestly believes one day she would do this.

"It will be yours if you don't shut the fuck up. The baby is sleeping," she snaps. "Oh wait, I forget you're a big bad mafia man now, so *I* better shut up."

She actually fucking rolls her eyes at me.

This woman knows how to rile me up.

Maybe it's time I gave her a taste of what happens when she pokes the bear.

I stalk toward her, and she takes a step back, her back hitting against the door. I slam my hands above her head. Her mouth parts in a perfect O.

"Don't fucking test me, sunshine."

She tips her chin up in defiance. Her eyes meet mine, and a sly smile passes her lips.

Oh, here we go.

"Coming from a man who doesn't even have the balls to talk to a woman after a kiss? Please, as if I'm scared of you," she huffs.

"Well, you should be," I whisper in her ear, and goosebumps form along her neck as I do.

"Whatever, Grayson. It was a mistake anyway." Her voice falters at the last part.

"Ouch, that hurts, baby." I trace my index finger along the soft skin of her cheek and all the way down her neck. "It's such a shame your body gives you away. I bet if I stuck my fingers under that tight little dress you have on, your pussy would be soaking for me."

Her mouth opens and snaps shut. I think I've finally shut her up without having to shove my cock in her pretty little mouth.

Maddie jumps as Keller clears his throat behind me. She sports the color of a beet with the same guilty look a kid would have when they're caught stealing sweets.

With a sigh, I straighten myself, and Maddie darts underneath my arm, awkwardly tugging at the hem of her dress. I stride straight past a flustered Maddie and wrap the dainty Sienna up into a massive bear hug.

"You look gorgeous, Sienna," I say, releasing her from my hug. Without even looking, I know Keller will be glaring daggers at me. He's never quite gotten over the fact I *technically* knew Sienna before him.

"Mr. Killer, is it beer time yet? I'm a little flustered," I say. Turning, I give a wink to Maddie, who returns it with a death glare.

Keller's deep laugh fills the room, and Sienna shoots Maddie a questioning look.

"Yeah, let's go," Keller responds with a laugh, then grabs his wife and starts to tongue-fuck her in front of us. I flick my eyes to Maddie and raise my eyebrows in amusement. She sucks her bottom lip between her teeth, trying to hold in a laugh.

And like that, my heart starts pounding. The way it does every time she smiles.

I take that as my cue to leave.

I fling my hand up to wave as I make my way into the kitchen.

"Have a lovely evening, ladies," I shout, encouraging Keller to hurry the fuck up.

"FUCK, THAT'S GOOD," I groan out as the ice-cold beer slips down my throat.

"Well, what the fuck was that with Maddie?" Keller questions, striding past me to grab the bottle of beer I got out for him.

"Just fucking with her."

"So, it isn't anything to do with the kiss?" Keller asks with a smirk.

I spit my beer out in response. How the fuck does he . . . ? *Oh wait, Maddie.*

"It was nothing."

"I can't believe you didn't tell me. So, how was your first kiss in, what is it, eight years?"

"Seven," I deadpan.

I should have told him; he's my best friend. Fuck, I've trained him nearly every day for the past six years. Together, we made him the undisputed heavyweight champion of the world. At this point, there isn't much we don't know about one another.

Yet it just didn't feel right talking about Maddie like that.

"It was just a kiss," I repeat, not sure who I am trying to convince.

"Yeah, that's why you've been avoiding her like the fucking plague for months. Come on, man, we know you want her. It's been obvious since you first laid eyes on her."

Yeah, I want her, and that's the fucking problem.

I never want a woman for more than one night. But Maddie has me imagining all the ways I could take her, fantasizing about her moaning into my ear and screaming my name. The only way I can stop myself is by avoiding her. The more I see her, the more I want her.

"Fuck off, Keller," I warn, tightening my grip around the bottle and taking another sip.

"Fine," he replies, raising his hands up in surrender. "So, how's things going with Luca? Seems like you're having a lot of fun."

"It's fucking carnage, I love it."

"Who'd have thought—my trainer takes my place as mafia hitman. I didn't know you had it in you. Looks like all that special forces training did come in handy. But, fuck, we need you back at King's Gym. We've got new sign-ups every day."

The King's Gym is our baby, our life's work. Since Keller became the undisputed heavyweight champion last year, amateur boxers have literally been lining the streets to join. To be trained by and fight alongside the best in the world.

"I'm on it. It's just been a busy week. You know I won't let you down."

He nods in response.

"Come on, let's watch Andre's fight," he says.

I pinch the bridge of my nose to relieve some of the pressure building, my mind still stuck on Maddie.

I need to make sure I'm gone before she and Sienna get home.

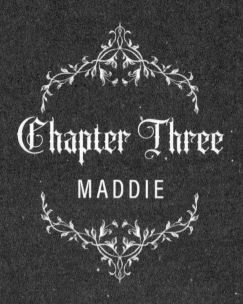

Chapter Three

MADDIE

It's a typical Friday night at the End Zone. It's packed, but one of the perks of Sienna being married to the owner is we always get our favorite VIP booth. I sink into the black leather and admire the array of shots laid out across the gold tables, with a magnum bottle of champagne taking center stage.

After the altercation with Grayson, I need all the alcohol I can get.

That man sets a fire within me, one I can't ever seem to put out. So here I am again, sexually frustrated over a man I can't have.

I toss back the tequila, the contents burning on their way down.

"What was that earlier with Grayson?" Sienna asks, pouring herself a glass of champagne.

"I have no idea, Si. The man is unhinged."

She knows about the kiss and that I was upset after. But

I think I've done a good job of hiding my true feelings ever since.

He wasn't wrong earlier when he said I'd be soaked. Just looking at him makes my panties wet.

"You've both been acting pretty strange since that kiss. You do know he hasn't actually kissed anyone in, like, years? Keller has no fucking clue why."

I almost spit my champagne all over the table.

"Don't be so ridiculous, you know as well as I do the man fucks anything with a vagina."

Well, anyone except me, it would seem.

"I didn't say *fuck*. I said *kiss*, Maddie."

Oh, here we go. Ever since I told her, she's been pushing me to admit my feelings and stop going on dates with Gregory. There's nothing to admit. Grayson is hardly the one who's going to give me marriage, a family, and unconditional love.

"You know as well as I do, Si, Grayson is not the man I'm looking for long term."

"Don't you think maybe, just maybe, you need to stop obsessing over making everyone else happy and do something for yourself? There might be a reason it isn't working with anyone, because that's not your story."

Well, shit.

I do what I do best and grab another shot and down it. I slide one to Sienna, hoping that snaps her out of her motherly advice phase.

"Come on, Si, it's our first girly night in forever. Let's forget about men for a minute, drink, and dance. That is what will truly make me happy right now," I say, sipping my champagne to wash down the taste of vodka still whirling around on my tongue.

She nods in defeat and downs the shot, spluttering. I chuckle as the buzz of alcohol finally hits me.

TWO HOURS LATER, the table of shots and the bottle of champagne are gone. I'm swaying in my seat and can't stop giggling. I haven't been this wasted in a long time. Sienna is busy, drunk-texting Keller while blushing.

"Hey, Si, I'm just going to go to the ladies' room real quick," I say, snatching my clutch bag from the seat. I'm not even sure how I can actually form a sentence, let alone walk straight. On wobbly legs, I make my way to the toilet, holding on to the wall for support.

Sitting on the toilet seat with the lid still down, I hold my head in my hand. My elbows are resting on my knees and I'm trying to focus on getting the room to stop spinning around me. I need to get out of here, and I need to get Sienna home too. She's even worse than me.

I fumble around the sticky floor, searching for my bag, only to realize it's already on my lap.

Jesus Christ, get a grip, Maddie. I dig out my phone, squinting to make out the buttons on the screen. I tap the green icon and start a text. Gregory will pick us up, he's a nice man. I'll text him.

I have his name picked out, and I start randomly typing, hoping for the best. I can't see what the hell I'm doing, so I'm going from memory.

ME
Hey babes, I am soooooo drunk and need a ride plsea.

That will do it.

I don't know how long I sit there, staring at the floor. My phone never pings, so I sigh and get up. The room seems to have stopped spinning. I run the tap and splash some cold water on my face and drink it straight from the faucet.

Once I make it back to the VIP booth, I stop. *He's* here. Sprawled out, his arms resting above the backrest, looking every bit the sex god he is. Even with him in denim jeans and a simple tight white T-shirt, I'm salivating over his muscles protruding out. Honestly, as much as it annoys me, he is fucking hot. I even love his hair; he's grown it out from the buzzcut. It's now longer on top with a wave in it. Delicious.

Sucking in a breath, I try to push down the desire bubbling in my core. I'm drunk and horny, and after earlier, I'm still turned on from his words. God, the way he owned my space. He obliterated me while barely touching me.

"Oh, here she is. You can stop staring and sit if you want, Maddie. I won't bite that hard," he mocks, tapping his lap. His eyes are eating me up, making me melt on the spot. Then I remember how he's everything I don't want, and I shake myself out of my lust-filled haze.

I ignore his request and squeeze into the booth next to Sienna. "What are you doing here?" I question Grayson.

"You texted me, sunshine. And here I am, at your service," he teases, giving me one of his sexy grins, his white teeth peeking out. Those damn lips I want to kiss.

Stop it, Maddie, you are drunk!

"No, I texted Gregory?" I reply, swiping my phone from my bag and pulling up my latest texts. Shit, I did text him.

"Hey, Maddie," a deep, masculine voice shouts from behind me. It's one I don't recognize. A guy I was dancing with a while ago walks toward me, a grin on his face as he gets closer.

I give him a sweet smile, all the while feeling Grayson's eyes piercing into me.

"Hey."

The man, whose name I can't quite remember, looks past me at Grayson and hesitates before speaking.

"Do you feel like getting another drink and a dance?" the man asks, giving me a soft smile.

The annoying sound of Grayson clearing his throat fills my ears. His jaw is clenched, and his fists are balled on the table. I cock an eyebrow at him, trying to tell him to fuck off without actually saying it in front of the man who wants to dance.

"She's leaving," Grayson declares, staring at me, which makes me shift uncomfortably in my seat.

"Am I?"

I look to Sienna for some help, who just shrugs and laughs, flicking her gaze between Grayson and me. *Great help there, Sienna.* Grayson slams his fists down on the table and stands. His height and strong build are making my dancing friend look tiny in comparison. Grayson strides over to me with that look that just screams *don't fuck with me right now.* And honestly, I don't have the energy to deal with his macho pissing contest right now. I sigh and turn back to my new friend.

"I'm sorry, he's right. I am about to leave. Maybe another time," I say, giving him an apologetic look.

He nods and exits out of the VIP area. "Or maybe the fuck not," Grayson grits out and holds out his hand. The way he acts and the things he says never quite match up. He avoids me like my dad avoids the divorce lawyer for the most part, and then gets all possessive of me with other men.

"Oh, fuck off, Grayson," I snap, getting up by myself and slapping his hand away. "Sienna, are you ready?"

She nods and hurries out of the booth, sliding up next to me and linking her arm in mine.

"You two just really, really need to fuck this out of your systems. Now." She giggles drunkenly in my ear.

I shake my head and carry on walking with her in tow to the back exit and toward Grayson's fancy white Audi, which flashes to life as we approach.

"Get in," Grayson huffs, storming past and opening the passenger door and the back door. He turns to us and gently brushes the hair out of my face.

"You. In the passenger seat," he demands and leaves. He almost makes me miss him crowding me. Sienna snickers as she slips in the back of the car, leaving me staring at the open door in front of me. *Why do I feel like this is a really bad idea?*

The drive is silent. Grayson grips the steering wheel so hard his knuckles are turning white.

As soon as we arrive, Keller opens the car door and plucks a now-sleeping Sienna out. "Thanks for bringing her home. Have fun, you two." He chuckles.

My eyes start to feel heavy. With the heat blasting on my face, it is really a struggle to stay awake. I rest my head in the palm of my hand and lean on the cool car window.

"Sunshine, have you got your keys?"

I am so tired I can barely lift my head, so I just nod. The next thing I know, I am floating, encased in his strong grip, the steady rhythm of his heartbeat almost sending me back into slumber.

"Mmm, you smell good."

"Thank you, sunshine, you don't smell too bad yourself. A mixture of sweetness and tequila," he whispers.

"I like it when you're not all grumpy and annoying," I say. The filter between my brain and my mouth has malfunctioned.

"Well, I like it when you aren't threatening to kill me or telling me to fuck off."

Once we make it up the steps to my apartment, he carefully places my feet on the floor.

"You got decent coffee?" he questions with a smirk.

"I live off the stuff, so yes," I say, opening up the front door. "Ahhhh, that is almost orgasmic," I moan at the relief of my feet finally being free from the heels as I kick them off.

Grayson coughs behind me as he tries to hold in his laughter.

"Sunshine, if that's orgasmic to you, I feel sorry for you."

"Oh, you have no idea." I make my way over to the coffee machine and grab two pink mugs on my way.

3:09 a.m. flashes on the oven.

Shit, it is late.

I yawn as the dark liquid fills the mug. I need a couple of minutes to rest my eyes.

"Come on, sunshine, time for bed."

I peel open my eyes and find myself nuzzled against his chest, *again.*

He delicately places me on the bed, and my head sinks into my pillow. A fuzzy feeling takes over me as he tucks the comforter under my neck and strokes the hair out of my face. I grab his wrist before he has a chance to move.

"Stay."

"You promise to keep your hands to yourself?" He smirks.

"I promise." I pout.

His arms bulge as he tugs at the hem of his shirt and brings it over his head, revealing his sculpted body. Dark tattoos, almost tribal, cover each pec. I knew he was well-built, but shit, his body is a frickin' work of art. All I want to do is trail my hands along that delicious V above his jeans.

"Eyes up here, sunshine." His deep voice snaps me out of my stupor.

He whips his jeans off, revealing tattoos that snake out of his boxers all the way down his thick thighs to his ankles. My eyes widen as I spot the outline of his cock straining against the fabric. *Holy hell, no fucking way is it that big.* He laughs and shakes his head while folding his clothes and placing them neatly on my dresser. He walks toward me with a hunger in his eyes.

"Oh wow, you're a big boy. Shame, I bet you don't know how to use it," I tease, pulling the comforter up to my neck.

Butterflies swarm my belly as he approaches the edge of the bed.

"Oh, Maddie. I know exactly how to use it. It's a shame *you'll* never know," he says, ripping back the duvet. "Scoot over then." I stare blankly at him. I can't concentrate on anything other than how sexy he is. My mind is just mush, and the throbbing of my pussy is making it even harder to think.

I roll over to the other side of the bed. The cold, never-slept-in half of my bed. The sequins of my dress are stabbing into my arms. I mean, if he's only wearing underwear to bed, it's only fair I do the same. A grin forms on my lips as I lift my hips up and unzip my dress, sliding it down over my ass and wiggling it off over my legs, then hurling it on the floor.

Shit, I wasn't wearing a bra.

A blush spreads over my cheeks, but it's too late to do anything about it. Plus, he's seen my tits before . . . by accident, but still.

He pulls the blanket back. My nipples instantly form into peaks.

He holds the sheet up, his mouth open as his eyes home

DETONATE ~ 31

in on my exposed chest. He runs his other hand over his face and groans. "Fuck, sunshine. You really don't make anything easy for me, do you?"

I have no idea what he's talking about. When he rejected me after the kiss, I assumed he wasn't into me. Yet his actions and words suggest otherwise.

"Just get in, it's cold," I say, suddenly feeling too exposed.

"Oh, is that why your nipples are so hard?" He bites his lower lip. His eyes still haven't left my tits.

The mattress dips as his powerful frame lands on the bed. He rolls to face me, our noses almost touching. The only sound in the room is our heavy breathing. Electricity sizzles as we just lie there, staring into each other's eyes.

"Sunshine, you need to get some sleep," he says. I sigh in disappointment. I don't know why I'm shocked; the man isn't interested in me like that. And I don't want him, right?

He inches forward, pressing a soft kiss on my forehead. His strong arms wrap around me, and he pulls me up against him. I wrap my leg over his and it lightly brushes against his rock-hard cock.

"Not tonight, sunshine," he sighs.

I know this is for the best, and I'm too tired to argue anyway.

"Goodnight, Grayson," I whisper, closing my eyes and snuggling into him. His steady breathing lulls me into a peaceful slumber.

Chapter Four

GRAYSON

Her soft waves of bright blonde hair brush against my nose as I breathe in her vanilla scent. The steady rise and fall of her chest indicates she's still fast asleep. I've had my four hours and I'm good to go, and apparently so is my cock.

I need to get out of here before we do something we regret.

I keep replaying the shift in Maddie's behavior with me. That distance was gone, and the fun Maddie was out to play. But she doesn't seem to hate me as much when she's had a drink, that's for sure. The way she licked her lips when I undressed . . . Fuck, her perky tits are ingrained in my mind now. It took all the willpower I had not to suck on one of those rosy buds last night.

Now here she is, cuddling up under my arm, her back pressing into my chest and my hand almost touching her tit. We've come a long way from her threatening to stab me.

I slowly pull my arm out from underneath her head, hoping not to disturb her. I need to get the fuck out of here. There is only so much restraint a man can have, especially when I have the woman I've dreamed of fucking for months, naked, with her ass pressed up against my cock.

As I roll over, she stirs next to me. I gently tuck her back in and press a soft kiss on the top of her head. "Bye, sunshine." I don't even know why; she's already shattered my one no-kissing rule to pieces. Now I just can't seem to stop. Her plump lips are the only ones I want.

And the only ones I can't have.

That's why this has to stop. I can't keep fucking with her anymore, especially now that I know she's in as deep as me. Last night, there was a complete shift in the air between us. Just one more argument could tip us over the edge of no return and break us both. That strange feeling I get whenever I'm near her, like my heart is pulling me from the inside, *almost* makes me stop getting dressed. But I don't. I throw on my clothes and walk toward the bedroom door without looking back.

"Are we going back to hating each other today?" Her groggy voice catches my attention.

Resting my arm against the doorframe, I lean into it and take her in. Her rosy cheeks give her away far too easily.

"You have no idea what it does to me when you get riled up, Maddie."

Her brows lift, and her lips part. I've effectively rendered her speechless.

"I'll see you around, sunshine. Don't make a habit of drunk-texting men and taking your tits out for them. You have much more class than that."

She picks up a pillow and hurls it at me. It lands a yard in front of me. My eyes dart between the latest attack object and her scowling face.

"Trust me, that will be the last time you will ever see my boobs again."

I wish it wasn't.

Amused, I say, "I'll have the image saved in my brain forever, don't you worry."

"Goodbye, Grayson," she huffs, hiding under the duvet.

"See ya, sunshine."

Last night, maybe I flew too close to the sun.

Chapter Five

MADDIE

I groan, rolling over to the cold side of my bed. I press my fingers against the bridge of my nose, willing the headache pounding behind my eyes to stop. I gently pull the quilt away from my body, and my nipples stand to attention when the cool air hits them.

A glass of water and two painkillers are sitting in the center of my bedside table.

Well, I didn't put them there. After a few drinks, Drunk Maddie wouldn't give a shit about Sober Maddie's hangover the next morning.

Grayson.

He's seen my boobs twice now. I slap the palm of my hand against my forehead in annoyance, which only makes me wince. The air seems to turn into a furnace as I sit, naked and wanting to die of embarrassment. Fuck, if he tells Keller, I'm never going to hear the end of this from Sienna.

He wouldn't, would he?

I snatch the tablets from the nightstand and swig them back with some of the water. I moan in appreciation as the cool liquid soothes my dry throat. But it's not quite the coffee my body so desperately craves right now. With a sigh, I push myself off the bed, slip on the black oversized hoodie that's been thrown in a heap on my dressing table, and wander out to the kitchen.

Since Sienna moved out, it's far too quiet here. Not that I need a roommate, but I wouldn't mind the company. I like to be distracted from life, from feeling lonely.

As I round the corner to the kitchen, I pause, shocked. Holy shit, did he clean? My counters are sparkling. The coffee machine is ready with a fresh mug that has a happy face on it. Way too cheery for me right now.

I mean, I should probably thank him. He took my drunk ass home, put me to bed, and apparently tidied my apartment in the middle of the night. I place the cup under the machine. It buzzes to life and the black liquid fills the cup. God, I can't wait for this. Fetching my cell phone out of my silver purse from the barstool, I check my notifications.

Twenty-five new matches on my dating profile. Maybe Mr. Right is one of these. I scroll through the onslaught of profiles, swiping along their pictures.

After a while, I sigh and shut down the app. I'm too tired and hungover to deal with this today, as if the hangxiety isn't enough with stripping in front of Grayson, *again*. I cannot handle stewing on the fact that I can't find "the one."

My phone pings with a message, and my heart rate picks up when I read its contents.

GRAYSON
Morning, sunshine. How's the head? Your earrings are in my car.

Now I remember why the man riles me up. He acts like God's gift to women. He sleeps with anyone *but* me. Not that I want to sleep with him. Although, the rejection does kind of hurt.

> **ME**
> Not my earrings, asshole.

His reply is instant.

> **GRAYSON**
> Oops.

Is he serious?
As I go to put the phone away, another text pops up.

> **GRAYSON**
> JOKING. Don't worry ;)

I shake my head when I realize I'm smiling like a teenager with a crush at my phone. *He's not a good man, Maddie.*

> **ME**
> Who you are with is not my concern. After
> all, you run away after a kiss anyway.

Sienna should have never told me about his no-kissing rule. I can imagine his face all scrunched up as he tries to come up with something to hit a nerve with. It's almost become a normal part of life now. Winding each other up until one of us is pissed off enough to stop.

> **GRAYSON**
> I haven't had any complaints about what I
> can do with my mouth.

> **ME**
> Me neither.

Is the heating on, or am I about to combust? I need to shut this down. Now. This text exchange alone proves he's a walking red flag, one I need to cross right off my list. If I'm going to find myself a man, prove to my parents I am respectable, I need to stop engaging with this idiot. He distracts me. That kiss distracts me. Then I can relax, I can be happy.

At least I don't have to see him for a while now. With that, I make my way to the shower and turn on the hot water.

Just as I slip out of my clothes, my phone pings again. I pop out of the bathroom to go and see.

GRAYSON
See you next weekend, sunshine.

For fuck's sake! I throw my head back, just as another text appears. Christ, can't people leave me alone in my delicate state?

MOM
We've booked a table at La Brasserie,
Friday, 12th Feb. You can bring a date,
seeing as it is near Valentine's. I expect
you must have someone by now?

I groan out loud at her text. Can't she cut me some slack? She's obsessed. I don't even have the energy to text her back. I can't handle the next lecture I'm about to get on being single and how my body's clock is ticking for children.

That discussion is for another day.

I chuck my phone on the bed and head off to the shower.

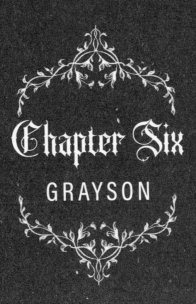

Chapter Six

GRAYSON

etween working my ass off at the boxing gym every day, whittling down our new recruits, and Luca having me keep watch over Marco Falcone's eldest daughter most nights, I am fucked. At the same time, I'm relieved to keep my brain busy with something other than Maddie. After spending the night with her slender and perfect naked body cuddled up to me, I fear I will never recover.

It confirms that I can never fuck her. If I do that, I am fucked.

That's why I have the no-kissing rule. Simply to avoid any intimacy. Since my bitch of an ex-wife screwed me over, I vowed to never let another woman into my heart. Yet every time I am in Maddie's presence, she seems to unknowingly chip away at that oath. Every damn time she licks those lips, I want them. I've had a taste, and it was fucking delicious.

The more I push her away, the more I rile her up. I can keep her at arm's length. Enough to sate my need for her without touching her. She's a temptress, and I don't know how much longer I can resist her.

I throw on a pair of denim jeans and a white shirt. I even style my hair and perfect the edges of my stubble. I always pride myself on cleaning up well. Knowing I will be in Maddie's presence tonight, I have to step it up a notch. I just can't help myself when it comes to her.

After parking my Audi in Keller's compound, I walk over to the door and knock. I wonder if she's already here. I have no clue how to act around her after last weekend. Hell, I can never predict how she will be around me. But today, I'm actually dreading it. Especially now that I know how her body fits against mine, how much I fucking love spooning her to sleep.

The door flies open, revealing a glowing Sienna in a flowy navy dress and gray cardigan. Little Darcy, cuddled up into her side, watches me.

"Grayson, you made it! Come in."

"Sienna. Little Darcy." I walk through the threshold and stroke the baby's mop of black hair, and she giggles. "Aren't you the cutest little thing in the world. I missed you," I coo. "You look beautiful, Sienna."

"Thank you, Grayson." She smiles. Over the last year, she's become part of my family. I will always be grateful to her for saving my best friend, even if it was from himself.

"Where's the big man?"

"In the kitchen. I got bored of him telling me how to do it, so I left him in there to fend for himself. Although, you should all be grateful; his food will be far better." Her face lights up as she talks about him.

I shut the door and walk through the living room, spotting Keller towering over the stove, wooden spoon in hand. Luca and Mrs. Russo are busy chatting in Italian across the dining table.

"Luca."

"Welcome to the chaos," he replies.

"Uncle Grayson!" Max shouts, jumping off of his chair and hurtling toward me, grabbing my legs.

"My favorite little boxing star!" I ruffle his hair.

"I've been practicing my uppercuts with Keller like you told me!"

"Good job. You can show me them on Thursday." I grin, and he scampers away.

Keller spins around, his black shirt splattered with white sauce. "Grayson, grab me a beer, please, I'm dying of thirst here," he says. I shake my head and chuckle, making my way over to the fridge and taking three bottles out.

"Keller, go sit with your friends, I've got this. Just take Darcy, please." Sienna bundles Darcy into Keller's arms and grabs the spoon out of his hand. As she goes to walk past him, Keller grabs her wrist and pulls her under his arm, kissing the top of her head. When he whispers in her ear, I purposely tune it out. The blush that spreads up her chest is enough to tell me what he's saying. I pop open the caps and walk to the dining table, taking the spare seat between Keller and Luca. I have Mrs. Russo at the head of the table to my left.

Tipping my head back, I take a long sip of beer. The front door crashes open, and Maddie barrels in.

"Oh my God, sorry I'm late, my client didn't like the shade of gold I used." She rolls her eyes dramatically. Rushing over to the kitchen, she wraps Sienna in a hug. "It smells delicious," she mumbles before her eyes snap up to the rest of the table.

She's a hot mess.

A fucking gorgeous one.

I shift uncomfortably in my seat, my cock twingeing against my zipper. Like it does every damn time when she's near me. There's just something about this woman that gets to me.

Her gaze flickers in my direction, but she soon diverts it to Luca and finally settles on Mrs. Russo at the head of the table. Her stilettos click along the marble floor as she does that strange penguin run that women do in heels toward Mrs. Russo.

"So lovely to see you again, Mrs. Russo." Her smile is so bright and genuine.

"Aaaah, Maddie. You look stunning. Have you been snapped up yet?" Mrs. Russo grabs Maddie's left hand, looking for a ring. The collar of my shirt suddenly becomes too tight as the green monster rears its ugly head.

"Not quite." Maddie nervously laughs. We all know it gets to her. I clear my throat, and her attention snaps to me. *Time to play,* sunshine.

Scooting my chair back, I tap my lap. "Want to take a seat? Come tell me all about it?" I ask, doing my best to hold back the laughter.

One thing I'll never get sick of is winding her up. The way her cheeks heat and she gets that perfect "fuck me" purse to her lips every damn time thrills me in all the right ways. I tell myself I'm doing it to make her mad, but in reality, she's fucking hot.

There it is . . . my favorite red color that flushes her cheeks.

She scowls at me. "I'd rather sit on the floor, thanks."

"Hey, I thought we were friends now?" I shrug, giving her puppy-dog eyes.

Her head snaps to Sienna's in horror.

"Wait! Have you two finally fucked?" Luca chimes in. "Keller, you owe me ten grand."

"Enough of that, young man," Mrs. Russo snaps back, her thick Italian accent enough to calm us all.

Resting my elbow on the table, I lean forward, cocking my brow at my best friends.

"Tell me more about this bet."

Before they can respond, Maddie interrupts, "No, we haven't, so, Keller, you can keep your money. Luca won't ever be getting that." She stomps over to the chair opposite me and yanks it out, plonking down. Her arms cross, and she's looking at me like she wants to kill me.

Perfect. Just how I like her.

I scoot my chair back in, and my foot grazes her calf. Before I know it, pain radiates through my shin as she slams her stiletto into it.

"Fucking hell, Maddie," I hiss, and now, it's my turn to glare at her. A mischievous smirk dances across her lips. I reach and grab the bottle of champagne in front of us and pour her a glass.

Her dainty hand shoots forward, the array of sparkly rings that decorate most of her fingers shimmering. Fuck, if she punched me, it probably would hurt. As her fingers wrap around the glass, my hand covers hers to stop her picking it up. As soon as our hands connect, blood rushes to my cock.

"I think there is a *thank you, Grayson* coming," I tease. She tries to free her hand, but I tighten my grip.

"Thanks," she says, giving me one of her fake smiles. The waft of garlic chicken makes my stomach rumble as Keller not-so-elegantly drops the plate of food down on the navy mat in front of me.

"Thanks, man." I nod.

I reluctantly let go of Maddie's hand. Huffing, she brings the glass up to her glossy, plump lips and tips her head back to take a sip.

Fuck, what I would give to taste those lips again.

A drop of champagne spills from the corner of her lips. She wipes it away with her middle finger. I can't help but bite down on the inside of my mouth to hold back the groan. Her eyes never leave mine the entire time.

What? she mouths with a smirk. Oh, she's playing a dangerous game.

I shake my head, pretending to be unaffected by her. Thankfully, she can't see my erect cock straining against my jeans. If she was any other woman on this planet, I would have fucked her by now. But I can't do that to her. She isn't a one-and-done. I would keep coming back for more until I broke her. I'd lose my family. Everyone at this table right now would hate me. So, if it means having an aggressive jerk-off in a freezing shower every time I see her, then so be it.

"You all right, buddy? You seem flustered," Luca asks. Without even looking at him, I know he's grinning from ear to ear, reveling in my agony. The man is clever, too clever. There's nothing he doesn't notice.

"Perfectly fine here," I reply, not taking my eyes off Maddie. Picking up my knife and fork, I dig in. I bite into the chicken and it melts in my mouth. "Damn, Sienna, this is amazing," I mumble through mouthfuls.

"Mrs. Russo has been teaching me a thing or two." Sienna gives me a proud smile.

Keller runs his tattooed hand through his wife's long dark hair, adoration evident on his face.

"Damn, I need to find me a woman that can cook like this." The words slip out of my mouth, so much so I nearly choke. I can't bring myself to look in Maddie's direction.

"Wouldn't that mean actually dating?" Keller says, flicking up an eyebrow in amusement. That fucker.

"I'm good then." I shrug, continuing with my food despite rapidly losing my appetite.

Maddie glances every now and then in my direction. Once we are all finished, she gets up from the table and starts collecting our plates. She goes around to everyone else first, then stops next to me.

Close enough for me to take in a breath of my new favorite scent.

Her.

Picking up my plate, I rest it on top of the others, purposely brushing her hand on the way down. A decision I regret as soon as our skin makes contact. Electricity shoots through my hand. The way her eyebrows flick up shows me she feels this too.

Luca shuffles in his seat next to me, rummaging through his pockets and pulling out a little white packet of cigarettes. He offers one to me.

"Thanks," I say, picking out one of the brown tips and tucking it behind my ear. Maddie turns her back and struts off into the kitchen. Luca stands, tapping me on the shoulder. I rip my gaze away from her reluctantly and follow him out into the garden.

He has a similar look in his eyes as the afternoon I first met him. Sitting in an Irish bar in Times Square, moping into a glass of scotch on his own. He'd looked how I felt, so I'd ordered two of their finest scotch.

"You look how I feel. Here," I say, placing the tumbler down next to his almost empty one.

He looks up at me through bloodshot eyes and nods at the seat opposite him. "Well, take a seat. We can be miserable in silence together."

I chuckle and pull out the deep-green chair, then toss down my sports bag, the one that holds the only contents of my entire life.

Luca spots the bag, eying me suspiciously.

"You aren't here to kill me, are you?"

What the fuck.

"Nah, if I was, you'd be dead by now."

He shrugs, tossing back the remnants of his drink.

"Wouldn't be the worst thing in the world."

"Oh, come on, it can't be that bad."

His eyes scan the room before he leans forward on the table.

"I've just lost everything."

"Trust me, I know how that feels. I moved here today, just after finding out my wife had been fucking my now-dead best friend."

He chokes on his drink. "I hope you're the one who killed him."

"Gunshot in Afghanistan. Told me on his deathbed."

"Absolute fuckers. Hey, well, if you want your wife killed, just give me a shout. You're speaking to the new mafia leader. I guess that's what I do now."

The conflict is clear in his eyes. He isn't a murderer by choice. Not like me. He doesn't relish taking someone's life with his bare hands.

"Why don't you look happy about it? I thought being the top dog is what everyone wants in that line of business."

He scoffs. "I didn't have a fucking choice. I was never in this world. I was on the street, fighting with my brother, try-ing to turn pro. Until my father's minions, the same father who abandoned me at birth, turned up and dragged me off the streets. Turns out my piece-of-shit father didn't only want to fuck up my childhood, he'd signed me up for a life of hell as an adult too."

"Street fighter, you say? I was a boxer, used to train up the guys in my corp."

He appears to be in deep thought.

"Do you want a job?"

For the mafia? Do I? I want to rebuild my life. I want to start again, try to curb this urge for blood. Calm this anger.

"Doing?"

"Training my brother. He's good, he just turned pro. Heavyweight. He won't fucking listen to you, I will warn you of that. But he can make it, I just know it. He just needs a decent trainer. He needs investment in his boxing gym, a co-owner. I'll put you up in one of my apartments."

I rub my palm along my stubble. I don't have other options. I've got the money to invest.

Fuck it.

He pulls out his phone, sliding it over to me. A guy, about the same build and size as me, fills the screen, walking out into a tattered boxing ring. Tattooed from neck to foot, a murderous look in his eye.

"I'll do it." I extend my hand out to him. "I'm Grayson, by the way. Grayson Ward."

He clasps my hand and gives me a firm handshake.

"Luca Russo. And that, on the screen, is Keller Russo."

Thirty minutes in New York and I'm tied to the mafia already. Fuck yeah!

Luca flicks open his Zippo and lights his cigarette, then passes it to me. I light my own up and inhale, the toxic chemicals burning into my lungs.

"You really haven't fucked her yet?" Luca asks, puffing away.

"No."

"I don't get it. Why don't you just fuck, get it over with, so you don't have to keep pining over her? You'll be doing yourself a favor. It's obvious." He shrugs. I can't ever talk about this too much with Keller. I can't risk Sienna knowing. And she can't keep a secret to save her life. So, Luca is really the only one who understands. For the past seven years, he's put his trust in me, whether it's training Keller or becoming his right-hand man. I trust the fucker with my life.

"We can't fuck. I don't want to hurt her."

"Yes, we know, Grayson, you have a big dick. I don't think she'd mind being a bit sore." He winks.

"Fucking hell, Luca. Not like that. We all know she's after anyone who's not me. I can't just fuck her once and leave her. I don't think I could do it."

"You don't seem to have a problem fucking and leaving other women."

"They aren't her, Luca."

"You let her kiss you," he says, stubbing his cigarette out.

"I'd murdered Christ knows how many men. I wasn't thinking straight."

"So it wasn't the best kiss of your life?"

"I just can't. Leave it at that."

"Your loss. Someone will snag her up and you'll regret it. I promise you."

"Hmm, maybe." The thought of someone else touching her, getting to have her in all the ways I never could, makes my chest constrict.

A ring breaks our conversation, and he says, "It's Nico. He's dealing with the Falcones. I'll be in in a second. Be ready to leave." Putting the phone to his ear, he walks off onto the grass, and I stub out my cigarette and head back in.

Maddie is busy humming away to herself doing the dishes, while the rest of the gang chatters away at the dining table. Without thinking, I head straight toward her.

"Need a hand?" I ask, sliding up next to her.

"No, thanks," she mutters, concentrating on the bowl in her hand. She bites her bottom lip, side-eyeing me.

She grabs the black cloth next to her and starts drying the bowl, then goes up on tiptoes to reach for the cupboard door above her head. I cage her in, and her ass rubs against my dick. *Oh fuck.*

"Let me," I rasp, reaching up and opening the cupboard door. Her ass wiggles against my cock.

"Stop it," I warn.

She turns around in my arms, her back now resting against the marble countertop. I take the bowl out of her fingers and shove it in the cupboard above us.

"Make me." She tips her chin up, her arms crossed, making her tits rise out of her top.

Desire flashes in her eyes. I tip my head to the side, eating her up with my gaze. She doesn't move an inch; she stands her ground.

Her peachy scent consumes me as I suck in a breath. God, she's fucking delicious.

My nose brushes against her jaw until I reach her ear.

"You don't want me to make you. Trust me, sunshine," I whisper.

I frown as a devilish smile dances across her lips. She arches her back; my eyes are glued to her tits. So much so that I don't notice her left hand snake behind her into the sink full of bubbly liquid.

Her hand smashes into my face, and she drags it down my cheek. The bubbles sting my eyes. I squeeze them shut and let out a hiss.

Maddie's hysterical laughter rings through my ears. She's doubled over, holding her stomach, struggling to breathe. I can feel all the eyes in the room on us.

I lean over her bent-over body, but she's too busy laughing to take notice of me. Picking up the soaking sponge, I step back, lifting my hand, water dripping through my fingers. I hover it over her head.

"Something funny, sunshine?" I tease.

"I can't . . ." she wheezes, holding her chest. My chest vibrates as I squeeze the sponge above her head. She gasps as water drips down her forehead.

Her palm connects with my chest when she pushes against me. I don't move. Her white shirt is now see-through. Her lacy white bra doesn't cover those erect rosy buds now staring at me. Tempting me.

She isn't pissed. The blush spreading across her cheeks isn't in anger. She's turned on. I follow her gaze as it roams over my body, settling on my throbbing cock. I know these jeans aren't going to hide the hard-on I have for her.

"Grayson, we gotta go!" Luca frantically shouts from behind me. Maddie's body sags against the counter. Fuck, I don't know what to do. So I do what I do best—avoid everything.

"I'll see you around, sunshine."

"Now!" Luca shouts, kicking my ass into gear.

Maddie nods, biting that goddamn bottom lip and turning her back. I grab my jacket from the back of my chair, giving Sienna and Darcy a quick peck on their heads.

"See you Monday?" I nod to Keller. His jaw tics as Luca rushes out of the house. I know he's worried about his brother. Keller was always the one to protect him. And now, I think he's struggling with not being there for him as much.

"I'll look out for him, Keller. You know that."

He gives me a tight smile, and Sienna encases his tattooed hand in hers.

"Thank you, I'll see you Monday." He turns his attention straight back to his wife. His reminder of why he can't be out protecting his brother anymore. I take one last glance at Maddie. She mouths, *Be safe,* and fuck me, I don't know what to do with that. I quickly wave to Mrs. Russo and sprint out.

Getting myself the fuck out of here.

Chapter Seven

GRAYSON

I lean on the black leather couch in the center of the room in Luca's gothic-style mansion. He paces around the room. The day of the dinner party, the Falcones somehow kidnapped Nico, our hacker, from his home. Since then, we've been busy scoping out all the places we could think of where they may hide him. So far . . . nothing.

It's been two weeks, but we haven't received a body *yet*, so it's likely he's still alive. The Falcones would never pass up an opportunity to gloat about the fact they finally got one over on us.

"We need to show them just how easy it is for us to pluck one of theirs off the street," Luca says, still storming around the house.

"So we do just that."

It won't be hard. Taking Nico probably took months of planning.

"We need to lure them out. Marco is fucking psychotic. I mean, where the fuck is he getting all these men from? Every time we take them out, they seem to fucking respawn." He seethes.

"Look, we can't underestimate them. Not after what they did with Sienna. They might be sloppy, but they have numbers. We've disarmed every attack up to this point. Now we need to show him we have access to anyone close to him. We send a threat, and in return, demand Nico?"

One wrong move and Nico's life will be at stake. The Falcones might be clueless, but they are more dangerous that way.

"How about you get close to his precious cousin, Amara? She's a wild card, mind you. Take her out on some dates, and that will lure them out. Then we can get our message across."

Great. Take a Falcone out on dates. Just what I need!

As if sensing my displeasure, he says, "It won't be that difficult for you. She is smoking hot."

I'm only interested in that fiery blonde bombshell who seems to steal all of my thoughts.

"Fine, I'll turn on the charm and see what I can do." I huff, reaching for my coffee on the table.

"Oh, come on, it won't be that bad. You look like you could do with a good fuck anyway." He chuckles.

He's not wrong. Even if I did, it won't change the fact it still wouldn't help. Not unless I can finally get Maddie out of my system. Which won't be happening.

"Any suspicious activities around the drug shipments last night?" I change the subject.

"No, it seems to have calmed down on that front."

Great. At least we have one part of the business under control.

Chapter Eight

MADDIE

The Friday before Valentine's. What a perfect evening to go to dinner with the parents. Still single. Not only that, but with a mother who's too obsessed with my love life, or lack of it.

I haven't seen Grayson since that awkward yet hot-as-fuck argument we had at Sienna's. That was over three weeks ago, so I've been concentrating my efforts on forgetting about him and that damn kiss. I've been on a few dates. None of which I had any instant spark with. They kind of bored me to death. I was listening to them drawl on about work and finances. *Yawn.*

I'm still cringing over the fact I told Grayson, the big bad mafia hitman, to be safe. I don't know what I was thinking. That was way too personal.

I quickly throw on a black turtleneck knitted dress, tights, and a pair of leather heeled boots. Then I flick some mascara on my long fluffy lashes, just enough to make my green eyes pop. I've already spent the hour straightening my hair, which is so damn long and thick it takes forever. But I can't have my mom looking down her nose at me. If I can make my appearance perfect, that's one less thing for her to comment on. Eurgh. *Why did I agree to this?!*

I tip the rest of my prosecco into my mouth, letting the bubbles tingle on my tongue. I'm going to need as much as I can tolerate to get through this. My phone beeps on the counter, telling me my Uber is outside. Better get this evening over with. I sigh, grabbing my purse and leather jacket from the barstool.

The ride to La Brasserie in Midtown is quick and uneventful. The cool air whips over my body, making me shiver.

I swing open the glass door only to be greeted by a bubbly teenager, far too upbeat for the mood I'm in right now. All I feel is dread and anxiety.

"Good evening, miss, do you have a reservation?" she asks, tapping away on her iPad.

I survey the room and it's impossible to miss my parents in the middle of the room. My dad beams at me and waves, while Mom pokes her head up over what I assume is the wine menu and drops her gaze straight back down.

Good start.

I give Dad a quick smile and wiggle my fingers, then turn my attention back to the server.

"I'm just here to meet my parents." I point.

The waitress pulls out the dark wooden chair, and I slide off my jacket and take a seat, carefully placing my purse and coat on the chair next to me. In the seat my date was supposed to be in.

"Hi, sweetie, you look lovely," my dad says, nudging my mom with his elbow as if to get her to pay me some attention.

"Hi," I say, trying to hide any hint of bitchiness in my tone.

"How's Gregory, any updates? Why didn't you invite him?" Mom asks in her high-pitched voice.

I pinch the bridge of my nose, waiting for the throbbing headache to form. Why did I bother telling her about him? Oh wait, because I'm constantly trying to impress her.

"We've been on a few dates, Mom, I'm not sure yet. He's fine. Nice."

"Oh, Maddie, get your head out of the clouds. Nice is good. It's stable. It's plenty good enough for you. I mean, come on, you're just a makeup artist yourself, for Christ's sake."

"Carol!" my dad scolds her and shoots me an apologetic look.

"What?" She shrugs, completely unfazed.

He's always had my back and tries his best to defend me. But she is relentless, I'll give her that much. There's only so much he can do. I don't want him to fight with her about it either. All he's ever done is love me for how I am.

"I have my own makeup studio and my own apartment. I'm doing well, thank you very much," I snap, my blood starting to boil.

The door opening creates a cool breeze right through the restaurant, followed by a fake laugh that catches my attention. I can't resist turning to look. My breath hitches as I spot him. Suddenly, the room is like a sauna. Every damn time I see him, my heart starts to race no matter how hard I try to stop it.

Grayson's date looks like a model, complete with a low-cut dress and fake boobs almost falling out. She's running her hand up and down his big, muscular arm. He looks gorgeous in his black tailored suit, and it's tight enough to see his muscles bulge through. His crisp white shirt accentuates his lightly tanned complexion and his short sandy hair. I want to look away, but I can't. I'm in a daze, watching his big frame lean down and whisper in her ear.

His eyes snap up to mine. I roll my eyes at him, and he smiles back. Enough to soak my panties. Not wanting to give him the satisfaction of knowing I'm drooling over him, I swivel back to face my mom. Fuck him and his stupid sexy smile.

I reach for the menu and open it, trying to hide my blush. That is a line of questioning I can't deal with right now.

Heavy footsteps pound behind me and so does that annoying laugh that makes my ears want to bleed. The closer he gets, the more the electricity bolts through my body. I stick my foot out under the table.

His foot connects with mine, and his hand thuds onto our table. The force of it causes the cutlery to fly into the air.

"What is going on?!" my mom shouts, all flustered.

I'm doing everything I can to hold in the laughter, still hiding behind the menu. I don't need to look to know he's wanting to kill me.

"Oh, I'm so sorry, sir, I don't know what you tripped on. Are you okay?" the waitress asks, shocked. I slowly lower the menu, coming face-to-face with my nemesis, my drop-dead gorgeous nemesis.

His jaw tics as he stares straight at me, cocking his brow.

"Well, hello, sunshine," he drawls out.

"Grayson," I say, keeping my tone neutral. I expect him to be angry, but instead, I'm met with his hungry eyes roaming along my body. He leans forward, his face just inches from mine. I can't breathe, and my heart is about to beat its way out of my chest. He brings his lips to my cheek and presses a soft peck. It takes fuck-all in my power not to moan. He stands up straight. I let out a sigh of relief now that he's finally out of my personal space.

"Sorry about that. I don't know what happened. I'll leave you guys to your evening." He grins, addressing my parents.

I rest my elbow on the table and put my chin on my hand, giving him a sweet and innocent smile. All the while fighting the urge to jump him and maybe smack that stupid grin off his face.

He stalks off, his date following him.

The flustered waitress takes our order. I go for a steak and fries with all the sides.

Every now and then, I steal glances at Grayson.

"Well, if you're going to be with men like that, you're never going to find a man to stay with you. I mean, how many dates have you been on now, and still nothing. I'm embarrassed for you." Mom scoffs, breaking my stupor. I don't have it in me to argue back right now. I'm too busy concentrating on not crying. She hates that.

"If you'll excuse me, I need to use the bathroom."

Which means I will have to walk past Grayson's flirting fest. God, I wish that man didn't get under my skin so much. I wish he wasn't the best kiss of my life.

My dad squeezes my hand as I walk past, that small gesture enough for tears to start forming at the corners of my eyes. After all these years, my mom still knows how to hurt me, and I let her. I'm so desperate to show her I am special.

I lower my head and rush past Grayson's table. I don't know how much longer I can keep pushing him away. I can't deny I'm jealous. Jealous he will fuck anyone else but me, apparently.

Once safely in the bathroom, I shut myself in a stall and lock the door, breathing a sigh of relief. I need a minute of peace before my next grilling from Mom. Dinner shouldn't be so hard. It doesn't help that Grayson's kissable lips have been taunting me this whole time. His lopsided grin while flirting with that woman who is almost the complete opposite of me. Is that what he's into? It shouldn't hurt, but it does.

The sound of the door slamming shut breaks me from my thoughts. My back is still pressed up against the stall door.

"Sunshine, are you in here?"

Goosebumps erupt throughout my body at his masculine voice. I can't let him see me like this. He better not have come in here to taunt me.

I slowly unlock the door, slipping on my usual bitch mask to face him. It's the only way to keep my heart safe.

"What do you want, Grayson?" I step out, running straight into his solid chest. I'm not short for a woman, but he's huge. Maybe six foot four. He towers over me. Every inch of him oozes strength and power.

I step away from him and tip my chin up to look at his face. I'm shocked when there's concern etched all over it.

"You looked like you were about to burst into tears when you left your table. I wanted to make sure you were okay." He flings his hands up in surrender. "Please don't shout at me, I'm already embarrassed enough after you tripped me in front of my date." He grins. God, he's a prick. A fucking gorgeous one.

That smirk just soaks my panties every time.

I clench my legs together and awkwardly cross one foot in front of the other. This is the effect he has on me, especially with him invading my space. His spicy scent is assaulting my senses. It's too much. Desire burns through my veins, which is dangerous, on top of anger and jealousy.

"It was an accident." I shrug, averting my gaze from his.

His index finger rests under my chin as he bends down so our faces are level. A hunger flashes through his eyes. My breathing gets heavier as he starts to lower his head to mine.

No, Maddie, he's on a date with another woman.

I snap my eyes shut and turn my head away from him. He takes a deep inhale and brings his lips to my ear, gently brushing my sensitive skin.

"I don't think it was an accident. I think you might be a bit jealous."

He's not wrong.

My brain is screaming at me to leave, to tell him to fuck off, and forget about him. But my mom's words repeat in my mind. *Nice is good enough for you.*

I turn my face back to his, his lips now hovering over mine.

"And what if I am?" I ask, rolling my bottom lip between my teeth.

"I thought you wouldn't fuck me if I were the last man on the planet? I remember those exact words at the dinner table last Christmas, just before you threatened to stab me with the carving knife if I touched you again." He chuckles.

"That's true." I know it doesn't sound remotely convincing as my voice breaks halfway through the sentence.

"Is that why you're blushing? Do I make you that angry? Or is it because you want to fuck me?"

"Both," I answer honestly, causing his eyebrow to raise.

I've never been honest about how I feel about him to this point. Over the past year, I've pushed and pushed, hoping he will leave me alone and my feelings will disappear. But they haven't.

His hands band around my waist, and he pulls me in.

"This is a bad idea, sunshine," he murmurs.

"I know." I lace my arms around his neck, giving him a sweet smile.

He licks his lips as he stares at mine. God, that mouth.

"You know I don't date."

"Well, seeing as you're on a date right now, I beg to differ," I retort.

"Maddie, you know what I mean," he warns.

Sighing in defeat, I slowly remove my hands from his neck, but he catches them before they even reach his pecs.

"Look, it's fine. Let's just forget this. Go back to not liking each other. It's easier."

"There's only one of us playing that game, sunshine. My feelings for you are the opposite. That's the problem. I haven't stopped thinking about those perfect lips or those perky tits. Every time you get angry at me, all I want to do is shove my cock in your pretty little mouth to shut you up. I've let you push me away. I don't think I'll be able to stop this if we start."

A chill runs up my spine at his declaration. This whole damn time, he's been pushing me away for the same reason. He likes to rile me up.

"I want this. Show me what you've got, big boy."

The next thing I know, my back is slammed against the tiled wall.

"You should be scared of me. You know who I am, you know what I do. Yet you still can't help but infuriate me. It's stupid, really," he taunts me as he hikes my dress up, grabbing my hips. His fingers pinch into my flesh as he lifts me up the wall. I wrap my legs around him as his erection rubs against my sensitive core.

A moan escapes my lips at the contact.

"Tell me to stop, sunshine. Tell me this is a horrible idea."

His eyes search mine, but he won't find what he's looking for.

"I can't. Don't you dare stop."

We stare into each other's eyes for what feels like a lifetime, his cock twitching against me, our heavy breathing filling the room.

"Don't say I didn't warn you." With that, the air is sucked out of my lungs and his lips crash down onto mine. The kiss quickly turns frantic, with his tongue possessing mine. I run my fingers through his hair. He groans. I can't breathe, but right now, I don't care. His rough hand cups my face, and he bites down on my lip.

"Ouch."

"Shut up, baby, you love it," he teases before slamming his lips back onto mine. My spine squishes against the wall. His other hand grabs my ass.

"God, your ass is fucking perfect. I can't wait to fuck it," he mumbles against my lips, and I whimper.

Mmm, he's an ass man.

He trails his fingers around to my front. The sensation makes me shiver as he reaches the hem of my tights. "Today, of all days, you actually dress for the weather." He chuckles, his hand sliding beneath the band and cupping my throbbing pussy through my satin thong.

"Fuck, sunshine, you are soaking for me," he growls, burying his head into my neck, leaving hungry kisses along my collarbone. I tip my head back to give him better access, forgetting all about where we are.

He shoves my panties to the side and parts my folds with his fingers. He starts to rub slowly all the way from my entrance to my clit. It feels heavenly. My eyes roll into the back of my head.

"Mmm, yes, keep going," I moan, rocking my hips with his rhythm. "Oh, fuck," I shout as he slides two fingers inside me. My walls tighten around them. His other hand shoots up and muffles my moans.

"Keep that pretty little mouth shut for once," he says, removing his hand, as I nod in response.

"I mean it, otherwise I'm going to have to find other ways to keep you quiet."

Those words, the demanding tone, send waves of pleasure straight to my core. He ups the momentum of his fingers. I have to bite down on my lip so hard to stop any noise coming out, I'm sure I'll pierce the skin. His thumb circles my clit. The sound of my juices as he slams in and out of me fills the room. I'm so close to the edge that it's on the tip of my tongue to tell him.

"I want to taste you. I'm fucking starving. The service is too slow here," he rasps.

He scans the room, as if sensing my inner struggles about where we are. His hands come back to my hips, and I tighten my legs around him. He walks us over to the main door of the bathroom, and my back slamming up against it. I shoot him a questioning look, and he gives me that grin of his.

As I stand on shaky legs, he drops to his knees before me, looking back to me with burning desire. I feel suddenly unsure of myself.

Not that he gives me much time to think as he shoves my dress up and rips my tights and panties down in one swift movement.

"Fucking hell, don't ever wear tights again," he growls, yanking up one of my feet and slipping the boot off and then the other, followed by my underwear, leaving my long legs on display.

"Hook your legs over my shoulders," he commands as he resumes his position between my legs, grabbing one and then the other, settling them on his shoulders. My body weight is resting on him as I lean back into the door. My hands are splayed either side of me against the door to keep my top half up.

"God, you don't know how many times I've imagined doing this," he says, peppering kisses along my inner thighs, sending me straight back into pure pleasure.

His tongue connects with my clit, and he laps it up. Alternating between licking and sucking, his fingers take me by complete surprise as they start thrusting in and out of me. I throw my forearm up to my mouth and bite down to muffle my moans.

The pressure builds, blood pumping in my ears, my whole body on fire. I snap my eyes shut and let the feeling roll through my body.

"Eyes on me. Watch me devour you as you come all over my face." His breath flutters against my pussy.

I snap my eyes back to him. His striking blues are filled with pure hunger as his mouth sucks on me. Everything becomes too much. He hits every right spot. My walls clench around him as he laps up my orgasm.

"Oh my God, Grayson," I scream out. Fuck the rules. I continue to ride my orgasm.

He slows up the pace as I pant up against the door.

Fuck.

An emptiness consumes me as he slips his fingers out and carefully guides me down onto my trembling legs. I'm a complete mess.

He yanks my dress down to cover me up and stands, but stays only inches from me.

He tucks my hair behind my ear and brings his lips down onto my swollen ones, the taste of my sweet juices still smeared over him.

"I-I—" Words fail me. He's literally fingered the words out of me. I cup his massive cock through his pants and ask, "What about you?"

"You think that was all just for your pleasure?"

His deep laugh echoes in the empty room and it makes butterflies erupt in my stomach.

"We're doing this again, sunshine. You can do whatever the hell you want with me." He runs his hand over his face, letting out a ragged breath.

What the fuck is going on?

I wrap my arms around his neck and pull him into me. I move to plant my lips onto his for a soft kiss, but he quickly turns his head to the side so my lips graze across his stubble.

"What the fuck, Grayson? You've just fucked the words out of me and are now turning away from a fucking kiss. Are you serious right now?"

Hurt flashes across his face as my hand connects with his chest to push him away from me. He doesn't budge, though.

"Move, Grayson. It's okay, we won't do it again. I get it, you probably have a one-and-done rule and I've just used my ticket. I won't cry about it. Go back to your date. You can stick your dick in her to finish yourself off."

I bend down and pick up my clothes and boots from the floor and storm past him toward the stalls.

"For fuck's sake," Grayson mutters behind me, but I just roll my eyes and continue on.

Flinging open the stall door, I waltz in and turn to close

it. Grayson's strong arm flies out and holds the door open. He looms over me like a madman.

"Get out."

"No," he says.

"We're done."

He crowds me.

"Maddie, I want you. Make no mistake about that," he says, stopping a breath away from me.

"So why not kiss me?"

"That's complicated, sunshine."

"Well, I don't do complicated."

"Oh, I think you do. But here, let me uncomplicate things just for you," he whispers against my lips, cupping my blushed cheeks in his hands and sending tingles down my neck.

I close my eyes and sink into the gentlest of kisses. Our mouths explore each other in the most sensual way.

I could stay like this forever.

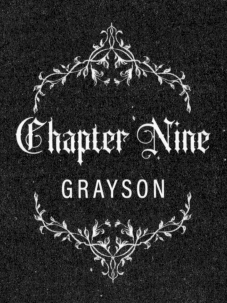

Chapter Nine

GRAYSON

The way her soft plump lips dance with mine, the way she hums in response. It's perfect, it's dangerous.

I don't know what possessed me to follow her in here. The way she scuffled past the table holding back tears gave me a weird feeling. I have to give her credit; the whole tripping me in front of my *date* was truly a masterpiece. I would expect nothing less from my blonde bombshell. We both know she doesn't hate me. Hell, she just let me devour her pussy against a door, for fuck's sake.

God, if that was the appetizer, I can't wait to have the main course.

She's going to erupt when I show her what it's like to be fucked properly.

I know I shouldn't be doing this, but after nearly a year of this sexual tension, it would always have come to this. There was no other endgame.

She shattered my no-kissing rule and now look at me,

gently caressing her lips and exploring her mouth with my tongue, lapping up the remains of that sweet prosecco.

When it comes to my sunshine, I think she's about to break every rule.

I break the kiss, leaving her looking at me with her brows furrowed. I rest my lips on her forehead and pull her slim frame into mine, distracting her so I can listen.

A feeling in my gut tells me something isn't right.

After years of training in the special forces, I know to always trust my gut. I can sense danger before it even arrives. I'm on my date with Amara, Marco's cousin. We knew this would lure them out, but I didn't plan on Maddie being here. She's the last person I want mixed up in this.

Frantic shouting in Italian has me reaching for the semiautomatic holstered in my suit pants. My fingers are itching to pull it out. Gunshots echo around the room. Maddie flinches against me as they ring out. I squeeze her tighter into me, looping my fingers around the handle of my gun.

"Grayson, what was that? My parents are in there," she says through a trembling breath.

Maddie shakes like a leaf against my body.

This is a normal day in my life.

"I'll make sure they are okay. I'm going to go. Under no circumstances do you leave this bathroom. Lock the door and do not unlock it for anyone other than me. Okay?"

She nods, tears streaming down her face.

"Sunshine, this is what I'm trained to do. I'm gonna go out there, eliminate the problem, and then I'm taking you home." I need her to stay strong. I can't have her walking into danger.

"What if you get hurt?" she whispers.

"I won't. They haven't got anything on me, baby." I wink and press a quick peck to her lips, removing the gun from my waistband. Her eyes go wide as she spots the semiautomatic in my hand.

I rush out of the bathroom and peer out toward the main door that leads to the restaurant, waiting and listening. I need to know how many of these cocksuckers are in here before I do anything in front of a room full of innocent civilians.

"Sir, please, we are going to have to call the police if you don't put your weapon down," a woman pleads to a man. I'm going on the assumption there is only one here.

"Amara, get the fuck over here. The fuck you think you're doing? You fucking stupid woman," a man shouts in his deep Italian accent. Gasps fill the room as he moves closer. This was the plan.

She's the wildcard that refuses to bow down to her cousin. I scoped this place out on many occasions. I picked the perfect table, past the restrooms. My plan was always to go to the bathroom but not with Maddie. She was a welcome distraction.

I stand quiet, listening for footsteps. Just when they reach me, I fling open the door and grab the short Italian man by the throat. Fear flashes in his eyes as he frantically draws his gun up so I'm staring straight into the barrel. His hands tremble as I tighten my grip around his neck.

He won't shoot me, for the same reasons I haven't killed him on the spot. Too many eyes on us.

"I don't fucking think so," I spit out, violence dripping from my tone.

As much as I'd love to blast his brains out, I can't. Not here, anyway. I'm here to deliver a message, because apparently burning their warehouse to the ground with three of their men inside and stealing back our shipment of cocaine wasn't enough. They were then stupid enough to retaliate by taking Nico.

I whack the gun out of his hand with my own, and it clatters on the floor. I draw my blade from my back pocket and bring it up to his forehead. I push it in enough to pierce the skin. Crimson drips from the wound. I drag the knife all the way along his forehead and down to his cheek, slicing his flesh as I do. He sucks in a breath, biting his lip. He's starting to tremble in my grip.

He's now blinking through the blood dripping over his eyelids as I drag him in closer while bending down to his ear.

"You tell Marco just how easy it was to pick up one of his family members, and you couldn't stop me. If he carries on, we will take every single person he cares about, one by one. He has twelve hours to return Nico, unharmed. If you don't, then say goodbye to pretty Amara over there," I say, nodding over to an unbothered Amara, biting on her manicured nails.

I kick his guns away and release him. He grabs his throat and gasps for breath. He nods, turns on his heel, and runs back out of the restaurant.

Maddie's parents look on in horror. From the two-minute interaction I've had with her mother, I can already say I don't like her. I gather she was the reason Maddie was running from the table in tears. I remember listening to Sienna going on to Keller once about how worried she was about Maddie. She seemed to think her mom was piling on too much pressure on her to find a boyfriend and get married.

I say she's had a lucky escape avoiding marriage.

I take a deep breath and plaster on a smile, for Maddie's sake. But like fuck am I letting her go home with them. They don't deserve a ray of light like Maddie if this is how they treat her.

As I approach their table, her mom gives me a tight smile, but her eyes give her away. She's fearful of me. As she should be.

"Mr. and Mrs. Peters," I greet them, extending my hand.

Blood drips from my fingers, so I quickly wipe them over my pants and put my hand back out. Maddie's dad, despite looking horrified, shakes my hand.

"Robert," he replies.

"Grayson, wasn't it? Do you know where Maddie is?" her mom questions in a patronizing tone.

"She's safe. I am going to take her home now."

"We can't let her go home with this madman. Did you see what he just did?" her mom shouts at Robert.

"I assure you, she is more than safe with me. It wasn't a question. Have a lovely evening," I say, needing to get away from this already-exhausting conversation and back to Maddie.

I turn toward the bathrooms, giving Amara a quick wink on my way past. Her hand flies out and catches my fingers. I immediately withdraw them from her touch.

"You know, I don't care what my cousin says. Come, sit, have a drink with me and then you can fuck my brains out later," she purrs, crossing her legs in some strange attempt to seduce me.

"No thanks," I reply, leaving her openmouthed.

I head toward the bathrooms and push open the door. A sudden urge consumes me to get to Maddie.

"Sunshine, it's me. You can open up now."

The lock clicks, and she slinks out of the doorway, her eyes puffy and red, makeup streaming down her face. Her eyes meet mine and then roam over my body, as if assessing to see if I'm really there.

"Oh, thank God, you're okay. I was so worried." She sags in relief, her hand pressing against her chest.

"You were worried about me?"

I can't remember the last time someone was this concerned about my safety.

"Ugh, of course I was worried about you. You went running out there when someone had a gun!" The panic is clear in her voice.

I open my arms out to her. "Come here, sunshine."

She runs and leaps into my arms, wrapping her legs around my middle, nuzzling her face in the crook of my neck.

"Can you see why this is a bad idea now?" The words are gutting me to actually say, but it's the truth. This is my life.

Her face snaps up to mine, a serious look masking her pretty features.

"I still want this."

My cock springs to life as her pussy rests against it. I swear I can feel heat radiating off her. My hands grip her ass cheeks and I bring my lips down to her neck and suck.

A moan falls from her lips, and I smile.

"Grayson, I want you, no, I *need* you to fuck me. But if you think you're fucking me in a bathroom, you have another thing coming."

Ah, there's my feisty girl.

"Well, we better get out of here before I bend you over the sink and fuck you then. Because I'm about a minute away from doing just that if you continue to grind your sweet pussy on me," I whisper, which earns me another moan.

I think we've officially passed the point of no return.

She slides her legs down, and I hold on to her hips as her feet land on the tiled floor.

"I need to say bye to my parents," she says, biting her lip.

"No need, I've already told them you are coming with me."

Shocked, she doesn't move from her spot.

"Come on, I can't wait to be balls deep inside you. Let's go." I hold out my hand to her and she accepts. A grin stretches her lips.

I head for the back exit and toward the parking garage. I open up the passenger door and guide her in with my palm on her lower back. It's almost weird for us, being so nice to each other.

She gives me a small smile through the passenger window, and that's enough to make me forget any doubts swirling around my mind.

She knows I'm a monster and wants to fuck me anyway.

Chapter Ten

MADDIE

We left the twinkling lights of Times Square a long time ago. I have no idea where he lives, but I assumed it wasn't far from there.

But what do I know about Grayson?

His heavy breathing is the only sound other than the hum of the engine. I don't dare to sneak a glance, for I might be unable to stop myself from pouncing on him and fucking his brains out. Even the way he was gripping the steering wheel, the veins protruding out of his hands, made me all hot.

"I didn't realize you lived so far away," I say, turning to face him.

"We aren't going to my place." His deep, husky voice makes my heart rate quicken.

"Right, so where are we going? A hotel?"

"Nope." His eyes never leave the road as he replies.

A few moments pass, and Grayson takes a sharp left, into almost complete darkness. Not even a single streetlight illuminates the surroundings. Fear tingles in my body when I remember who I've actually gotten in a car with.

A man who works for the mafia. Shit, a man who *kills* for the mafia.

"This isn't funny, Grayson, you're scaring me now. Just take me home." Panic laces my voice. He smirks, as if he's relishing my fear.

He slows the car as we approach what looks to be the remains of an industrial unit. I squint to assess, but the only thing lighting the place up is the car's headlights.

I'm alone at shit knows where.

He shuts off the engine. The silence is almost deafening.

He's staring at me with an intensity. With a carnal hunger in his eyes that rips deep into my soul. He brings his fingers up to the side of my face and gently strokes down. I flinch in response but the desire builds in my core, causing me to clench my legs even tighter.

"Grayson, what are you doing?" My body's on high alert as the interior lights go out, blanketing us in darkness.

"Do you want to know where we are?"

I nod.

"Well, this is the warehouse I burned to the ground the day I saw you at Keller's. Over there are three burned corpses." His voice is steady.

Should I be more scared of him? Probably.

No matter what he says or does, my heart has this weird pull toward him.

"And? You know I know what you do. You know I'm not scared of you. So, why?"

"I need you to realize I'm not your Prince Charming, sunshine. There's no sugarcoating here; I want to fuck you. I've wanted to fuck you since the moment I laid eyes on you last year. But I can't ever love you. And I really don't want to break your heart either."

I let the words sink in. His words do hurt, but I know he's right. My body shivers as the cold air filters into the car. For once in my life, I'm going to do something for myself. I want this.

"Then just fuck me—" Before I can finish my sentence, he yanks the back of my head and slams his lips to mine. He consumes me completely. His tongue swirls around mine, laced with the remnants of scotch.

I wrap my arms around his neck and pull him closer, and he smiles against my lips. He breaks away from me. His fingers softly trace my lips, pulling down my bottom lip with his index finger.

"Suck," he commands, then thrusts his finger into my mouth, almost hitting the back of my throat. I bite down on his finger, and he draws in a breath.

"I said suck, not bite, sunshine." His breath brushes against my cheek and sends shivers down my spine. His soft lips press wet kisses along my jaw, and I suck on his finger.

"That's a good girl. Now imagine that's my cock. Think how full your pretty little mouth is going to be when I fuck it," he whispers and bites down on my earlobe, instantly drenching my panties.

He pulls out his finger slowly with a pop. He has that lopsided grin painted across his gorgeous features.

I reach over the center console and undo his trousers as he leans back, giving me better access. I unzip them, displaying his thick shaft that's straining against the fabric of his boxers. I lick my lips, then give him a seductive smile. He rakes his hand over his face and groans as I wiggle his trousers and boxers down to free his cock. I wrap my fingers around the shaft and start to tug up and down, using my other thumb to swipe up the little bit of white liquid coming out the tip, bringing my thumb up to my mouth and licking the juices off. The salty pre-cum swirls around my tongue.

"Fuck, sunshine," he groans as I continue to pump his cock. His head slams back against the headrest, his eyes squeezed tightly shut.

His left arm shoots out, his fingers lacing tightly around my neck. I let go of his dick and grip his muscular forearm, uselessly pulling his hand that's closing my windpipe. I try to lean back, away from his grip. He smirks as I try to back away, then nuzzles his face into my neck. Part of me wants to run away. But most of me is turned the fuck on. All I can think about is him slamming his cock inside of me, making me scream out until I can't take anymore.

He loosens the hold around my throat, and I gasp in a deep breath. Relief washes over me, replaced with pure desire.

I need him. Now.

"I thought you said you were going to fuck me, Grayson?" I say through a shaky breath.

He twirls a finger around a lock of my hair, then pulls, sending piercing pain right into my scalp. He forces my face up, my neck completely on display for him. "My dirty, filthy girl wants to be fucked." His gravelly voice beats against my sensitive skin, sending tingles through my entire body.

Fuck, he called me his.

I grab his face and suck on his bottom lip. His hand grasps the back of my head, pulling my hair to the point that it burns my scalp. The pain only intensifies my aching desire for this man. His hands ride up my dress to the hem of my tights.

"These fucking tights . . ." he moans in annoyance, then

rips them off. My shoes are next, and then he bunches up my dress around my waist. "It's too fucking cramped in here. For what I have in mind, we need space," he says, lifting himself off me and sitting back in the driver's seat, leaving me half naked, panting, and ready to explode.

"Are you fucking serious right now?"

He chuckles and opens the driver's door, slipping out and slamming it shut.

What the fuck?

The next thing I know, the passenger door I'm leaning against flies open, sending me hurtling backward.

"Grayson!" I scream, bracing myself to smash my head against the rubble. His strong arms grab hold under mine, and he pulls me out of the car. His expression is full of mischief. I lace my legs around his torso, his rock-hard cock digging into my ass.

He walks us around the hood of his car, the headlights still the only source of light in this dump. He gently places my bare ass down on the warm hood, the engine still rumbling, vibrating against me. He lays me down and covers my body with his.

"Much better. Now, I can fuck you properly," he whispers, pressing a soft kiss to my lips and stroking my cheek with the front of his hand.

"Please, Grayson," I beg.

He tuts and traces his fingers over my dress, finally reaching my panties. I close my eyes and tip my head back. He rips off my thong, the freezing air assaulting my skin as he pulls apart my legs, leaving me exposed to him.

"God, you're fucking soaked and ready to take my cock, aren't you, sunshine?"

"Hmm . . ." I hum.

He traces his fingers along the inside of my thigh, just brushing over my sensitive pussy, which causes me to moan in frustration.

"A greedy girl, I see." He slides his index finger from my clit down to my entrance, and just that sensation alone has my legs trembling.

He chuckles and slams his fingers into me.

"Oh, fuck yes, Grayson, more!" I moan, arching my back away. The ferocity of his movements almost tips me over the edge.

"Is my pretty little whore ready for my cock yet?"

I've never been spoken to like that, and fuck, I like it. I'll be his whore any day of the week.

"Please . . ."

He whips his fingers out of me, leaving me with an emptiness. His strong hands grab my waist, flipping me over to my stomach. My hands fly out in front of me to take the impact against the warm, rumbling hood of his car. His cock slides up and down my slit, and I bite down hard on my bottom lip to contain myself.

He curls my hair around his fingers, yanking my head back, exposing my neck, making me shout out in pain as it rips at my scalp at the same time he slams his cock into me, sending waves of pleasure straight through me.

"Holy fuck, Grayson."

He bends over my back, bringing his lips to my sensitive neck and biting down hard, while thrusting in and out of me with ferocity. The sounds of his hips slamming against my ass cheeks and our heavy panting are the only noise. My whole body begins to tremble around him; as he nips and sucks at my throat, his other hand finds my ass cheek and grabs tight, yanking my body back onto his dick.

"Fuck, you are perfect, sunshine," he grunts out between thrusts.

"I'm so close," I pant out, squeezing my eyes shut as waves of pleasure barrel through me.

With that, he flips me onto my back to face him. He pulls me toward his cock, entering me and leaning his muscular frame to cage me in, his hands on either side of my head.

Bringing his face to mine, he whispers, "I want to see your pretty little face as you come, sunshine," before his lips collide with mine, which finally tips me over the edge. Blood pumps in my ears, and my heart almost beats out of my chest as he fucks me and devours my mouth at the same time. I'm moaning into his mouth, biting at his lip. "Scream for me, sunshine, I want even the demons in hell to hear you scream my name," he says, and I grab both sides of his head as I come undone, my body violently shaking, screaming his name from the top of my lungs. "Fuck!" he roars, reaching his own release, filling me up.

He slows down the pace, now gently rocking in and out of me, my legs still trembling around his frame.

"Fuck, sunshine. That was . . . fuck," he says. I whip my gaze to his. He's running his hand over his face, letting out a ragged breath. He gives me a smile and presses a soft kiss to my forehead.

"Come on, let's get out of here." He holds out his hand and I take it. I can't believe we did that here of all places. My thoughts lead me to the dead bodies, and I snatch my hand back and duck under his arm. He cocks an eyebrow at me in confusion. With a roll of my eyes, I head toward the passenger door, flinging it open and getting in.

He jumps into the driver's seat and slams the door with a wild look on his face.

"What was that about?"

"Nothing." It all hits me like a ton of bricks. That was by far the best sex I have ever had. However, sadness consumes me as I realize . . .

We can't do this again. He could never be the man I need him to be, so I can't let my heart get attached.

Chapter Eleven

GRAYSON

Holy fuck.

I knew sex with Maddie would be incredible. But that? That was world-shattering. Everything about her draws me in. She fucks like she was made to fuck me and only me.

Now that I've had a taste, I know I won't be able to give this up. I can't.

As I'm driving us back to my penthouse, I can't help but keep glancing at her. She's not spoken a word since we got in the car; she's staring out of the passenger window, her bright blonde hair all wavy and messy, half of her clothes still off. She basically looks freshly fucked and perfect.

I should have known after that damn kiss, she would change my world. I rest my hand on her thigh, and she sighs. Her eyes are all puffy and red.

Like earlier tonight, seeing her in any pain feels like a knife through my heart. Fuck, I'd even say it's worse than discovering your wife has been fucking your best friend. I *knew* that wasn't love. The day Maddie kissed me only solidified the fact. Never once had I felt any real sliver of love when my wife kissed me. I've stayed away from Maddie because I can't risk hurting her. My black heart isn't capable of loving her the way she needs, the way she desperately craves being loved.

But I'm a selfish dick, and for as long as she will let me fuck her, I'll keep taking it.

I wipe the tear away, and she gives me a sad smile.

"Sunshine, what's up?"

"It's just been a bit of a day. It's all too much. Can you take me home?" she says.

"No. I want you in my bed tonight. It's closer and I'll take you home in the morning. Okay?" The words come out before I even know what I'm saying. I sound like a sappy dick, but a big part of me wants to wrap her up in my arms and fall asleep.

She nods and leans into my hand.

"Good girl."

Gone is the sadness in her eyes, replaced by the hunger that dances behind them. I smirk and slide my hand down her body, landing back on her thigh. My dick twitches against my pants. I grip the steering wheel and slam my foot on the accelerator. I need to get us home before I fuck her in another parking lot.

NERVES DANCE IN my stomach as I pull into the underground garage of my building, nodding to the two security guards to open the barrier.

Something about letting Maddie into my home scares me.

"You know you live somewhere fancy when a security guard has to let you in." She chuckles.

"Damn right it's fancy, just you wait," I reply, giving her a wink.

Leaving Chicago and coming to New York, meeting Luca and Keller, changed my life. I park the car in my designated spot and kill the engine.

"Come on, let's get you to bed," I say. Her laughter fills the car. I open the door and slide out, making my way around the front of the car to the passenger side. I fling open the door and bend down, grabbing her by her waist. Her legs wrap around my middle and her arms loop round my neck, her breath hitting my throat.

"Do you have to? You know I can walk, right?"

"I saw how shaky your legs were, sunshine. Thought I'd do you a favor."

"Asshole."

I roll my eyes and slap her ass. I can't help but notice the little moan that escapes her lips, giving her true feelings away. I stride over to the elevator and jab the button, and it quickly pings open. I walk in and press for floor 52, and the doors close behind us.

Maddie's head flings up from against my shoulder as she looks around the mirrored elevator. Her eyebrow cocks, and she gives me a seductive smile.

Before I know it, the elevator doors slide open, and I let out a breath, putting her back on her feet.

"Oh wow, this is . . . it's so you." Maddie says, taking in her surroundings. The penthouse is open-plan with floor-to-ceiling windows that look out on the twinkling skyline. The interior is dark, just how I wanted it. Black and white monotones. It's clean and tidy. Placing my hand on the small of her back, I lead her through the lounge and to the kitchen. She jumps up on one of the barstools at the counter, placing her elbows on the side, resting her chin in her palms, just watching me as I grab a couple of glasses.

"Drink?" I ask, holding up one of the crystal glasses to her.

"Water, please."

I grab a glass and fill it with some cold water and place it down in front of her.

"Mmmm," she moans as she downs the glass, little droplets dribbling across her chin. My hand darts out and I cup her jaw. Moments pass between us, our breathing heavy, but no words are spoken.

I have no fucking clue what I am doing.

But those luscious, sparkling lips are screaming at me to kiss them. I bend down and grip the back of her head, forcing her face into mine and claiming her lips. It's like being a teenager and having your first kiss all over again. Now I can't seem to stop.

I deepen the kiss and my tongue swirls around the inside, which is still cold from the water. She moans into my mouth. Everything I do, she responds so perfectly to. My dick painfully strains in my pants. I want to fuck her badly, *again*. I trail my fingers along her dress until I reach the hem, breaking the kiss and pulling it over her head.

I take a minute to admire the view in front of me. The one woman my heart has ever skipped a beat for, the one woman who I never thought I would get to taste, to fuck, is here, in my penthouse, waiting for me to fuck her. Again.

This is what I wanted, right? Then why do I feel like shit, taking something from her when I know I can't give her what she wants? My mind spins, but her voice snaps me back into reality.

"Grayson, are you okay?"

I shake my head and pull my fingers through my hair. She cocks her brow and huffs in annoyance, snaking her arms behind her. The straps of her black bra fall down her biceps as she rips it off, holds it out in front of her between her thumb and index finger, and drops it on the floor.

She knows damn well how much I love her boobs.

A mischievous smile spreads across her lips as she crosses one leg on top of the other.

"Are you just going to stand there staring at me, or are you going to fuck me? If it's the first option, I suggest you take me to the bedroom."

It's enough to bring me back to her. I want her like I've never wanted anyone else in my life. But this nagging voice in the back of my head just won't shut the fuck up. Without saying a word, I lift her into my arms.

I walk us toward my bedroom and kick open the door. Lifting the covers, I place her gently on the bed and tuck her in. She flicks me a confused look. I quickly shuck off my clothes and fold them neatly on the stool in the corner of the room. Sliding under the covers, I wrap my arms around her, bringing her back tightly against me. Her luscious ass teases my cock. Cupping her breast in one hand, I bring my lips to the back of her neck, giving it a kiss. The sweet sounds of her raspy moans fill the room.

I don't want to just fuck her.

I want to consume her. I want to take it all. But also, I want her to have all of me.

I start peppering kisses all the way down her spine, her back arching slightly as I make my way down. Until her ass is in my face. I bite down on her ass cheek, hard. Enough to make her squeal. I chuckle, rubbing where I bit her. She rolls on her back, and I spread her legs, positioning myself between them, kissing and licking along the inside of her thigh. She thrusts her hips up in response and I push them back down.

"Grayson, please," she whines, moving her hips back up toward my face again.

Placing a firm hand on her stomach, I lick all the way up from her entrance to her clit and back down again, as delicately as I can. A single swipe has her legs twitching next to my head.

I quickly slide my index finger into her. I know it's not enough for her. I get some of her juices smothering my finger and slip it back out, running it slowly toward her back entrance. Her body goes still as I tease the hole, waiting to gauge her reaction.

When she bucks her hips up again, giving me full access to her ass, that's it. I slam my mouth over her clit and suck as my finger slips into her ass.

"More, Grayson, I need more!" she moans as I fuck her ass with my finger. I thrust three digits in her pussy, keeping to the same pace as the one in her ass, lapping her up at the same time. My dick threatens to explode as she now fucks my face, screaming my name from the top of her lungs. Her legs hook around my neck as her body shakes.

I know she hasn't finished, so I take my opportunity. I remove my fingers and climb over her. She opens her legs even wider to give me room. Grabbing her left thigh, I bend it toward her chest, and using my free hand, I line my dick up. With one swift thrust, I slam into her.

"Oh my God, Grayson!"

"Fuck," I hiss. "Tell me you're close," I pant out through gritted teeth.

"So close."

She writhes, combusting around my cock. I let go, spilling everything I have into her, shouting her name so loud I sound feral. Without leaving her, I bend down and kiss her. She smiles against my lips, and I stroke a stray hair from her face. Reluctantly, I slide out of her and roll off the bed, heading straight for the en suite. I need a minute to compose myself.

Turning the tap to cold, I splash my face with the water, hoping it calms me down. My heart is still racing. *Why does she have to be perfect for me? Why couldn't I have just left this alone?* I know damn well I wouldn't be able to stop myself. Since the moment I first laid eyes on her, I knew she was it for me.

And now that I've had her, there's no going back—not for my heart, anyway.

The one she will rip straight from my chest when she finally finds a man worthy of her, a man who can give her everything I never could.

With a final splash of cold water, I grab a cloth and head back into the bedroom.

Maddie's breathing is steady, and she doesn't even flinch as I enter. I quickly clean her up and she stays sleeping the whole time. As quiet as I can, I get into bed and snuggle up to her. This has to be the last time this ever happens.

A dark cloud settles back over me as I close my eyes.

"Good night, my gorgeous sunshine," I whisper.

Chapter Twelve

MADDIE

The sunlight burns my eyes. I roll onto my side, expecting to find a sleeping Grayson. Instead, all that's there is a pillow, and a feeling of loneliness consumes me. Sleeping with his strong arms wrapped around me was nice. I felt safe.

Sitting up, I stretch out my arms and let out a yawn. I have no idea what time we actually went to sleep. Hell, I can't even remember going to sleep.

All I know is I was fucked into oblivion by Grayson. And now here I am, in his bed under his silky black comforter. I slip out of the covers and head over to the drawers. His clothes are all folded in color-coordinated piles, and it's actually very pleasing to look at. After living with a messy Sienna for years, I'm used to everything being a bomb site. But here is a man who does laundry and folds neatly. Maybe I was wrong about him.

I throw on one of his black T-shirts. I'm not short, but it hangs off me like a dress. Oh well, he's seen me in worse.

I head to the en suite only to be greeted by a sparkling white bathroom. It has floor-to-ceiling windows that look out onto the pretty skyline. I had no idea Grayson was this rich. I spy a stunning waterfall shower in the back corner. Not wanting to overstay my welcome, I settle with a quick face wash and brush my teeth.

Then I make my way to the kitchen. The banging coming from there piques my interest.

"For fuck's sake, where's the fucking spatula," Grayson shouts as I jump up on the barstool and watch him. He hasn't even noticed I'm here yet, being busy bent down, yanking open drawers and cupboards.

"Morning," I say chirpily.

He pops up from the counter, looking flustered, in just a pair of shorts. I scan his body, taking in every ripped muscle, every dark tattoo that spans both of his arms and his pecs. Wait, he has his nipple pierced? I lick my lips as I imagine biting his piercing. God, he even has that perfect V.

"Morning, sunshine." He gives me one of those panty-dropping grins, the ones I so used to hate.

"Oooh, so I get breakfast as well," I tease. "I thought you didn't do sleepovers, let alone breakfast. God, I must be special." I give him a cheeky smile.

"Mmm," is all he says before turning his attention to the frying pan.

Weird.

A phone vibrates on the countertop.

"It's yours," Grayson calls out.

God, I hadn't even thought about my phone. I lean over and grab the phone. Gregory's name flashes on the screen. Shit.

I answer.

"Hey, Maddie, how are you?"

"Hey, I'm good, thanks. You?"

"I'm fine."

Grayson's head jerks around, his eyes boring into mine.

Oh, shit. He coughs, that little shit. He knows exactly what he's doing.

"Where are you?" Gregory asks.

"Uh, I stayed at a friend's."

"What friend?"

I don't like where this is going.

"Grayson."

"I thought you couldn't stand him?"

I lie, "He ended up giving me a lift home, and I was so drunk I crashed at his place."

"Right. I thought you went out for dinner with your parents?"

Oops.

"I did. I'll see you later?" I ask, feeling guilty.

He sighs. "Yeah, how about Italian?"

"Italian sounds good. I'll see you then," I respond and cut the call.

As I'm debating how to face Grayson now, he says, "You still hate me, sunshine? I think the number of times you screamed my name last night tells me different."

"Don't remind me." I reply.

He tuts, placing the plate of scrambled eggs in front of me. The smell makes my stomach rumble, and I remember how famished I am.

"Thank you," I say and dig in.

As soon as the buttery goodness hits my tongue, I moan.

"Yes, it was just like that. *Mmm, Grayson, more, please,*" he mimics me.

He grabs his own plate and pulls out the barstool next to me. Within minutes, he's already hogged it all.

"I feel guilty," I admit, lowering my gaze to the floor. I'm not with Gregory; we've had a few dates but that's it.

"What for?"

"I guess, sleeping with you when I should be putting effort into getting to know Gregory."

He stiffens.

"Are you fucking Gregory? Do you want to keep fucking him?"

I haven't fucked him, nor do I want to. Not that Grayson needs to know; ours was a one-time thing.

He jumps off the barstool, his eyes filled with rage. He grabs my waist and yanks me up, my butt crashing against the island counter, my face now level with his. My breath hitches as he brings his mouth to my ear.

"Let's get one thing straight here, sunshine. If you want me to keep fucking you until you see stars, no other man touches you. I'll keep it simple. I. Don't. Share."

How the hell is this turning me on?

His warm breath hits the sensitive skin below my ear. It takes everything in me not to wrap my legs around him and beg him to devour me.

But I know I can't do this.

A man like Grayson isn't going to want to keep me around. I close my eyes and sigh. I can't believe I was stupid enough to give in to this. I should have known that after that kiss, I wouldn't be able to stop.

"Well then, I guess it definitely was a one-night thing," I whisper.

"Fine." He pushes himself off the counter away from me.

His jaw clenches as he looks at me, just for a moment, before shaking his head and storming off down the hallway.

I pick up my phone from the counter and quickly type out a text to my receptionist, sending a location pin to where I am.

EVIE
I'll be there in fifteen minutes. I have SO many questions, Maddie!!

Oh, shit.

"Grayson," I shout. I don't have the energy to run after him today. My body is sore and my head is throbbing.

Nothing.

"I'm going now. I'll see you around."

When no response comes, I sigh and grab my bag, throwing the phone inside. With slow, hesitant steps, I make my way to the elevator. I'm about to press the call button when suddenly, a hand slams over mine and pulls me backward.

"What the fuck?"

He whips me around to face him, a pained expression flashing across his features. He almost looks tortured.

"It's not fine," he says.

"What?" I ask, tipping my chin up to him. I don't have time for his mood swings today.

"I don't think I can let you walk away. I can't let you fuck anyone else, Maddie." He rests his forehead against mine.

His confession hits me straight in the heart, stealing the air out of my lungs. Deep down, I know I don't want to stop this either. I know Gregory isn't the one. He's nice, he's reliable. But he's not mine. He doesn't set off a spark in me like Grayson. And what's wrong with a girl taking what she wants, anyway?

I cup his cheeks.

"I'll make you a deal. We keep doing whatever this is, exclusively. We *both* don't fuck anyone else. But I will keep dating. No one will touch me, but I'll date. If and when I find someone good enough, we stop this." I gesture between us.

"Does that mean I can fuck you anywhere and anytime I want?" he asks, hovering his lips over mine.

I nod.

"Now?" he says, taking my bottom lip between his teeth, his fingers skimming the hem of my T-shirt.

Shit. Evie.

He cocks his eyebrow at me as I push him away.

"I need to text my friend," I say, rustling through my bag and snatching my phone. I shoot her a text telling her not to worry. I'll deal with the grilling from her later.

My phone pings with a text, and Grayson leans over.

> **GREGORY**
> I've booked us a table at Rico's, 7pm.

"How original." Sarcasm drips from his tone.

"Oh yeah, where would you take me if we were dating?" I instantly regret asking this as his eyebrows raise, as if he's deep in thought.

"Where's the one place in the world you've always wanted to go?"

"London."

"There's your answer."

"Grayson, that's not how dating works. You don't just fly your date around the world. A restaurant works fine."

"I think that's where you're wrong, sunshine. If a man wants you, he won't stop until you are completely his. He will put the world at your feet and stop at nothing to see your smile light up the room. He will worship you." He closes the distance between us, my back flush against the elevator door.

"He will want you in every possible way. He will claim you, own you, and fuck you how you're supposed to be fucked."

Heat courses through my insides at his bold words.

"That's exactly how I would do it" is the last thing he says before he slams his lips over mine. He commands every inch of me, takes what he wants, and I let him.

The loud ringing from his pocket makes him break the kiss. "For fuck's sake," he mutters, sliding his phone out of his pocket.

"Two minutes. I have to take this." He presses a kiss to my nose.

My cheeks start to hurt from smiling so goddamn hard.

"Luca," he greets.

I stand there, my back still pressed against the door, breathing heavily as he walks away from me.

Grayson shouts, "What do you mean he's fucking dead? How?" making me jump. For a few moments there, I forgot who he is, what he does. How dangerous his life is.

All I can hear are muffled whispers now. God, I need to leave. Grayson strides back toward me, his eyes full of fury.

"I have to go. I'll drop you home on the way."

"Okay."

His eyes roam over my body. The next thing I know, he's scooping me up into his arms.

As we enter the elevator, I ask, "Are you okay? What's going on?"

"Nico's been murdered. They just dropped his mutilated body outside Luca's gates."

"I'm sorry. Nico was the guy who came and found me the day Sienna was kidnapped, right? The one who brought me to you."

He nods solemnly.

"What are you going to do now?" I ask, my curiosity getting the better of me.

"Hunt them down and give them slow, painful deaths."

"Just be safe, Grayson. Promise me."

He cocks his brow.

"Don't worry about me. I know what I'm doing."

"Promise me."

He sighs, his grip on me tightening slightly.

"I promise you."

"Thank you," I say and press a kiss on his stubbly jaw.

———————————•———————————

WE RIDE OVER to my apartment in silence. He slows the car down as we approach my building. I reach for the door handle, but he grips the back of my neck, turning me to face him.

"I'll text you later, okay?"

I nod.

Reluctantly, I turn away from him and open the car door. The cold breeze blows my T-shirt, reminding me that I'm not wearing any panties.

"Hey, do I not get a kiss goodbye now?" he says with a cheeky grin. I clamber back across the passenger seat on all fours and press my lips against his. He inhales as our lips connect.

I break the kiss and grin, shuffling back out of the car and slamming the door shut. I can feel his gaze on me the entire time I walk into my building. I open the door and head in with a quick wave to him. I need a shower, a nap, and some ice cream.

I have no clue what we're doing.

I have a date with another man, but all I want to do is rush back to be fucked by Grayson.

I can't stop the smile as I remember all the ways Grayson made me orgasm last night.

I can't resist him.

Maybe I'll take a little break from dating anyway.

Chapter Thirteen

GRAYSON

The moment Luca told me Nico had been murdered, my mind flashed back to Casper. The second he took his last breath in my arms when he ripped my life apart. It's all I see; the hurt stabs me through the heart as painfully as it did that day. Enough to take my breath away.

The anger, the torment, the burning urge to kill had taken over. I'd clocked out of life. Until Maddie asked me to promise her I would be safe. The concern on her face and the tenderness of her actions literally dragged me back from the depths of hell.

That's why I've kept my distance from her this week. It isn't fair that she worries about me and my safety. In reality, especially now, I want Maddie as far away from this as possible. I can't have her getting hurt.

We've had intel from Carlo, who handles our drug shipments. For now. Since he dealt with the Falcones, he has learned his lesson and is proving to be a handy source. He's informed us that the Falcones reached out to him this morning, asking for a meetup to discuss future shipments again. Luca told him to agree, so we set up a trap. They take the life of one of ours; we retaliate by taking two of theirs.

I drive over to the Falcones' warehouse in silence. Every time my mind veers off into the darkness, I think of Maddie's bright smile. She keeps me from falling off of the cliff.

I spot Luca's silver Bentley when I enter the parking lot. Pulling up next to him, I kill the engine, leaning over and opening the glove box to retrieve my gun and blade. Luca is already next to my car, puffing on a cigarette, the smoke wafting straight up my nostrils as I exit my car. He takes one long drag, the cherry illuminating bright red before he tosses it on the floor and stubs it out with his black leather loafers. Frankie stands behind him, arms crossed in one of his signature navy suits. With slicked-back black hair, he and Luca could pass as brothers.

"Boss," I say to Luca and nod to Frankie.

Luca nods in response, blowing smoke above his head. "You ready?"

"Always. These fuckers need to die."

"It seems every time we kill one, another two respawn from somewhere." There's an annoyance in his tone. He's been trying too hard to solidify his position as the boss in the organization. This isn't the life he chose; this is the life forced on him.

"We've got this!" I reassure him, but truly, I don't know where this ends.

Frankie claps Luca on the shoulder. "We, together, are unstoppable. Let's show these fuckers."

"Let's get this done, then we go and drink," Luca says, pulling his gun from his Armani suit jacket, turning his back, and marching over to the battered warehouse door. I follow his lead, my fingers tightly wrapped around my gun, my blade in my back pocket. Before we reach the door, I grab Luca by the elbow. If he had it his way, he'd go storming in without even scoping out the headcount in there.

"We can't trust Carlo. You hold still here. We'll scope it out and confirm there are only two Falcones in there." Then I address Frankie: "You take the right side of the building, I'll go left."

"Got it," Frankie responds, and Luca rolls his eyes at us.

Ten years of military training; there is no way I'm walking myself into a death trap.

Aiming the gun out in front of me, I creep toward the door just as voices echo throughout the building. They're talking in hushed Italian; I can only distinguish three people so far. The metal side door is slightly ajar. Leaning in, I peer through the gap. Immediately, I spot Carlo and his right-hand man, Dimitri.

There are two others, wearing gray suit trousers and white shirts. Looks like Carlo is working his way up our good books.

Spinning on my heel, I raise my hand and motion for Luca to come. A smirk forms on his lips as he pulls out his gun and stalks toward me, brushing straight past me. Frankie rounds the corner to join us. "All good on my side."

Luca kicks open the door. "Knock, knock, motherfuckers," he shouts, tapping his gun against the metal frame.

"For fuck's sake," I mutter, shaking my head. Honestly, he wouldn't have lasted ten minutes in the military. I follow closely behind him, my gun aimed at the Falcone on the left, Frankie's to the right.

"You motherfucker!" one shouts, lunging toward Carlo and grabbing him by the throat.

Carlo flings his head back, his eyes pleading with me. For a fucking drug dealer, he's a complete pussy.

Falcone's other man whips out a gun, pointing it straight at Luca. Before he even has a chance to aim it properly, I line up my shot and pull the trigger. The bullet goes straight into his forehead, and blood splatters out of the back of his head as he thuds to the floor. Carlo is dropped to the floor as the remaining Falcone grabs his gun from his waistband.

"I fucking wouldn't," I warn, my gun now aimed at him.

He doesn't move, but I'm not taking any chances.

I fire the gun at his chest. I don't want this to be a quick kill. The color instantly drains from his face as he clutches at his chest, crimson now staining his bright white shirt. He collapses to his knees. I stride over toward him, the barrel of my gun connecting to his temple.

"Please," he begs.

This is for Nico.

I grab the blade from my back pocket and hold it up against his throat, slowly swiping across from left to right. Blood pours out in the wake of the knife, dripping down his neck. He gurgles, now clawing at his throat. I lift my left foot and slam it into his chest. He tumbles over in a heap, bleeding out on the rubble.

I turn my attention to Carlo. "Make sure they are delivered to Marco tonight."

He frantically nods, his eyes wide, staring at the two dead bodies on the floor in horror.

"Pleasure doing business with you. We will see you next week for our shipment," Luca addresses Carlo.

"Come on, we have scotch to drink and women to fuck," he says, heading straight for the doors. Frankie laughs and follows him. I nod at Carlo before following behind.

"I'll meet you there, boss. I'll go freshen up. Keller will kill me if I go in there covered in blood."

With a snicker, Luca drives off.

AFTER QUICKLY STOPPING at home, I showered and changed into a charcoal-gray suit and white shirt. I've left my hair messy on top but sharpened the edges of my stubble. The End Zone doesn't get lively until around 10 p.m.

I park outside the back entrance of the club and unlock the door with my key card.

I make my way through the hallway, past the black office doors, toward the VIP area. I nod at the two security guards positioned by the door, who usher me through.

I spot Luca right away, his crystal tumbler against his lips, throwing his head back and downing the contents before slamming the glass back down on the table.

Shaking my head, I reach the booth and sprawl out. The blonde waitress returns quickly, placing our scotch on ice in front of us, with a shot of some clear spirit next to it. She gives me a shy smile and twiddles with her hair. God, all I want to do is pick up Maddie and bury myself in that perfect pussy. I let out a ragged breath and pick up my scotch, letting it burn all the way down.

Frankie returns from the bar with a tray of shots and a mischievous smirk on his face.

"You ready to get fucked up, Grayson? I've heard you're an

animal on a night out." Frankie winks, placing the shots on the table and thrusting one toward me.

"I'm an angel," I smirk, downing the shot and raising it in the air to Frankie. The licorice sambuca literally rips at my throat. Fucking disgusting.

Frankie slips in the booth next to Luca, downing his shot.

Luca nudges my ribs with his elbow, sporting a cheeky grin. I follow his line of sight and see three barely dressed women with their fake tits on display walking toward us.

"Really, Luca?"

"Since when aren't you up for getting laid?" Luca asks, his eyebrow raised.

Good point. Since a certain sunshine barreled into my life. Since that kiss, I can't say I've been too interested in entertaining other women. I've tried, but no matter what I do, I can't get Maddie out of my head.

"I'm just not feeling it tonight." I shrug, avoiding eye contact.

"Bullshit. It's Maddie, isn't it?"

"No," I lie, keeping my face straight.

He whacks my arm and laughs. "Grayson's pussy-whipped. Who'd have thought?!"

Frankie's head jerks around to me, and he chuckles.

"Who is she? Has she got any hot friends?" he questions, wiggling his eyebrows.

"Shut the fuck up," I spit out.

"Oh well, more for me." Luca turns his attention to the girls as they approach our booth, and the two brunettes instantly jump on Luca and Frankie. They're lapping the attention up as they drape themselves over their laps.

The blonde stands next to me, wearing the tightest,

shortest dress known to man. Her tits pop out of the top. She bites her lip as she slinks into the booth next to me.

"Sorry, sweetheart, not tonight," I say, and she pouts. Ignoring my request, she straddles my lap, her fake breasts now right in my face. Yes, she's attractive, but the only blonde I want on my lap isn't here.

"I can change your mind," she purrs into my ear, and I actually turn my nose up.

The temperature in the room changes. My heart starts fluttering like I'm having a fucking heart attack. The only time I've ever felt like this is when . . . Shit. Maddie.

"I said no. Now get the fuck off me."

I squeeze my eyes shut and pray Maddie hasn't just walked through that goddamn door. The woman finally gets the message and clambers off me. "Fuck you," she spits as she storms off, brushing right past Maddie.

Maddie's expression is . . . detrimental. She gives me a sad smile, turns on her heel, and leaves.

Fuck. Fuck, fuck, fuck.

I slam my fists on the table, the glasses spilling alcohol everywhere.

"For fuck's sake, Grayson. Go and get your girl before you end up killing someone." Luca waves me off.

I jump to my feet and sprint after her. I can take a pissed-off Maddie; I can even deal with a furious one. But a hurt one, that I can't deal with.

I push my way through the crowd, searching for those shiny bright blonde locks. It doesn't take me long. Her head is tipped back, mouth wide open, as another man pours a clear spirit into her mouth. All the while his other hand is on her ass.

Furious, I stalk over to her, my fists clenched, using every bit of willpower I have not to strangle this prick who's touching what's mine.

Once I reach them, I cough loudly.

"Hi, Grayson, this is . . ." She raises her brow at the prick.

"Mason."

"Yep, Mason. And this is my *friend*, Grayson."

He gives me a nod and pulls her closer into him.

Not a fucking chance.

"Come here, Maddie," I growl.

Her eyes widen, but she stays still. That little black dress does nothing to hide how she feels.

"Not now, Grayson," she snaps, and there's a slight shake in her voice.

"It wasn't a question, sunshine," I say as I move closer. The prick gets the message and releases his hold on her, stepping out of the way. Her back is up against the bar now as I close the distance between us. Putting my hands on either side of the bar behind her, I cage her in. That sweet, flowery scent calms me.

"With me." I shoot her a look. "Now."

She rises up on her tiptoes. "Make me." *Oh, here we go.*

"You'll regret that." I keep my voice low, and she tips her chin up, but the red flush creeping up her neck gives her away.

My bad girl wants to be punished.

Fuck it.

Grabbing the back of her head, I pull her in and shove my lips over hers. Tequila swirls around my tongue. She moans into my mouth, biting down on my lower lip. I hiss in response. My cock's already throbbing for her. I don't give a fuck that we're up against a bar in a nightclub. When I'm with Maddie, she's all I can focus on.

She's become an obsession. The light I crave at the end of a dark day. She's the one and only person on this planet whose happiness means more than anything.

"No one else touches you, Maddie. We literally made this deal a few hours ago."

Her lips turn up into a mischievous smirk. "I think you need to get that memo too, Mr. I-like-strippers-straddling-me."

I'm glad she feels the same way as me.

"Trust me, there's no other woman I want touching me." I brush my lips along her jaw. "And if you don't touch me in the next five minutes, I'll have to drag your ass out of here and fuck you down an alleyway. Your choice."

Her eyes light up.

She gives me one of her infectious grins and a quick peck. "Good boy. Now don't piss me off like that again." I can't help but laugh and shake my head. Relief washes over me. "Well, what are you waiting for?" she purrs, and that's all I need. Snatching her hand, I race past the VIP area, swiping the card and entering the office.

A large oak desk sits in the center with a black leather chair.

This will do fine. I drag her in and kick the door closed with my foot, slamming her back up against the door.

Her breathing turns to little pants as I grip her wrists and lift them over her head. My other hand slides down her perfect curves to the hem of her teasingly short little black dress.

Dipping two fingers in, I brush along her bare pussy.

"You mean to say, you let another man have his hands that close?" I grit out, slamming two fingers inside.

"N-no, I wasn't thinking."

"Did you want him to do this to you?"

Her head snaps to mine. "What? No. Never."

Relief washes over me.

"Good girl." I up the momentum, sliding in a third finger and tightening my hold on her wrists. Her back arches against the door. Her exposed skin tempts me.

Biting down on the sensitive flesh above her collarbone, I suck hard.

"Oh my God, Grayson!" she moans, her chest rising and falling frantically.

When I remove my fingers, her body sags against mine in frustration. Picking her up by the waist, I walk us over to Keller's massive desk that's scattered with paperwork and glasses. In one swoop, my hand clears the contents of the desk, and glass shatters all over the wooden flooring.

There's a bottle of Macallan in the array of drinks on the table next to me. I bring the bottle to my lips and take in a large mouthful.

"Delicious," I rasp, "but not as delicious as your sweet pussy."

Placing the bottle on the desk next to her, I bend over and unzip the side of her dress. She lifts her hips up into the air so I can drag the garment off her body, tossing it to the floor next to me.

"Beautiful," I say, my gaze scanning all the way up her body, her legs now spread to give me the full view of her pussy, drenched and ready for me. Her rosy buds are erect, demanding my attention.

I take her nipple in my mouth and suck. Then, I pick up the bottle and line myself up with her pussy.

"Pour. Let it roll down your stomach. I want to taste you at the same time," I command, placing the bottle in her trembling fingers.

She does as I say. I hover my mouth above her clit, my

eyes focused on the amber liquid rolling between her tits toward me.

"Keep pouring."

Keeping my eyes pinned on hers, I start to devour her, twirling my tongue around her clit, letting her sweet juices mingle with the scotch, drinking her up like a man fucking starved. The more I fuck her, the more drenched she gets.

"Fuck, baby. There is nothing more satisfying than knowing I can get you this soaked for me." I barely recognize my own voice. "Do you want a taste?"

Those dazzling emeralds pierce into me as she bites down on her lip and nods.

With one final lick, I stand, taking the bottle from her hand and knocking back the scotch. Placing the bottle back down, I bend over her, my hands lacing around her throat, my mouth full of liquid.

She licks her lips and opens wide, tipping her head back. Her silky blonde hair cascades down her back. I pour the liquid from my mouth into hers. The muscles in her neck tense under my fingers as I squeeze tighter.

Her throat bobs as she swallows.

"My two favorite flavors," I whisper.

She brings her middle finger up to her lip, catching the drop spilling from the corner.

"Now that's how a man should pour a drink into a woman's mouth," she says.

I cock a brow.

"Now it's my turn," she says, grabbing onto my shirt to pull herself up.

"Sit." She points to the black leather chair, pushing me away with her palm.

And fuck, having her boss me around is by far the sexiest thing I've ever experienced.

I spread my legs out and she steps between them. Her fingers frantically undo my belt and zipper and release my throbbing cock. She straddles me and laces her fingers around my shaft, lining it up with her entrance.

"Ride me, Maddie. Prove that pussy is mine."

Her eyes sparkle as she sinks down on my dick. Her walls clamp tight around me.

"You are perfect," I grit out. My hands squeeze the arms of the chair as she rides me, thrusting herself up and down. Biting down on her bottom lip, she cups my jaw.

"Fuck me like you own me, Grayson."

Grabbing her by the ass, I stand and back her into into the nearest free wall. I collar her throat tight, and she sucks in a breath. Her fingers grip my forearm as I start to fuck her. The faster I go, the tighter my grip gets around her neck.

Squeezing my eyes tight, I crash my lips over hers, loosening my grip around her throat so she can kiss me properly.

"Mine," I grit out between the kisses.

Tingles spread through my entire body as her walls clamp down on my cock. A few more thrusts and I erupt.

"Fuck!" I shout, pouring into her. She reaches her own release as her body violently thrashes against mine. She screams out my name and it's like music to my ears. I let her take everything she needs from me as my chest heaves.

I rest my forehead against hers, and we try to steady our breaths. Stealing a quick kiss, I regretfully pull myself out of her.

"Stay with me tonight?" I ask.

She rolls her bottom lip between her teeth, staring at me.

"Fine, but you owe me at least five orgasms before bed."

I brush my lips against her cheek.

"Let's call it six and you have a deal." I smile against her soft skin and nip at it, moving back and offering my hand to shake.

She stares at my outstretched hand, then places her dainty hand in mine and shakes with a grin.

Chapter Fourteen

MADDIE

We ride over to his penthouse in silence.

I steal a glance at him. Shit, even the way he drives, those veins popping out of his forearms as he clutches the steering wheel . . . I lick my lips.

"Admiring the view, sunshine?"

"No," I lie, rolling my bottom lip between my teeth.

His large hand smacks down onto my thigh, grabbing it tight.

"Are you lying to me?"

"N-no," I squeak.

"You, sweetheart, are a horrendous liar."

We pull into his building and he parks. As I'm about to exit, he rounds the car and bends down and scoops me up, flinging me over his shoulder, his hand firmly gripping my ass.

"Really, Grayson, it's about ten footsteps to the elevator." I roll my eyes.

"I saw you yawning. I'm conserving your energy. Now,

don't be mad, but I took the liberty of buying you a few supplies to keep here, like women's products."

"That's sweet, thank you."

After the quick elevator ride, we enter his apartment,
not even stopping as he takes us straight into the bedroom. Darkness envelops us. He places me on his soft bed.
Stretching my arms above my head, my eyes flutter closed.
His knuckles graze my cheek, and I melt against the softness
of his touch. As soon as he removes his hand, I feel empty.
He turns the bedside lamp on, and a warm light fills the
room. Standing up, I unzip my dress and let it fall to the floor.
Grayson's eyes never leave my exposed breasts. He scans my
entire body until his hungry eyes meet mine. My eyes inevi-
tably home in on the erection straining against his pants. The
way he eats me up gives me confidence.

I flick off my heels. He cocks his brow as they tumble
across the floor. If I had to guess, he hates mess. Everything
around him, even down to his clothing, his stubble, is immac-
ulate. And here I am, throwing my shit around the place like
I live here.

I pad over to him, rising up onto my tiptoes, rubbing up
against his clothed frame. My body tingles with desire. I nip
at his bottom lip and he groans. I trail my tongue along his
sharp jawline, his stubble tickling my tongue. "Touch me," I
purr in his ear, and he stiffens against me.

Running my hand up his body, I undo each button, starting from the top and working my way down. My fingertips
graze his rock-hard abs on my descent. His breath hitches as I
reach the buckle of his belt and unclasp it. Stepping back, he
shrugs off his suit jacket and shirt, leaving me drooling over
his defined body. I frown as he sits on the edge of the bed, his
pants still on, legs sprawled out.

He taps his thigh. "Sit."

Desire floods straight to my core as I close the distance between us. Hoisting my leg over his to straddle his thigh, my wet pussy throbs against his smooth suit pants. I start to grind my hips against him in slow movements, the friction from the fabric hitting the right spot. He cups my breast, and I arch my back, giving him better access. He takes my nipple in his mouth, his teeth biting into my sensitive flesh. The pain only accentuates the pleasure rippling through me. He switches between licking, kissing, and biting.

"More, Grayson," I moan.

"You're soaking my pants, sunshine. Absolutely fucking drenched for me."

I search for his dick, but he snatches my forearm to stop me. "You don't get to touch. Not yet."

"What, why?" I whine like a complete needy bitch. But I don't care; I need him.

With a final suck on my nipple, he removes his mouth. "On all fours and grab the headboard." His deep voice sends shockwaves straight to my pussy. *Jesus, this man and his mouth.*

"Don't make me repeat myself."

I shuffle off his lap and crawl around him, gripping the leather headboard with shaky hands. I suck in a breath as he swiftly removes his pants, finally freeing his cock. He stalks toward the bed, which dips as he climbs on, positioning himself behind me.

"Fuck, sunshine," he mutters. I jolt as his tongue connects to my clit and starts to make small circular motions while his fingers trail up the inside of my thigh toward my pussy. His fingers slam into my entrance.

"Oh God, Grayson," I pant, my chest heaving. My hips

buck of their own accord, meeting his rhythm, as he continues to lick and suck. My body sags as he removes his fingers, only to trace them around my back entrance. My pussy convulses around his mouth. I inch my hips back, and he inserts a finger. I quickly get over the alien feeling, which is replaced by euphoric pleasure.

"I can't wait to stick my cock in this tight hole."

"Mmm, yes."

He ups the pace, his tongue now lapping me up. "I'm so close, Grayson." The burning sensation from one end, mixed with the delicate motion in my pussy, is tipping me over the edge. My legs start to tremble as I dip my shoulders toward the pillows.

"Keep those hands on the headboard."

"Grayson, please, please just fuck me." I can't take it anymore. Before I can ask again, he's removed himself from me and is rubbing his cock along my slit.

"More, Grayson."

"Jesus," he hisses, then slams into me. The headboard bangs against the wall. His palm connects with my ass cheek with a slap, while his other hand grips so tightly.

"Grayson!" I shriek, my lungs now burning. The second his hand connects to the same spot again, I lose it. I come so hard, stars fill my vision. I can about make out the cursing coming from Grayson over the ringing in my ears. With a few final thrusts, he reaches his own climax, roaring out my name and draping his sweaty body over mine.

"Holy fuck, sunshine."

He presses a light kiss at the center of my spine before rolling off me. I collapse onto the bed, squashing my face into the plush pillow.

As my breath returns to normal, Grayson clambers over

me. I tip my head to the side, and he spreads my legs, warm liquid spilling down the inside of my thighs.

His finger trails up my leg, wiping up his cum from my skin. He slides his fingers inside me and leans over. "My cum stays where it belongs—inside you."

Holy. Fuck.

"Mmm, that feels nice," I whisper.

"Tomorrow, sunshine. Don't worry. Now, we need to sleep," he says, stroking the hair out of my face. He pulls back the duvet and tucks me in, snuggling into me. He snakes his arm under my pillow, and I use his chest as my own. The rise and fall of his chest bring me comfort.

"Good night, Grayson," I say. He gives me a soft kiss on my forehead. The kiss is something a loving boyfriend would do. Not a fuck-buddy.

"Sweet dreams, baby." I give him one last peck and nuzzle my head into his chest. His strong arm tightens around my waist, and I drift off to sleep.

I BLINK A few times to unblur my vision. Lifting my head off Grayson's chest, I prop myself up on my elbow. Dark ink covers both of his pecs and all the way down his arms. I trace my fingers along the tattoos, picking out what I can. A lot of it seems tribal. I stop on a date. 08/22/2015. Hmm, seven years ago . . . Shit, does he have a kid? I mean, not that it is any of my concern. But it kinda would be nice to know.

His cough startles me. I turn to find him staring at me with puffy eyes and one eyebrow cocked up.

"Morning, gorgeous," he says in a rough tone.

"Good morning."

"Question . . ." Unable to help myself, I start, intrigue getting the better of me.

"It's a bit early for that, but shoot."

"This date—2015. What's that for?"

He squeezes his eyes shut.

"Fuck, it really is too early for that." He chuckles awkwardly.

"Hey, it's okay. Maybe another time. You don't have to spill your life to me, Grayson. I'm not really anyone to you."

His large hand covers mine, stopping me from tracing the tattoo.

"It's the date my best friend, Casper, was killed in action."

Shit.

"Oh my God, I am so sorry." I squeeze his hand, and he gives me a sad smile and sighs.

"It's okay, sunshine. That was also the date I found out my best friend had been fucking my wife."

Holy fuck.

"I-I don't know what to say. That is awful." I slip my hand from underneath his and cup his cheek.

"They never deserved you, Grayson."

The realization dawns on me as to why he's so against relationships.

Stroking his face with my thumb, I press my lips against his. I close my eyes and kiss him with everything I have, wanting to kiss the pain away. To prove to him that not everyone would stomp on his heart like that.

He breaks the kiss, his eyes searching mine.

"You know you're special to me, right, sunshine? You aren't just 'anyone.' You're quickly becoming *everything*."

I can't stop the smile that spreads across my lips, and that's enough to make my cheeks hurt. He's everything I want. I've never felt this connection with anyone else before in my life. As I stare into his eyes, taking in this beautiful man in front of me, my smile quickly slips as my brain churns.

Why couldn't this happen with anyone else but him? The man who can't make my dreams come true. He doesn't need fixing. Love isn't going to change him and pull him out of the darkness. He thrives there. Can I let him pull me in to his world?

"Hey." He tips my chin up. "I lost you for a second there. What's going on in that pretty little head of yours?"

"N-nothing."

"You really think I can't tell when you're lying to me? I've studied you long enough now to know pretty much everything about you," he growls, rolling over the top of me, pinning my wrists above my head with his hands.

I'm at a loss for words.

"Come on, Maddie. Tell me, what's the matter?" He pouts, giving me a devilish smirk as he starts to slowly grind up against me.

"Not fair, Grayson," I whine, tipping my head back. He takes that as an opportunity to suck on the sensitive skin of my throat. I moan the instant his lips connect with mine.

"You can't have my cock until you tell me."

"You fucker." I try to wriggle out of his grip, but that only rubs his cock harder against me. Desire fills me.

"Sunshine, you know you want it." There's a playful tone to his voice, which makes me smile.

"Fine," I huff.

"I'm confused how we got here, how I feel about you. I'm scared of what this actually is between us. We want two completely different things out of life, Grayson. But we're so perfect for each other. It's like life sent you to me as a cruel twist of fate." I sigh, avoiding his eyes.

Even though we'd texted a few times and had calls last week, I missed him. All I wanted was to cuddle up in his arms.

"People change all the time, sunshine. We need to do some thinking." It's his turn to sigh as he brings his forehead to mine.

"But—"

"I'm not giving this up. I want you. I know that much will never change. It hasn't from the first time I set my eyes on you. So, we work this out . . . together."

Maybe . . . just maybe he's right.

"Who knew you were so philosophical, Mr. Ward."

"Mmm, you can call me that again," he says, closing his eyes.

This is the first time I have ever seen him look carefree. That darkness behind his eyes is gone.

"Do you have plans this weekend?" he asks.

"Nope."

"Stay here with me? I want you all to myself for the whole weekend."

When I nod, he beams.

Chapter Fifteen

GRAYSON

Maddie stayed that weekend and every other night since. I can't get enough of her. Even the way she has to steal food off my plate every time we eat, just to *taste*. The way she sings to herself when she's cooking. For a man that refused to kiss anyone for the past seven years, I'm certainly making up for that now. I don't let a single opportunity pass by where I can't have my lips on hers.

But reality calls. The past couple of weeks, we've been planning our retaliation. I warned Luca to keep his head; I know he's broken about Nico. But we can't act on emotions, not in this world.

Luca stares out the passenger window. Nico's murder has erupted a new level of fury within him. I know war zones. I know the easiest way to get yourself killed is by letting your emotions rule you.

I glance into the rearview mirror, and Frankie mouths, *Is he okay?*

Nodding, I shrug my shoulders and let out a cough to try to snap Luca out of it. His focus is much needed in this predicament.

The kidnapping of Marco Falcone's daughter. Rosa. His little princess.

It's a bold move. Just showing we can access his family wasn't enough.

If this operation goes to shit, not only are we in more danger, I might be dragging Maddie into this now too. If they know about her, they won't think twice about hurting her. I know they're capable of it. I saw what they did to Keller and Sienna. And I sure as shit am never letting one of those fuckers so much as breathe in the same space as my sunshine.

Every night for the past week, Rosa's either been out drinking with her roommates or out for dinner. I could have taken her at any point. Two guards track her from a distance. My bet is that she's whined to Daddy about wanting personal space.

Tonight, we're going for a simple snatch and grab operation. It's a Friday night. Of course she's going out clubbing.

Enzo tapped into her phone. He runs the most prestigious security firm in the country. But that doesn't stop him going rogue for us. He owes us after leaving his post with Sienna. He texts us the location and the names of the girls she will be with. The same two she's always with, Jasmine and Olivia.

Piece of cake.

Rosa's long black hair bobs out of the white Mercedes. She waltzes toward the entrance of Trance. I roll my eyes at the thought of stepping foot in this pompous nightclub. Her bodyguards follow suit.

"Boss, she's heading in."

Luca nods, lighting another cigarette. He gives me a sadistic grin, blowing out the smoke.

I pull up to a slow stop at the rear of the club. Frankie scratches at the stubble on his jaw in the back seat.

"Let's do this," Luca says, flicking his cigarette out of the window. Gone is his usual cheeky demeanor.

All three of us exit our car, courtesy of Enzo, and Frankie slips into the driver's seat.

"Remember, we have twenty minutes max in here. Any longer and we risk alerting the Falcones and them accompanying us. The last thing we need is a bloodbath in a nightclub," I say.

"Got it."

I nod and close the driver's door. Tapping my earpiece, I connect the call to Enzo. Turns out security firms can tap into just about any CCTV camera.

"Enzo, we're entering now." I eye Luca as he holsters another gun.

"Copy. The target is at the bar. A guard is stationed by the main entrance, the other by the bathroom."

"Got it."

Fuck, the bathroom leads to the fire escape, and that's our only route out. Rosa is a wild child. All Luca needs to do is dangle that little bag of white powder and she'll follow him just about anywhere. To the bathroom, mainly. However, she's not a typical junkie. Maybe I'm reading too much into the situation. *Fuck, focus!*

"Luca, stick to the plan. I'll take out the guard by the bathrooms."

He nods. "You ready, Grayson?"

My fingers lace around the knife in my pocket. It's my first

122 ~ LUNA MASON

kill in a while, and I can't fucking wait. Smirking, I say, "I was born ready."

He heads toward the red door. As we approach, the door clicks, and Enzo says, "Fire escape now open and bathrooms clear."

Luca creeps the heavy door open, the waft of sweat and cheap alcohol pouring out of the room. We walk along the corridor, past the women's bathrooms to my right. The music blares, pounding through my body.

I stop when we reach the men's bathrooms and press my back into the door. Luca continues and swings open the double doors into the club, fiddling with his zipper. God, the guy could have been an actor. He nods to Rosa's bodyguard and waltzes straight past him.

"Lights," I whisper in my earpiece.

As soon as I mutter the words, the corridor goes pitch black. Now I just have to fucking pray that no one comes in or out of this bathroom in the next five minutes.

Showtime.

When I yank open the door, the guard, dressed in a black suit and tie, doesn't even flinch. His eyes are focused only on Rosa and Luca. Her arm's draped over his forearm at the bar as he whispers in her ear. The guard's jaw clenches at the exchange. I take this window of opportunity. I bring my knife up in my right hand and sweep my left arm around his neck, using my forearm to press his chin up. I slice from left to right across his throat with pressure. He tries to grasp my arm in a poor attempt to free himself, but in vain. Tightening my grip around his neck, I drag him backward into the corridor.

His blood smothers my arm as I drag his unmoving body. His feet squeak against the flooring.

"Exit is clear."

"Copy. Cleanup crew en route," Enzo replies.

My muscles burn as I hold the dead guard in one hand, opening the fire exit door with the other. Resting my weight on my left foot, I hold the door open with my right to maneuver us out of the building. As planned, I drop his body behind the blue Dumpster outside the exit.

"Luca is exiting the building with the target."

Immediately, I take my position back up against the brick wall. Rosa's high-pitched voice gets closer and closer.

Our car rumbles to life just a few yards away. As soon as the fire exit door swings open, I pounce. Her pale gray eyes widen in fear. I clamp my palm over her mouth and pull her petite frame into me. When I hold my hand over her nose and mouth, she flails frantically in my arms, her warm breath hitting my palm, until she goes limp.

I lift her into my arms and stride over to the car, then lay her across the back seat. Frankie grabs the rope and leans over between the front seats, binding her wrists.

Mission accomplished.

Chapter Sixteen

MADDIE

I push open the door to my little makeup studio and flick on the lights. Notes of fresh paint still burn my nostrils.

My mom might not think being a makeup artist is a good career, but I am damn good at what I do and I am busy with clients. So, she can suck on that.

I head over to the messy reception area and re-stack the paperwork. I love Evie to death, but God, is she chaotic. I have another thirty minutes until my client arrives for the day.

My studio has one chair and an LED mirror and a little waiting area with a plush gray velvet sofa to match my dark pink and gray color scheme. I do have a tiny little kitchen out the back which has a coffee machine and mini fridge.

As I wait for the coffee machine to pour, I grab my phone out of my bag. I have never been so sore in my entire life, although, I have never been fucked that hard and so many times in my life.

Hmmm, no new notifications. I sigh, placing it down on

the counter. I don't know why I am expecting Grayson to suddenly behave like my boyfriend. We're just fuck buddies. Exceptional, mind-blowing fuck buddies. But it's not as if he's suddenly head over heels for me and can't get me out of his mind. *Why can't I get him out of my mind then?*

The last couple of weeks have really changed my whole perception of him. He's not just a brutish hitman, nor is he the playboy I thought he was. He's damaged, hurt. But when he's with me, he worships me like a princess.

My phone pings just as the coffee finishes pouring. My heart rate spikes. Snatching up the phone, I see the G, and butterflies swarm my stomach.

I haven't heard from him since he slipped out of bed last night. We've almost found a *normal* routine. We spend every evening together, have dinner with wine and watch TV. It almost feels real, too real. I don't want to seem like a nagging girlfriend. That's not what he signed up for. It eats away at me a little bit.

It's Gregory. Disappointment clouds over me.

I swipe open the message and read.

GREGORY

Hey, Maddie. It seems like ages since
I saw you last. Do you want to do
something Friday night? Maybe you could
come to my place for a film and takeout.

My fingers hover over the buttons. I really need to cut this off. I know he isn't *the one* for me. He is nice enough, but he just isn't Grayson. My brow furrows as I contemplate my response. Maybe, if I go, I can have the conversation face-to-face with him.

I quickly tap out a response before I talk myself out of it.

> **ME**
>
> That sounds great. I will be at
> your place around 7pm. Can you
> text me your address?

He texts back immediately with his address.

The door flies open, and Evie barrels in with a bright smile, her pink highlighted hair bouncing around her face.

"Morning, Maddie," she chirps and throws her coat off and tosses it on the coat rack.

"Morning," I hum, giving her a smile.

"Are we still going out Friday for David's birthday?"

Shit.

"Crap, yes, did you want to get ready at my place?" I ask, and her face lights up in response. I don't think she has many friends. If she isn't at work, she's studying to become a makeup artist to work alongside me.

"OMG, yes please!" she shrieks, spinning around in the desk chair with her feet in the air, chewing on a pen.

I type a quick text out to Gregory.

> **ME**
>
> Will have to make it later? I have David's
> birthday drinks to go to.

> **GREGORY**
>
> No worries, you could always stay at my
> place if you want?

I cringe at his reply.

> **ME**
>
> No, that's okay, I have a busy day the
> next day. I have to be at Sienna's early.
> Thank you though.

The studio door dings. I walk out of the kitchen area with a bright smile.

"Hi, Francesca, so lovely to meet you." I extend my hand to the stunning model standing before me. She doesn't need makeup to be glamorous.

"Hi, Maddie, thank you for booking me in so last-minute. Your work looks stunning. I had to give you a try!"

"Aww, thank you. Let me take your coat. Go, grab a seat. I will be with you in a sec!" I say, helping her out of her black puffer jacket and hanging it up on the rack.

My phone pings from the back room. Evie eyes me suspiciously, still chewing on that damn pen. I dart over, silencing the noise. I glance down at the screen and Grayson's name fills the entire lock screen.

> **GRAYSON**
> You left these here, so I'm taking them to the gym with me today.

I cock an eyebrow, scrolling to open the picture he sent.

My hand shoots to cover my mouth as I stare at a picture of Grayson's gorgeous face, my bright pink panties between his perfect white teeth.

A burning blush spreads across my cheeks.

> **GRAYSON**
> I'm keeping them, btw.

I squeeze my legs to try to calm the ache forming.

> **GRAYSON**
> Are you working all day today?
> Sunshineeeeeeeee.

I don't notice how much I'm smiling at my phone until my cheeks physically ache.

Evie coughs and brings me back to reality.

I type out a message and hit send.

> **ME**
> I finish at 1. Why?

GRAYSON
Lunch?

> **ME**
> Sounds good. Call you when I'm finished.

GRAYSON
Don't miss me too much.

> **ME**
> Sounds like you're the one missing me.

GRAYSON
Ain't that the truth. See you in a few
hours.

THE REST OF the week flies by. Every day, I meet Grayson for lunch. Most days, he jogs over to my studio. Every client has swooned over him. They can't even hide their attraction to him. I don't blame them either. That man is something else. Him in his gray sweatpants is enough to make any woman's panties drenched.

A pit forms in my stomach as I rifle through my wardrobe. Since Sienna moved out, I've used her room as a second wardrobe. Just about the only benefit of living on my own.

I need a pretty dress for a night out for David's birthday, but not so nice it gives Gregory any ideas. Considering I'm about to tell him I don't want to see him anymore. As the week passes by, my mind is solely taken up by thoughts of Grayson. If he isn't invading my personal space, he's invading my every thought.

Grabbing the metallic silver dress, I slip it on, the plunging neckline and spaghetti straps accentuating my cleavage. I've already straightened my hair and applied some fake eyelashes with a matching glittery silver eyeshadow. The fact that I lied to Grayson is heavy on my mind. I told him I was going out for David's birthday, but failed to mention the fact I was going to Gregory's after. I was relieved when he texted to say he couldn't meet me today. He said he had "work" to attend to with Luca. I don't question him; I don't want to know. As long as he comes back in one piece. I have an Uber booked to pick me up from the End Zone at 10 p.m. and another to collect me from Gregory's at 11 p.m. I don't want to stay long, and this nagging voice in the back of my head is telling me not to go.

Sitting back on the edge of the bed, I tie up my diamanté stilettos. My phone buzzes on the bed with Grayson's name flashing on the screen. I swipe to accept the call and put him on speakerphone.

"Hey," I say, trying to keep my tone neutral. I'm a crap liar, especially with him. He's the one person in the world who can read me like a book.

"Hey, sexy," he drawls, his deep voice making my legs clench together.

"Everything okay?" I ask, twiddling my hair.

Fuck, I'm nervous.

"I'm just on my way to the End Zone. Luca is insisting on a drink. We've had a hell of a couple of days. I thought, maybe, I could have you to myself after?"

"Uhhh—"

Shit, Maddie, think!

"I just started my period," I blurt out.

"And . . ."

"W-well, it's not as if we can actually do anything . . . you know, sex related."

He chuckles.

"Do you really think that's all I want you for?"

"No, but—"

Wait, do I?

He cuts me off before I can even finish my sentence. "No, there is no 'but.' I just want you. I've missed you."

My eyes flutter closed at his words. I want nothing more than to snuggle up with my giant and sleep.

"I missed you too." I sigh.

"Look at us being nice to each other."

I open my mouth to reply, but he beats me to it. "Plus, there are other holes I could use to my advantage in this situation."

My eyes go wide as I realize what he means. As if he's reading my mind, he adds, "Yes, sunshine, I'm talking about fucking that fine ass of yours."

"Grayson!"

"I gotta go, I'm outside Luca's and if I think about your ass anymore, my cock won't be able to take it, since he's already throbbing. The last thing I need is the boss seeing me with a hard-on."

I can't help but laugh picturing the scene.

"I can't say I'd be opposed to the idea."

He sucks in a breath and growls, "Fuck!"

"I'll see you soon then," I say in the most seductive tone I can muster and cut the call.

Letting out a deep breath, I run my fingertips through my hair.

How the hell am I getting out of this one?

———————•———————

BY THE TIME I arrive at the club, I'm a sweaty mess. It's chilly out, but the leather jacket I have on is sticking to my arms.

I'm a sweaty mess because I'm nervous.

I slam the car door of the Uber, having spent the entire ride playing over conversations with Grayson in my mind, trying to plan how to tell him I won't be going home with him.

"Maddie!" David's voice shakes me from my chaotic brain.

I didn't even notice him outside the entrance, puffing on a cigarette. I quicken my pace, my stilettos clicking against the sidewalk.

"Happy birthday, Davey!" I squeal, failing to notice all of his friends around him, watching our interaction.

"Thank you," he whispers, blowing the smoke into my face as he speaks.

"Come on, let's go get a drink," David's tall blond friend shouts, flicking his cigarette on the road and walking into the club.

"Where is Evie? I thought you were bringing her tonight?" David asks, and I sense a slight interest in my bubbly receptionist.

"She's meeting us here. She had to take her dog to the vet's. It sounds like someone might be interested in a certain pink-haired receptionist." I wink, nudging him with my shoulder. Not that it budges him in the slightest. David is a six-foot, athletic man, complete with a six-pack. Although I've always had my suspicions it's not just women he's into.

His cheeks flash a rosy pink color.

"Oh, shut up, Maddie." He chuckles, taking one last drag and dropping the butt to the ground.

"I'm only teasing. Come on, the birthday boy needs a tequila and so do I."

He loops his arm in mine, and we walk over to the bouncers. I've been here enough times now for them to know me.

"Do you want to tell me what's up?" David asks before we go throught the double doors into the club. I shake my head and take off my jacket, handing it to the bored-looking redhead at the desk.

"Maybe later." I shrug.

I am not sure I can even explain the predicament I have gotten myself into.

I'm about to tell a perfectly nice man that I don't want to see him anymore, because I want an ex-Marine mafia hitman to fuck me into next week.

After all the years I've gone on and on about finding Mr. Perfect to marry, David is going to laugh in my face when I tell him. And right now, I don't think I can stand it.

David pulls open the doors. Blaring music and crowds greet us. The sweat and booze waft through the air. My body heats as soon as we step in and head toward the bar. I divert past the busy dance floor, keeping my eyes focused on the bar as David grabs my hand and pushes us through the crowd. Bodies bash against my shoulders as we walk.

I scan the room, just waiting for Grayson to appear. I doubt he'd be out here with the rest of us. I've never really seen him outside the VIP area. I know he will be watching me. Those booths have a direct view over the bar and the dance floor.

I need a drink. My mouth is so dry I can barely swallow.

We finally reach the bar. I prop my elbows up on the sticky surface. The young, dark-haired bartender gives me a sexy grin and walks over, leaning over the bar. "What can I get for you?" His breath hits my cheek.

"Two shots of tequila, one sex on the beach, and a rum and coke, please."

He nods and makes our drinks, his eyes never leaving mine. I shuffle uncomfortably on my feet as he pours the shots and slides them across the bar. I grab mine and down the contents in one. I let the alcohol burn its way down. When I try to pay through my card, he places his hand over mine. "Drinks are on me tonight," he says, giving me a wink.

Oh, hell no.

"Thank you, but no. I want to pay for my drinks, please."

He leans over the bar.

"I can think of other ways you can pay."

I immediately take a step back, gritting my teeth. "Are you fucking serious?! What makes you think I want to have sex with you for a fucking drink! In fact, what gives you the right to even ask me that? You are an absolute asshole."

David grabs my arm and pulls me back.

My cheeks heat as everyone eyes me. "Oh, and don't expect to have a job tomorrow morning. After I tell Keller about this, you won't be stepping a foot back in here."

"Fuck tomorrow morning. He's leaving now," a deep, husky voice booms behind me.

The bartender pales as he looks behind me and backs away.

My Grayson.

I spin around to face him, and my nose brushes against his shirt.

"One second, baby," he says, pressing a quick kiss to my lips before leaning across and grabbing the horrified-looking bartender by the throat and dragging him over the bar. I gasp as he slams his body to the floor.

Seeing Grayson get all authoritative and caveman on me makes me hot. He looms over him and picks him up by the throat.

"Get the fuck out of here before I strangle you to death, you piece of shit," Grayson seethes. The barman quickly scuttles off, clutching his throat, without so much as a glance back. Grayson cups my jaw and brings his lips over mine.

"I had that under control."

"I know you did. I was simply reiterating the message for you. I know firsthand how scary you can be. But I can't have you stabbing a man in the eye with a stiletto tonight."

"I save that just for you."

"You have no idea how hot it makes me when you get all riled up." His index finger trails across my jawline and down my neck. The only person I can focus on is Grayson. He leans in, his lips skimming past my cheek. "I want to do very naughty things to you, sunshine. For being such a good girl."

The burning desire has me on the edge as he speaks. At this point, he could just touch my clit and it would send me spiraling over.

"And what if I've been a bad girl?" I take his bottom lip between my teeth and pull it.

"Then I'll have to take you home and show you."

"I promised I'd celebrate with David tonight. How about you go back with Luca and I'll meet you in the VIP area at 11? Then we go home? I need to at least have a few drinks with them to celebrate."

I have no intentions of following through; I need to slip out of here somehow without him seeing me. I know trying to trick an ex-Marine is not the best idea, but it's the only one

I have right now. I just need to get this over with and deal with the consequences later.

"Fine, I can't leave Luca until Frankie turns up anyway."

I press a kiss to his lips. I just need to tame the monster for a couple more hours, and maybe he won't even know I'm missing. I can hope.

"See you in a couple of hours, sunshine. Remember, be a good girl. And no one touches what's mine."

Chapter Seventeen

GRAYSON

This booth has the perfect view of the dance floor. I can't take my eyes off her. She's captivating, and not just to me, to every man in here. I grip onto my scotch that I've been nursing for the last half hour. Flitting between sexual frustration watching her ass sway to the music and anger every damn time she has to move away from a guy gyrating up against her.

"You're gonna shatter that fucking glass in a minute if you squeeze any tighter." Luca chuckles.

"Come on, lighten up. We all know she's coming back to you at the end of the night."

At some point, she's going to realize I'm not the man for her, that I'm not the man to give her everything she wants.

"What are you going to do with Rosa?" I ask.

"She's locked up in my basement. For now, she's safe. Plan is to draw them out using her and . . . poof"—his hands fly up to mimic an explosion—"bye-bye, Marco."

"So the big plan is to get them to a meet and blow the building up?"

A sadistic grin spreads across his face as he nods.

"Just tell me a time and place. You know I'll be ready."

"Count me in," Frankie says, before sinking another shot.

Luca's brows furrow as he watches the dance floor.

Maddie.

She's on the edge of the dance floor, concentrating on her phone with a frown.

10 p.m.

I slip out my phone and text her. I've done my two hours of watching her. There is only so much self-restraint I can show when she is looking drop-dead gorgeous in that silver dress.

Her head spins around in my direction. I can see the flush from here. Oh, she's ready for me. I can't get enough of this woman. I also need to remind her that this isn't just about sex. Not by a long shot. When she tried to fob me off earlier that she was on her period, it made me realize something.

I genuinely missed seeing her. It was twenty-four hours. Sex wasn't even on my mind when I called her up; I just wanted to hear her voice. I might be pussy-whipped. But I couldn't give a fuck. She can do what she likes to me.

I'm all hers.

And it's about time she understood that.

Chapter Eighteen

MADDIE

I grab my phone out to text Grayson. I know I was planning on "dumping" Gregory later. But after seeing
Grayson looking all sexy in a suit, like he wants to eat
me up, I can't resist.

Gregory is a no-go for me now. I might as well bite the
bullet and do it now that I've got the Dutch courage anyway.

ME
Hiya, I won't be able to make it over.
Actually, I've been thinking. We're better
off as friends. I'm sorry, I was planning
to tell you later, but something came up.
Sorry for wasting your time.

My phone beeps immediately with Grayson's message.

GRAYSON
Are you ready to go? I can't stare at your

ass any longer without wanting to drag
you into the bathroom and bend you over
the sink. You are killing me, woman.

"Maddie!"

Oh, fuck.

Gregory.

What the hell is he doing here!

He approaches me with a wide smile, his dark hair spiked on the top. He looks cute in a navy polo and jeans, but he doesn't make my heart flutter and my pussy throb.

"Hi, Gregory."

He wraps me up in a friendly hug, tapping my back as he does.

"What are you doing here?"

"I thought I'd give you a lift to my place."

I give him a tight smile, chewing on the inside of my mouth.

"Did you not get my text?"

Awkward. He rummages through his back jeans pocket.

Without turning, I know Grayson is behind me. The air crackles between us. Gregory is too busy messing around on his phone to notice the new arrival.

"The second your lips touched mine, you became mine," Grayson whispers in my ear, pushing my hair away from my neck. My body shivers against his touch. "Now be a good girl and tell him who you belong to, before he loses his fucking hands for touching you."

His arms lace around my stomach, pulling me in tightly against his frame.

Gregory's eyes shoot to mine, focusing in on the big burly man behind me, basically claiming me as his. He nods at me.

"I get it," he says, holding up my message on his phone.

"I'll see you around, Maddie."

He turns to start walking away. I spin in Grayson's arms, placing my palms on his pecs.

"I need to talk to him. He deserves an explanation. Just trust me, okay?"

"I trust you."

I flash him a grin and pull his head down to mine, giving him a kiss. I spin on my heel before I lose the courage, and sprint.

"Gregory, wait!" I shout. Gregory stops in his tracks. God, I'm sweating.

"Can we talk?" He nods, and I follow him out of the exit. The chilly air gives me goosebumps all over my bare arms.

"I'm sorry about that back there. It's not me. I didn't want to hurt you. I wanted to tell you the right way. I know we weren't together, but you deserved a proper explanation. I'm seeing Grayson, and it's complicated, but I think maybe, it could be something. I would regret it forever if I didn't at least try. I hope you can understand. You're a great guy. You deserve someone's all. And I can't give you that."

"Hey, I get it. I'm surprised, though. I thought you hated him?"

"Yeah, me too. I don't really think it was ever hate, though. It was irritation, yes. And the fact that I wanted him and couldn't have him."

He nods in understanding.

"Hey, no hard feelings. I wish you all the luck. You're an amazing woman. You deserve to be happy, however you find it."

"Thank you."

"I'll see you around, Maddie."

"See ya."

He walks off down the sidewalk. I turn around to face the exit door and cock my eyebrow. Of course Grayson's already there, holding my black leather jacket up for me. I walk over to him and turn around, sliding my arms in the sleeves.

"All okay?" he asks, and I nod in response.

"I'm yours, huh?" I bat my lashes at him.

"Damn right, woman." He bends and tosses me over his shoulder. The cold air shoots straight up my short dress.

"Grayson!"

His hand grips my ass, so I squeeze his butt cheeks as he walks. Damn, they are solid. He walks us around the side of the club to his parking space.

He guides me down his body, holding on to my waist.

"Thanks for the ride."

"Anytime." He winks.

He leans around me and opens the passenger door. "Time to finally claim what's mine," he rasps, biting down on the sensitive skin just under my jaw.

"Are we really doing this?"

I want this. I want him.

"Baby, I wasn't joking earlier. I'm fucking obsessed with you. Every single part of you. I can't keep letting you push me away. I want this. All of this." He pauses, searching my eyes. "The question is, do you?"

Without even a second of hesitation, I fist my hand through his hair and drag his mouth down to mine.

"I've always wanted you. What we have with each other . . . It's special. It's not something people find in their lifetimes. Why do you think I kissed you in the first place?" I brush my lips against his earlobe. "Now take me home and claim me. I've been a good girl for you."

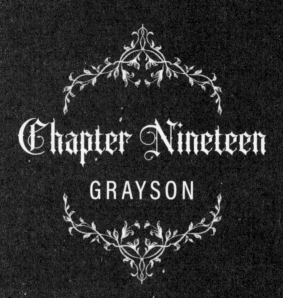

Chapter Nineteen

GRAYSON

Since the night at the club, a day hasn't gone by where I haven't seen Maddie. We are both busy with work. At times, I have to slip out of bed at midnight to oversee Luca's shipments. He can't risk any more being stolen. So far, so good. Between me and Frankie, we make a good team.

She didn't stay over last night, so she was gone by the time I wrapped up training the new recruits at King's Gym with Keller. I was fucked. All I wanted to do was snuggle on the sofa with her. *Who am I turning into?*

Maddie was going for dinner with Sienna after work and went back to her apartment after. I *almost* drove over there. I didn't want to sleep on my own. For the first time in seven years, I can finally sleep a full night when I'm with her.

Like hell am I going another night without her, so I decided to surprise her today by turning up at her studio after work. Well, I thought she'd be finished by 6 p.m., but it turned out models need makeup any damn time of the day. So I sat there, watching her work her magic for over an hour.

Evie kept me entertained with a round of twenty fucking questions. We covered my age, childhood, how many people I'd killed in the special forces, my dating history. That made Maddie's head spin around pretty quick.

Now, finally, I have her to myself.

Maddie puts her feet up on the couch, flicking through the TV, while I pull out a chilled bottle of sauvignon blanc. It's like the most natural thing in the world.

Just having her in my space brings the place to life. I pour out two glasses and make my way back over to her. Her hair is pulled up into a ball on the top of her head. Not a scrap of makeup on her face. Quite honestly, she is stunning. She gives me a bright smile, holding out her hand to take the wine from me. I take the seat next to her and bring my glass to my lips.

She takes a sip, closing her eyes and letting out a moan as she swallows. She has no idea just how perfect she is.

"God, I needed this," she groans, taking another sip. I join her. The sweet liquid almost makes my mouth itch. I'm more of a scotch man. The only sweet thing I need in my life is Maddie. Well, with the exception of my kryptonite—chocolate milkshakes.

"Rough day?" I ask, placing my glass on the coffee table.

"Just so busy. Evie double-booked me, so I had to squeeze two models in back-to-back." She rolls her eyes and puts her glass on the table. I place her legs on my lap and start massaging the bridges of her feet.

"Mmmm, that feels so nice," she groans, tipping her head back against the armrest.

"Have you always wanted to be a makeup artist?" I don't

know the little things. In the last seven years, I've never wanted to know anything about anyone, really.

With Maddie, I find myself always looking for more about her. Last night, I researched her star sign after seeing her Aquarius tattoo. I've never read a horoscope in my life, yet there I was, at 1 a.m., checking if Aquarius and Taurus were compatible.

I got mixed results.

"Ummm, not really. I studied sociology at Columbia with Sienna. Because my parents wanted me to go there, since that's where they met. I picked the subject that looked the least dull. But I practiced makeup on all of our roommates. As soon as I left, I decided that's what I wanted to do. Plus, there was good money in it. I worked at a salon first, which was great. But since Keller gave me the chance to open up my own studio, I haven't looked back. I love the freedom. I can take a nap when I want. I can take days off. I answer to no one but myself."

Her face lights up as she speaks.

"What about you? What made you want to join Luca? Was being a famous boxing trainer not enough?"

"It's all I've ever known. And I fucking love it. I'm damn good at it. If I can help Luca, I feel like I'm being useful. Boxing is great, but we've done that now. I suppose it doesn't quench my thirst as much as I thought it would. Everything changed the day I saved Sienna. It was the first time since leaving the forces I felt like myself again."

Not to mention the same day her kiss brought me back to life.

She smiles sadly, then clambers onto my lap, resting her head on my thigh.

"If I'd never have left her that day, this all might never have happened."

"It wasn't your fault, baby. I'm glad you left. What if you were there and he hurt you? Jamie was unhinged."

She nods against my thigh.

"Plus, it all worked out okay in the end. I mean, look at us. You would never have kissed me otherwise."

It's true, though.

That day changed our lives in more ways than one. We shattered the barrier between us.

"True, nothing like a good kidnapping to bring a couple together." She smirks.

"How every love story should start."

She hums and nuzzles her head against my thigh.

"How would you like a proper first date tomorrow night?"

She pushes herself off me to face me with a smile.

"I'd love that."

She wiggles her butt and unhooks her legs, swinging her right leg over to straddle me.

She rolls her hips just slightly, sending all my blood straight to my cock.

"I was trying to deepen our emotional connection," I murmur, reciting a line I'd read in my horoscope research.

"The only thing I want deeper is your cock. Inside me."

Who am I to deny my woman anything?

I haven't had my dinner anyway. And she's my favorite meal of the day.

As I slip my white T-shirt over my head, her eyes roam over my body, and fuck, the way she looks like she wants to eat me turns me the fuck on.

She follows my lead, seductively unbuttoning her black shirt. My eyes stay pinned on her tits as a lacy red bra peeks out from the gap. She shrugs the shirt off her shoulders. My hands settle on her bare waist, just above her leather skirt.

"Fuck, sunshine. Do you have any idea how sexy you are? I'm obsessed."

The flush on her cheeks deepens, and I trail my index finger along her warm skin just below her collarbones.

"I need a taste, Maddie."

My fingers squeeze her throat. My other hand slips under her skirt, brushing against her bare pussy.

I pull her in, so our noses touch. "Don't tell me you've been walking around New York with no panties," I growl.

"You'll find them in your car. It was meant to be a little surprise for you."

"I want the whole collection. What color were they?"

"Red. To match my bra."

When I swipe her bottom lip with my thumb, she moans against my touch.

"So fucking responsive."

Moving my attention to the exposed skin on the side of her neck, I bite down. When I slide a hand to cup her tit, she starts to grind her bare pussy against me.

A little whimper leaves her lips. Foreplay was never really my thing. Well, neither was kissing. With Maddie, everything is so different. I want to draw it out, watch her body writhe as she fights an orgasm.

Eating her out has become my new favorite pastime.

"Are you ready to ride my face, sunshine?"

"Damn right," she purrs.

"I want these lips first," I say, grabbing the back of her head and thrusting her face into mine, capturing her lips.

"Every inch of you is delicious." Lifting her up by the waist, I settle her back down on the couch next to me and sink to my knees on the floor. She looks down at me, her legs wide open, her eyes twinkling. I position myself between her legs, gripping her thighs, pulling her pussy toward my face. I lift her skirt up so she's fully on display, glistening and ready for me.

Her fingers run through my hair and she pulls me in. My greedy girl. She hooks her smooth legs around my shoulders and my lips cover her throbbing heat. Her sweetness bursts all over my tongue. Her back arches as I lick all the way up to her clit, biting down on it and pressing down on her stomach at the same time.

"Oh my God!"

Buzzing interrupts our moment. I try to ignore it as I lap her up, her hips rolling to meet my rhythm. She lifts her hips off the sofa, and I cup her ass, biting and sucking like a man starved.

That fucking irritating vibrating starts again. She doesn't seem to notice, so I carry on. There is nothing sexier than having her riding my face like this and smothering me.

As soon as the phone buzzes again, I growl, "For fuck's sake." Her body sags as I move back and then lean over to grab the phone.

"Mom" flashes up on the screen. Maddie eyes me suspiciously, her cheeks flushed bright red. I hold out the phone to her. "Fucking answer this before I smash it to pieces." With shaky hands, she brings the phone to her ear, her breathing erratic. All the while, she doesn't take her hungry eyes off me.

"Hi, Mom."

I sink back on my heels. She tries to close her legs, but I grab her knees, pushing them as far apart as they'll go. Her eyes widen in horror.

"I'm fine, I just jogged up the stairs to my apartment."

I give her a smirk before repositioning my face between her legs and so slowly licking all the way up her slit.

She squeezes her eyes shut, biting her lip.

"I can't, I'm busy Saturday night."

I reward her by sliding two fingers inside her while sucking on her clit.

"No, it's not a date."

I hum against her pussy, reminding her it fucking is.

"No, it's no one special and I'm not bringing him to Sunday lunch."

Her words stop me. Turns out that's the one way she could ever turn me off. I look up at her, and she gives me an apologetic smile.

What the fuck.

Why does this feel like being punched in the gut? I'm not her dirty little secret. I'm done hiding from the world. I don't even hear the rest of her conversation as my mind reels.

She's still rambling away. I pull out my fingers and move away from her, then stand.

I'd be so fucking proud to bring her home to my parents if I had that kind of relationship with them. Hell, I haven't seen my parents in seven years. We talk on the phone occasionally. After I left Chicago, I left them behind too. They are both retired and spend their time traveling the world. I was always a hindrance to them, hence why they rushed me off to the army at the first sign of trouble. I'd even thought about reaching out to them to see if they'd be home soon to meet her.

How fucking wrong I was.

Chapter Twenty

MADDIE

The hurt in Grayson's eyes as he backed away from me sends me into a panic.

I don't even know what my mom's rambling on about now. I just need to get to Grayson and make it right. *Fuck, why did I say that!*

I don't want to put Grayson through a grilling from my mom. Not yet. I don't think either of us are ready for that. The words came out before I could stop them. It's almost by instinct with her now. I'm so bothered about her opinion. I clearly don't care who I hurt in the process. It's toxic.

"Look, Mom," I cut her off, "I have to go. I'll see you Sunday." I don't give her a chance to reply and cut the call.

The bedroom door slams shut, making me jump.

Oh, he's pissed.

I pad over to the bedroom and hover by the door as he's slamming the drawers shut. Taking a deep breath, I turn the knob and open the door.

"Grayson, I'm so sorry about that."

He doesn't even turn to look at me; he just rummages through his T-shirts.

"Grayson?"

"It's fine. Just go get dressed, I'll take you home. I think we could do with some space."

I sigh and lean against the door frame, watching as he shoves a black sweater over his head. I swallow the lump forming in my throat.

"Okay."

Reluctantly, I make my way back into the living room, picking up my black shirt that's tossed on the floor. As I do up the last button, Grayson storms past the couch and heads toward the elevator, jabbing the button.

Wow, he really does want me gone.

"I can call a cab, don't worry."

"Just because I'm pissed off doesn't mean I won't get you home safe. Okay?"

I nod and grab my phone off the couch and snatch my bag from the floor. The elevator dings and the doors slide open. I follow behind him and we stand in silence, staring at the sliding doors.

I can almost hear his brain ticking from the other side of the elevator. I let out a breath as the doors reopen into the parking lot. The cold air makes me shiver. I follow him to his Audi with my eyes on the ground.

I slip into the passenger seat, and he's already turned the engine on, his hands gripping the steering wheel.

This is bad.

As we go past the security barriers, I turn to him. His sharp jaw's clenched. I rest my hand on his thigh, and he flinches.

"I'm sorry." I slide my hand off his thigh. He catches my hand and laces his fingers through mine, squeezing them.

"If you aren't ready for this, that's okay. I can wait. I'm not the most patient man, but for you, I'll try. I don't think I'll ever be a man you want to take home to your parents, though, Maddie."

Before I met him, well, before I kissed him, he would have been right. I would never have even considered a relationship with him for that reason.

But now, I don't want to let this slip away because of what my judgmental mom thinks. Tonight proves that. I can't see him hurt like that because of me again. He might be a powerful, strong man. But underneath that, he has been hurt deeply. I need to earn his trust. I need to prove to him love still exists.

"I am ready. When it comes to my mom, it's difficult. No one would be good enough in her eyes. I really like you, Grayson. I don't want her ruining it before we've even started. She has this weird way of instilling doubt in everything I do."

"You let her control you."

That raises my hackles.

"That's not true," I snap back.

"Oh really, Maddie? Go on, why have you spent the last fuck knows how many years, relentlessly dating to try to find your prince to whisk you away into the sunset? Thinking you live in some sort of fairy tale?"

"How dare you." I snatch my hand away from his.

"So I'm lying?"

He's pushing me. And it's working.

"What's wrong with trying to find love, Grayson? You know, someone to spend the rest of your life with."

He laughs.

The asshole.

Fine. If he wants to push me away, two can play at that game.

"Maybe I should have just invited Gregory to meet them instead. At least he gets me," I mutter, staring out the window at the dreary graffitied streets.

"What the fuck did you just say?"

My head thrusts forward as he slams the brakes, stopping dead in the middle of the road.

"What are you doing?"

"Get the fuck out of my car."

"W-what?" I choke out.

My eyes scan the area. I haven't taken any notice of where we are. The street lights flicker, and a group of guys with their hoods up loiter across the street. No way am I getting out here.

He sighs, leaning over me, not touching me at all, and grabs my door handle, pushing it open.

"Get out. I can't listen to any more of your bullshit tonight. I get it, I'm just a fuck. I'm not good enough for precious princess Maddie. Well, call Gregory, get him to pick you up. I don't care anymore. You've made it clear where we stand."

"Fuck you, Grayson. I just want a decent human being. Clearly, that's not fucking you. So, gladly. Gregory would never do something like this to me."

I grab my bag and get out of the car, slamming it shut behind me, flicking him the middle finger as I walk off down the street. I keep my head held high, despite the tears rolling down my cheeks.

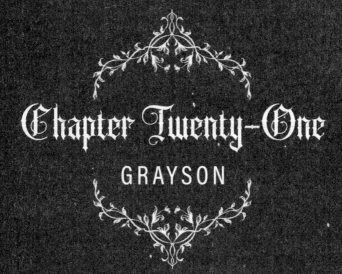

Chapter Twenty-One

GRAYSON

My mind whirls as I drive around in circles. The anger starts to subside. Scratching the stubble along my jawline, I replay that conversation back.

Fuck.

Fuck, fuck, fuck.

I'm a complete fucking idiot.

I slam my fists against the steering wheel, hitting my foot on the brakes. The car behind me beeps frantically at me.

"Fuck off!" I shout, turning the car around as fast as I can.

The Audi takes off as I race back to where I left her.

It's only been a few minutes; she will be fine.

I pull up to an abrupt halt in the exact spot I left her, but I don't see my blonde beauty anywhere.

Shit.

Pulling open the glove box, I snatch my gun. Even if I do shoot someone here, no one will give a fuck; it's a daily occurrence anyway. The cold air burns my face. I turn my nose up as the stale stench of weed assaults my senses.

I keep my gun close to my side; right now I don't need to draw unwanted attention to myself.

Walking down the sidewalk, within just a few steps, I've already passed two homeless men wrapped up in sleeping bags.

"Get off me!" a woman's voice screams.

I assess where the noise came from. Following the sound, I turn to my right and look across the street. There's a dark alleyway on the other side of the road. I jog over there, slowing my steps carefully as I approach.

"Give me your fucking phone!" a voice shouts.

As I round the corner, Maddie's silver stilettos shine in the light. The man, dressed all in black with a balaclava covering his face, is attempting to snatch her handbag. Whipping my gun out in front of me, I walk toward them, careful not to startle him. Fuck knows if he has a weapon.

I put a finger to my lips as Maddie spies me out the corner of her eye. She flicks her gaze away from me as the barrel of my gun presses against the back of this asshole's head.

"Get the fuck off her. Now!" Violence oozes off of my tone.

When he produces the slightest glimpse of silver—a knife—from his back pocket, I react on instinct and squeeze the trigger, blowing his brains out. My ears ring from the gunshot, followed by Maddie's screams.

Chapter Twenty-Two

MADDIE

"You're a fucking monster, Grayson. I hate you!" My voice rises an octave as my body trembles.

He steps over the dead man and wraps himself around me. I push against his chest with all the strength I can muster, but it's no use. He doesn't move, he doesn't let me go. He'll never let me go.

"You're right, sunshine. I am a monster. But I'm your monster."

"I'm so fucking sorry," he adds, closing his eyes, like he doesn't want to look at me. I know he's not apologizing for the dead body.

"If you're sorry, get the fuck off me and take me home." My arms are still glued to my sides, my fists clenched.

He sighs and releases me. I dart under his arm and run. He catches up with me, grabbing my arm. Without a word, he walks us to his car and swings open the door. I get in, and he slips into the driver's seat. I stare out the passenger window and all I can hear are his ragged breaths. It's making me feel stabby.

The car ride passes in silence. I can feel every time he glances over at me as my skin prickles. I suck in a breath when his hand skims my thigh.

"Get. The. Fuck. Off. Me." I spit out each word without looking at him. My blood boils at his touch. Not able to stand the noise of him breathing any longer, I turn the volume of the music up to full blast.

We pull up outside my apartment, and before he even fully stops the car, I fling open my door and get out, almost stumbling on the curb.

"Fuck it," I hiss, straightening my spine and running to my building without so much as a look back at him.

I sprint up the stairs, my lungs burning as I reach my apartment door. I go to get my keys out of my bag—

No, no, no.

Fuck.

I don't have my bag. I slam my hands against my apartment door and rest my forehead against it. I can barely catch my breath. Tears spill from my eyes like a waterfall. The fear, the anger, it all merges into one explosion of emotions.

The air suddenly shifts behind me. My hair stands on end. He's here.

I don't have the energy to even turn around. I don't want him to see me like this. A fucking mess. I don't want him to know how badly he's hurt me.

He spins me around, holding me steady around the waist. His touch burns deep into my core. His icy blue eyes search mine.

He leans over me and the click of the lock fills me with relief. I jolt out of his hold, snatch my keys, walk into my apartment, and slam the door shut. I slide along the door, falling to the floor and cradling my knees into my chest.

The room starts to spin as I let it all out. Barely able to catch my breath between sobs, almost hyperventilating.

The door rattles against my back.

"Sunshine, let me in," he shouts.

I don't move. I just can't.

My heart beats so ferociously, a lump forms in my throat. *Fuck, am I dying?* Panic grips me as I bring my hand to my chest and press hard. Stars form in my vision. I bring myself onto all fours, my lungs heaving.

"Help me!"

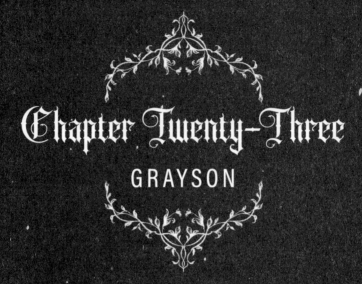

Chapter Twenty-Three

GRAYSON

My heart was in my throat the moment I heard her slide down the other side of the door. Every wail punches me in the chest.

I've never felt guilty before for any of the horrendous things I've done. But this is eating me up. I'm the last person she wants right now. I know that. She's furious and hurt. If she wanted to stab me all the other times I've wound her up, now she will be murderous.

Her cries become more and more frantic, hysterical even. She's losing it. I know the feeling all too well. The moment reality starts to slip, the darkness that creeps in and consumes your entire body. Once you enter that pit of darkness, it's hard, so fucking hard, to claw yourself back out. That's why I live in hell now. I've learned to thrive here. She's right; I am a monster. But I won't let the darkness steal my sunshine.

"Sunshine, let me in."

Nothing.

Pressing my ear to the door, I listen. I wince as her sobs get progressively louder. It's almost as if she's struggling to breathe through them. There's a wheeze in every breath.

Fuck.

There's some muffled movement, her hand slapping against the tiled flooring. Good, she's moving away.

I take in a sharp inhale.

"Help me!"

"Sunshine, move away from the door!"

I lift my left foot and slam it with all my force into the door. It flings open and smashes against the wall. She's lying in a heap on the floor. Her chest moves frantically up and down.

Fuck.

I dart over to her, dropping with a thud onto my knees. Her warm breath hits my face. Good, she is breathing. I stroke the soaking strands of hair out of her face and gently lift her head off the floor.

"Baby, come on, come back to me," I whisper in her ear, stroking her ice-cold cheek. Her body shivers against me. She's fucking freezing. Placing her head on my lap, I grip under her arms and pull her body up to my chest, cradling her like a baby. The fact that she still hasn't woken worries me. I check my watch; she has thirty more seconds before I call an ambulance.

"Sunshine, please. Come back to me." Tears sting in my eyes. What the fuck have I done to her?

I lift her up and get onto my feet.

"Grayson . . ." It's barely a whisper.

"Hey, sunshine."

I walk us into her bedroom and lay her down on the bed.

The bed dips as I sit on the edge next to her. Mascara runs down her face. She doesn't move, just stares at me.

"How are you feeling?" I whisper, not wanting to startle her.

"Fine."

"Do I need to take you to a hospital? What happened back there?"

"It was just a panic attack. I've never had one like that before, not enough to pass out." The color starts to come back to her face; I bring two fingers to her neck and check her pulse. It's steady, a little fast, but not concerning.

"Do you want me to get you anything? Some water?"

She shakes her head.

"I need you to leave. I don't just mean here, I mean me. Whatever this was is done."

I bite my bottom lip so hard a coppery taste drips on my tongue. I can't leave her like this, but if me being here sets her off, I can't stay.

"I can't leave you tonight, Maddie. Not after that. I'll run you a bath, tuck you in bed, and I'll sleep in the spare room. I'll be gone by the time you wake up. I just need to know you're okay."

She lets out a sigh and nods, still looking past me.

She's slipping away from me, and I can't do a damn thing to stop it.

Chapter Twenty-Four

MADDIE

I wake up with a start. My duvet is tucked around my neck. I don't remember much after Grayson ran me a warm bath last night.

My chest pangs. I already feel empty without him. I'm not going to find another man like him to satisfy me completely. I was hooked after one kiss. But I can't forgive him for this.

It's one thing having an argument, but tossing me out on the street in the middle of a gang war zone is totally over the line. I pad into the bathroom. Cringing at my reflection, I brush my teeth and slather on some moisturizer.

Making my way to the kitchen, I buzz the coffee machine to life and stare as the black liquid fills the cup. I didn't eat last night. I'll end up with the shakes if I don't get something inside me soon. Lifting up on my tiptoes, I open the cupboard above my head, jabbing my hand around toward the back in search of the brown sugar.

I know it's here somewhere.

My fingers hit against something metal. What the fuck is that?

I wrap my fingers around it and grab it. My eyes focus in on the small silver gun in my hands. It falls from my fingertips, clattering against the counter and making me jump backward.

What the fuck?

I whip my head around as Grayson clears his throat.

The asshole.

"Out!" I shout, pointing toward the door.

Hurt flashes across his features before he shakes his head. He prowls closer, and I instantly snatch up the gun from the counter, aiming it straight at his chest.

My hand shakes as he quickly closes the distance.

"It's loaded." My voice quivers.

He smirks at me, towering above me.

"I know. I loaded the damn thing."

He wraps his fingers around the barrel of the gun and presses it further into his chest.

"Get out," I whisper.

"No."

"Killing me is the only way you'll ever get rid of me. So if that's what you really want, do it. I deserve it. I am a fucking monster. I might have a black heart, but you own all of it. Until the day I'm summoned back down to hell, and even then, it will always be yours. So do it. Fucking shoot me."

"We should never have started this," I choke out, my hands shaking like a leaf.

"You're wrong, Maddie. I'll never regret this. I know I don't deserve you, but for what it's worth, I want to give you everything. I'm so fucking sorry about last night. I will *never* hurt you again. All I know is, I can't live without you. I want you. All of you. And I can try to be a man you deserve. That, I can promise you. Just . . . please don't leave me, sunshine."

His words hit me in the chest. I unhook my fingers from around the gun, and he takes it out of my hand. I'm so confused right now. I just can't help but burst out into a fit of laughter. Doubling over, I rest my hands on my knees, trying to catch my breath.

"You're a fucking idiot, Grayson. Why would you leave a gun here when you know how pissed I get at you?"

"I never really expected you to point it at me. But I mean every word, Maddie." He holds the gun up between us, and my lips part in surprise. "I will never hurt you again. Until the day I die. If you are the one who sends me there, then so be it."

He trails the tip of his gun along my collarbone, the cold metal forming goosebumps along my skin.

"It was kind of hot, though," he rasps and moves the gun between my breasts. I can't stop looking at this loaded killing machine, sliding down my skin.

He pulls the waistband of my shorts away from my body.

"I can think of something even hotter to do with this gun, though."

If his reaction to last night is anything to go by, he won't hurt me.

"Spread your legs for me, gorgeous," he whispers, and like the complete whore I am for him, I do.

The icy barrel of the gun rubs against my heat as he slides it back and forth slowly. He bends, grazing his teeth against my earlobe. I suck in a breath, too scared to move, yet so turned on at the same time.

"I'll never be able to use a gun again without picturing you like this."

The cold sensation against my pussy, mixed with the pure adrenaline, runs through my veins. My body sags as he removes the gun. He brings it up to his mouth, keeping his eyes pinned on mine. He runs his tongue along the barrel.

"Fucking delicious," he moans.

The gun clatters against the counter. I just stand there, openmouthed, staring at him. *Holy shit.*

"Kiss me." The words fall from my lips before I realize what I'm saying.

His brow furrows.

I need one last kiss. The chances I find a man who knows how to pleasure me the way Grayson does are slim to none.

"Please." I pout, licking my lips. Tempting him.

His lips slam over mine, making my pussy throb. Fuck, he's good. My tongue finds his as I wrap my arms around his neck and pull him closer, deepening the kiss. He moans into my mouth, which sets the sparks off in my body.

"If we don't stop this now, I'm going to have to bend you over the counter and feast on that delicious pussy for breakfast."

"Do it," I say, tipping my chin up. Sliding my hand along his chiseled abs, I move lower and lower and cup his erection through his jeans.

"I'll have my breakfast first, then." I lower myself onto my knees, undoing his jeans and freeing his cock. I wrap my hand around the base, which just makes it look huge. Licking my lips, I take him in my mouth, his salty pre-cum slipping down my throat.

"Fuck," he hisses.

"Take all of me, like the greedy whore you are," he groans, so I go deeper, the tip hitting against the back of my throat. I try not to gag. Tears stream down as I push my head further onto him, opening my throat to allow him in.

"Mmm, my good girl."

He thrusts into my mouth, hitting at the back of my throat. Over and over again.

"Oh fuck, suck harder."

My hands grab his muscular thighs, my nails digging into the skin. He tenses against me; I know he's close. He yanks me up by the hair, and pain sears through my scalp. But I'm too turned on to care right now.

He lifts me onto the counter, my ass hitting the cool surface.

"I need to be inside you. Now."

He pulls down my little shorts and panties, discarding them onto the floor. Stepping between my legs, he pushes them open and pulls me toward him.

His fingers trail up the inside of my thigh and then he swipes them along my seam. "Jesus, you are soaking for me. Am I going to need to add guns to our bedside drawer?" He pinches my clit, and I scream out. He slams his cock into me in one thrust. His lips crush mine, his tongue swirling around my mouth. "Mine," he mutters in a primal tone. He fucks me into oblivion. The sound of our skin slapping against each other fills my ears. Freeing my breasts, he takes my nipple in his mouth.

"Oh fuck, Grayson," I moan, throwing my head back.

"Scream my name louder, sunshine," he growls, biting at my neck. His fingers circle my clit as he fucks me with ferocity.

"Eyes on me." His voice is commanding. I snap my eyes back to his.

"Come for me."

That sends me over the edge. My body trembles against him as I scream his name.

"Fuck, sunshine." He releases into me. His lips find mine then, and my hands cup his cheeks. It's an intimate moment.

He rests his forehead against mine.

This is all too much. I want this man more than anything, but I can't live my life like this.

I'm going to miss this. I'm going to miss him.

"I need you to leave," I whisper. His cock is still twitching inside me. It's not what my heart wants, but it's what my brain is screaming at me to do.

His Adam's apple bobs as he nods.

"I'll give you time. But that's all you're getting. I meant what I said. And I promise, I will make this right." His voice is soft. He brushes away my tears with the pad of his thumb.

"I hate it when you cry, baby."

I look into his eyes through blurry vision. He presses a soft kiss to my forehead. As soon as he breaks away, he tugs on his jeans.

"I'll see you soon," he says. His hands engulf mine with a reassuring squeeze. I'm holding everything in. I can't move, I can't speak. I know if I do, every emotion will erupt out of me and he will never leave. He walks out of the kitchen. I hold my breath until I hear the front door open and click back closed. My body sags as I let everything out.

How has my life come to this, and why does it feel like my heart was stomped on the second he walked out of that door? Hopping off the counter, I run to the bedroom and grab my phone from the side.

I hover over Sienna's name. Biting on my lip, I hit dial.

"Hey, Maddie!"

"Hey, Si. Do you have a minute?"

"You know I do for you. Is everything okay?"

The moment someone asks if you are okay, when you

really aren't, always hurts. "Not really, Si. I really need my bestie."

"Keller! I'm going to Maddie's, can you come and take Darcy for me, please?" she shouts.

She carries on her muffled conversation with her husband while I sit and pick at the skin around my fingernails.

"Right, I just need to get changed and I will be around, okay?"

"Thank you, Si." Relief washes over me. I really don't want to be alone.

"Don't thank me. You do remember everything you did for me last year? We are best friends, no matter what. Please don't ever hesitate to call me. Just because we don't live together does not mean I'm not there for you. Do you hear me?"

I laugh at her motherly tone, but right now, it's what I need. I just need someone to wrap me up and tell me it's okay.

"I got it."

"Right, see you soon. I love you, Mads."

"I love you too." I sigh, cutting the call and flopping back onto the bed.

I really need to get a grip.

Chapter Twenty-Five

MADDIE

After a long, scalding hot shower, I have to say I feel better. Since the second Grayson left the apartment, my mind hasn't stopped thinking about him. At one point, I cried with laughter thinking about the fact I held a gun up to a professional hitman. What the hell was I thinking? Then my body heated up when I thought about what he did with that gun after.

I have no idea where I stand with him right now. We've both fucked up. We aren't right for each other. I drop into the leather sofa, covering my hands with the sleeve of my hoodie. Flicking the TV on, I scroll through and click on the news. I have about twenty minutes until Sienna arrives.

I don't even hear the front door open as Sienna wraps me in a warm embrace. She grabs the phone out of my trembling hands.

"Maddie, are you okay?" She cups my face in her hands and studies me. I sniffle and shake my head.

"Right, I'm going to make us a hot chocolate with extra cream. And then you are going to tell me what's been going on. I've just left Grayson at mine with Keller, and he looks just as awful as you do."

The tears fall harder the second she mentions his name.

She hands me a tissue and strokes my hair. "I promise you. Everything is going to be okay."

A few minutes later, a steaming hot chocolate is thrust under my nose. "Thank you, Si."

She sits beside me, crossing her legs on the chair as she blows into her drink.

"So, spill. From the beginning."

I take a deep breath. For the next few minutes that feel like hours, I let it all out. From the kiss we had last year, all the way up to this morning. I don't need to leave any details out; Sienna is more than accustomed to the mafia lifestyle.

"Maddie, do you think maybe it's not so much about what the other person can offer you? It's about how much you love each other. It's pretty obvious that you're madly in love with one another, disguised under the fighting. You have a man who would literally burn down the earth to be with you. To love you. Underneath all that craziness, he's obsessed with you."

I squeeze my eyes together to ease the throbbing headache forming at my temples.

"Just think about it. It's your life, and only you can decide. Not me, not your mother, or your family. Only you. Go with your heart. I just want you to be happy. And I think this hunt for Prince Charming is getting in the way of what you really want. *Who* you really want."

She's right.

This whole obsession boils down to my quest to please my mom.

I wanted my mom not to look down on me for once; I wanted her to be proud of me. And the only way I knew how would be to find a respectable husband.

"Come here," she says, opening her arms out to me. I launch myself into her arms, and she squeezes me tight, stroking my hair.

When everything else goes to shit, I'll always have my best friend.

Chapter Twenty-Six

MADDIE

After a weekend with Sienna, eating ice cream and binge-watching rom-coms, I feel better. I keep searching for men who I think my mom would approve of, who would give me this idea of a life I'm not even sure I want anymore. I'm actually in a place right now where I am happy on my own. I have an apartment and a studio with a thriving career. Why the hell have I been so obsessed with needing Mr. Perfect?

I spend the entire week keeping busy with work. The place is pretty much sparkling at this point. All my supplies are re-organized into neat containers; I even stacked Evie's pens in color gradients. Anything to keep my mind off him.

My mom called me yesterday to tell me my cousin, Masie, who as she reminded me is four years younger than me, is getting married at the end of the year. I've been invited with a plus one. Or rather, she's trying to force me to find a plus one. Alas, the only man I will ever want isn't the man for me.

Sometimes, things just aren't meant to be.

But this has been the longest week of my life without him.

Sienna beams at me as I approach the VIP booth area in the End Zone. A possessive Keller has his arm wrapped around her waist. Giving her a wave, I quicken my pace.

"Maddie." Luca nods, holding his glass of amber liquid up to me.

Frankie nods. His gray eyes are striking against his dark features and olive skin. I can't lie; he's very attractive. Not Grayson, but has that Greek god vibe, powerful and shrouded in darkness.

Maybe that's what I'm into.

Luca pats the seat next to him, and I join him. Keller pours me a glass of champagne and slides it across the table to me.

"Everything okay, Maddie?" he questions, raising his eyebrows as he speaks.

He knows.

"Yep." I swipe up the flute and down the contents. Luca chuckles next to me. Great. They all know.

I can feel all of their eyes on me as I sip my drink. The air in the room shifts then, and the hairs on the back of my neck stand.

"Evening." His voice sends electricity straight through me.

Grayson.

Everyone greets him, but I keep my head straight.

He slides in the booth next to Sienna, opposite me.

"Sunshine."

"Hi," I reply with a tight smile, trying my hardest not to squirm in my seat.

A barely dressed barmaid rushes over and drops a glass of scotch in front of him. Her fingers brush against the black shirt clinging to his bicep. My hand tightens around the glass. All the while, his eyes never leave mine. His Adam's apple bobs as he swallows, and I can't help but lick my lips.

Luca leans into me. "Hey, calm down with the glass. You'll shatter that in a second."

Immediately, my grip on the glass loosens.

"You're unusually quiet, Maddie. What's up?" he asks. It kind of stuns me. I've been to plenty of events with Luca, but we've never really struck up much of a conversation. He always chips in with jokes and comments, though.

But he's always watching. Taking everything in.

"I just have a lot going on. I don't know what I'm doing, to be honest."

I can feel Grayson's stare burning into the side of my face.

"He's been in the same mood this week—fucking painful." He chuckles.

We really are miserable without each other.

I whisper into Luca's ear. His strong sandalwood aftershave mixed with cigarettes assaults my senses.

"I'm pretty sure I've pissed him off to the point of no return."

"I don't think you could ever push him away. He's obsessed with you; he has been since last year. You did hurt him, though. Just think about what happened to him before. He's a softie deep down there somewhere. But he's also a hothead." He grins, side-eyeing Grayson.

"Maybe if you both just accept you fucking love one another, it might make life easier for us. Stop pushing each other away."

Love.

I've never felt anything so all-consuming, so passionate, so pure in my twenty-six years on this planet.

"Maybe. I guess we will see."

"Just think about it." He shrugs.

My eyes meet Grayson's thunderous expression and my cheeks heat. God, he's sexy when he's angry.

I cross my legs under the table, purposely brushing against his shin.

His face morphs from anger to hunger, his eyes flashing with desire, burning straight into my core.

He stands. I tilt my head up as he towers over me, holding out his hand. "Dance with me?"

The guys around the table shoot their heads around to us. Luca nudges my thigh with his own, prompting me to move.

I slip my hand in his, and the second I do, warmth swarms in my veins. He leads us toward the dance floor, barging past the crowds of people.

He doesn't say a word as he spins me in front of him and wraps his strong arms around my torso, his head resting on my shoulder. We sway to the music, my ass grinding up against him.

Everyone around us fades into the background. It's just us. I turn in his arms, lacing mine around his neck. We don't say anything, just stare into each other's eyes.

He was right; there was never any going back once we started this.

"Meet me tomorrow? At my gym? Say, 1 p.m.?"

"Wait, are you not staying?"

"I came to get Frankie. I promised you space and I want to give you it, Maddie. Last weekend was a lot, even for us. You need to work out what it is that you truly want. I don't want part of you. I want all of you. Every single inch. Nothing less. So, have fun tonight. Tomorrow, you make the decision. Okay?"

The words are on the tip of my tongue, to tell him to just take me home. I want it all. But something stops me.

He's right in a way, but the thought of losing him, being without him like I have been for the last week, gives me all the answers I need.

"Tomorrow." I cup his stubbly jaw. This moment is so raw.

He presses a kiss to the top of my head and releases me. Frankie strides in our direction.

"No matter what, it will always be you." Grayson takes my hand and squeezes before turning on his heel. He and Frankie head for the exit, and the next thing I know, Sienna is wrapping me up in a hug.

Can I do this? Can I really give him everything?

"Let's go get a drink, Mads. You look like you could do with one."

"Hmm, yeah."

Chapter Twenty-Seven

MADDIE

The wind whips my hair across my face. I'm standing on the pavement, staring at the front door to his boxing gym. Shit, I'm really doing this.

Pulling up my big girl panties, I push open the door. I'm hit with the scent of sweat and leather. Grunts followed by the thuds of punches echo through the room. The door slams closed behind me. Suddenly, all movement stops, and all eyes are on me.

There are muscles everywhere!

"Back to fucking work," Grayson commands, and everyone gets back to punching immediately. He's leaning over the red ropes on the boxing ring in the center of the room. His hair is drenched with sweat, his biceps tensed, glistening under the lights.

He's naked . . . well, his top half, anyway. His defined muscles are emphasized by the shimmer of sweat.

"Come here, sunshine."

He ducks under the ropes and climbs down the stairs, closing the distance between us. I tip my head up as he reaches me. I fiddle with the sleeve of my cardigan and stare at his bright red boxing gloves down by his side.

"I missed you so fucking much," he whispers.

"I missed you too."

My face is squished against his sticky, hard chest as he pulls me into him, wrapping his strong arms so tight around me I can barely breathe.

"I'm sorry. I promise I will never, ever do anything to hurt you again." His voice quivers. He's hurting just as much as I am. No, he shouldn't have left me and driven off. But I shouldn't have used his insecurities against him like that. If he had spoken about me with his parents like that, I would have wanted to kill him with my bare hands.

"I'm sorry for hurting you." I sigh and rest my head against his chest, the erratic beating of his heart hammering against my ear.

"You have nothing to be sorry for, baby. This is all on me. Now, let me make it up to you?"

"What are you up to?"

"It's a surprise. I promise it's a good one. I just need to finish this session and then I'm all yours." He plants a kiss on the tip of my nose. I grab his cheeks and pull him down, claiming his mouth.

The room erupts into wolf whistles. He smiles against my lips.

"You've got all evening to fuck each other's faces, Grayson. Get your ass up here and let me punch you. I've got ten minutes of my session left," Luca rumbles.

"We both know you won't be landing any punches on me, give me a minute."

"I can't show you up in front of your girl," Luca retorts with a wink.

Grayson's laughter draws my attention back to him. "Are you okay to wait while I knock that cocksucker out?" he says. "Then, I'll show you your surprise."

Excitement bubbles in my stomach. "Can I have a clue? Please?"

"Chop fucking chop, Grayson," Luca grunts.

Grayson rolls his eyes. "Patience, baby," he whispers. "Go, take a seat and watch your man fight."

"Got it, sir." I wink, tapping him in the center of his chest.

He turns his back and stomps back into the ring. I step over to the mats just to the left of me, next to the punching bag chained to the ceiling. I plop down onto the floor and spread my legs out straight in front of me, leaning my back up against the wall.

"Come on then, show me what you've got," Grayson taunts Luca.

Luca throws a punch, and Grayson ducks out of the way. "Really, Luca? Fucking sloppy. Hit me," Grayson demands. Luca launches his left hand straight at Grayson's cheek. As it connects, my man's head jolts back. He shakes his head and grins at Luca. "Better, but still not hard enough."

Ten minutes fly by. Grayson and Luca are bent over with their hands on their knees, breathing heavily. Sweat drips down Grayson's forehead. "I'm off, I'll see you next week," he says, saluting Luca and ducking back under the ropes. He stalks toward me, pulling off his gloves. "Are you ready?" He holds out his wrapped hand. I grab his hand, and he pulls me to my feet.

We exit through a wooden door at the back of the gym.

Pictures of Keller and Grayson at Keller's world title fight are framed on the wall. A smile forms on my lips as I remember that day. That was the first time since *the kiss* that I'd seen Grayson. He avoided me for as long as he could, up until the wedding.

A large oak desk sits in the center of the room, scattered with paperwork. My brows furrow as I spot two small suitcases, one baby pink, one black.

Grayson circles behind me, wrapping his arms around my stomach, leaning his head on my shoulder. "Where's the one place you've always wanted to go?"

"Russia?" I lie.

"Not quite."

"London?" I try to hold in my excitement, but it still comes out more like a squeak.

"I'm about to give you the best date of your life, baby."

"Oh my God!" I shriek. "Thank you, thank you, thank you." I pepper kisses all over his neck.

"When are we going?"

"Now."

"Wait, what, I haven't even packed!"

"All taken care of, everything you need is there." He nods at the suitcase.

"How?"

"I'm a very resourceful man, sunshine."

"Well, go get showered. We have a flight to catch." I push against his shoulder.

"It's a private jet, baby."

He lifts me up, and I wrap my legs around his waist. His lips slam onto mine, his tongue plundering my mouth. I moan into his mouth. His hard cock rubs against my panties, sending bolts of electricity to my core.

"Fuck, sunshine," he growls. "I never want to go a single week without you again."

"Me neither."

The door rattles as he slams my back into it. "Are you ready to join the mile high club, baby?"

"Fuck yes."

Chapter Twenty-Eight

GRAYSON

Excitement radiates off her in contagious waves. Last weekend was the realization I needed. I can't lose her.

Every damn day, I made sure my lunchtime jog included her studio on my route. If I couldn't be with her, I still needed to see her. She's my drug. My heart belongs to Maddie. I'm sure it has since the first time she threatened to stab me in the eye last year. But now, I know what I need to do. I *have* to be better for her. Give her everything she deserves.

I'm addicted to everything about her. Her strength, her bright personality, her sass. Every damn thing. And I will do everything in my power to keep her. Even if that means slipping on a mask in front of her parents to keep them off her back.

I've never felt like this about anyone. Just one week of no contact almost sent me off the rails. I couldn't concentrate on anything other than how to get her back and keep her. This woman deserves the world, so here we are, thirty-five thousand feet in the air, on our way to the bright lights of London for the weekend.

She's busy sipping her champagne and reading on her Kindle. I don't know how many times I've seen the word *cock* flash up on that screen. She's about to ride one in a minute. I'm patiently waiting for the air hostess to stop fiddling around us.

Maddie's pink dagger nails stab into my forearm before she politely tells her to "Fuck off." The air hostess looks at me in horror, but all I can do is shrug. I'm not apologizing for Maddie being possessive of me. It's fucking sexy.

The air hostess finally retires to the cockpit. I saw the way the pilot eyed her up earlier; I bet they'll be busy for a while. I take my opportunity.

"Hey! I was reading that," she whines when I pluck away her e-reader. I bring my mouth to her neck, and she tips her head toward the window. I lick her silky skin all the way up to her jaw. A small moan escapes her lips.

"You don't have to read about cock when you have one ready and waiting for you here."

My hand brushes along her bare legs, all the way up to the hem of her tight black dress. I slip my fingers underneath, expecting to find a lacy thong. She opens her legs, just slightly, enough to give me access to her bare pussy.

"Mmm, no panties for me today?" I rasp, and she shakes her head. I'm starting to acquire quite the collection of her panties in my car. I bite the flesh on her neck, and her floral perfume swirls around my tongue. "On my lap," I whisper.

"Here?"

"It wasn't a question, baby. Straddle me. Now."

She licks her lips, hiking her dress up slightly, enough to cover her ass at the back, but giving me the full view of that soaking pussy. The blood rushes to my cock. She clambers over my lap, settling her legs either side of mine, resting on the leather chair. Her arms wrap around my neck, her tits now directly in my eyeline. My hand moves underneath her, and I slide three fingers inside her. Using my other hand, I pull down her dress to reveal her tits. Taking one of her nipples into my mouth, I suck at the same time as I fuck her with my fingers. Her hips roll in rhythm. She pants as I continue to suck and bite. Her breathy moans spur me on. She leans forward, and I slide my fingers out and reposition them so my index finger rims her asshole. My middle and ring finger push back into her pussy. Her lips part in an O as my index finger slowly slips in.

"Fuckkkk!" she rasps. I muffle her moans with the palm of my hand. She shoots me daggers as I slow the pace. I give her a smirk and slip my fingers out of her.

"If I don't get my cock inside you in the next twenty seconds, I'm going to explode," I grit out.

Her hands shoot straight to my jeans, scrambling at my belt and finally releasing my aggressively hard dick. She brings her hands back up to my shoulders and lifts herself up, settling right above my dick. Then, she slowly sinks down. The sensation erupts tingles throughout my entire body. Her walls clamp around my dick, squeezing, as she chokes on a breath, reaching the base. "Jesus fucking Christ. You are going to kill me, woman!" I growl as she lifts herself back up and slams down. My eyes almost bulge out of their sockets. Her pussy brushes up against me every time. I pinch her clit, causing her to throw her head back.

"Kiss me," I groan, barely able to contain myself.

Without missing a beat, she brings her lips to mine hungrily, moaning into my mouth as she rides me. I slam my hips up to meet her rhythm. Our teeth clatter against each other's. I grip the back of her head and push her further into me. Every single muscle in my body tenses. "Now!" I growl. A whimper escapes her, so I press my lips to hers to silence her. I jolt violently, spilling into her.

Damn.

A few moments pass, her forehead resting against mine as our breathing regulates.

"Well, how was your mile high service, Miss Peters?" I tease, stroking her swollen bottom lip.

"Hmmm, perfect. How many more hours have we got left on this flight?" She smirks, slipping my hand from underneath her.

"About three hours."

"Well, Mr. Ward, I might need your mouth on my pussy after that. Shall we say in about an hour?"

"You know you can sit on my face whenever you want, sunshine."

She lifts herself off me and plops back down into her own seat. I bend over and pick up her Kindle and hand it to her.

"Better than the book porn?"

"God, so much better." She chuckles, resting her head on my shoulder and lighting up her screen.

I rest my head atop hers and close my eyes, sliding my arm behind her back so she can cuddle into me.

"Hey, hold it up a bit, I want to read," I say.

"I have to say, I think you're better with your mouth than this guy."

"Oh, really? In that case, I'm not waiting an hour for a taste." Her body vibrates against mine, my favorite red blush creeping across her chest.

This might be the best flight of my life.

Chapter Twenty-Nine

MADDIE

A s soon as we touched down in London, Grayson had us whisked off in a black limousine outside Heathrow Airport. I have no idea where we are staying or what he has planned, but I don't care.

The limo drives through the busy streets of London, and I'm pretty sure we stop at every single set of traffic lights on the way. Not that I mind; I'm happy sightseeing from the window. Grayson is busy tapping away on his phone, his other hand encased in mine. London is pretty gray this morning . . . well, it's the afternoon, according to my phone. Time zones aren't my thing; it hurts my head just trying to work that out.

The streets are bustling with people. Much like a smaller version of New York. The big wheel catches my attention. Sienna always went on about how stunning the view is over sunset. Grabbing my phone, I snap a quick picture and send it to her.

"Hey, Grayson."

"Yes, baby?" He rests his phone down on his lap.

"Could we go on the London Eye?"

"We are going to fit in as many tourist attractions as we can in forty-eight hours, or, well, whatever we can manage between me fucking you overlooking the skyline, that is." He winks, and I have to bite my tongue, literally, not to squeal in excitement.

"Thank you for bringing me here. Best. Date. Ever."

"Anything on top of your sightseeing list?"

"Buckingham Palace. The Tower Bridge lit up at night. Ohhh, and maybe a little bit of shopping on Oxford Street." I pout.

"I take it Sienna has given you an extensive list."

"I might have texted her."

"How about whatever we don't fit in, we do next time?"

Next time.

My stomach flips at the thought.

"Deal."

THE CAR COMES to a stop outside a red-carpeted entrance. Flashy cars are lined up along the street. "This looks amazing, Grayson."

"Only the best for my woman," he replies, getting out of the limo. The serious-looking, black-suited driver holds my door open, and Grayson comes into view, holding out his hand for me.

Two men dressed in black uniforms with the funny hats remove our luggage from the trunk. Grayson whips out his wallet and hands a wad to the driver, who gives him a nod.

"You ready, baby?" he says.

I nod, unsure what else to do. As we walk toward the glass revolving doors of the Shangri-La, I'm completely overwhelmed being surrounded by glitz and wealth. I don't belong here. My biker boots squeak against the shiny gray marble floors. The essence of bergamot wafts through the reception area, which is perfectly detailed with gold against the marble.

Grayson checks us in, and I wait behind him. He takes my hand in his, giving me a reassuring smile, before walking us over to the elevator, passing huge displays of bright red flowers with impressive crystal chandeliers hanging above.

An empty elevator greets us. I stay cuddled up against him as we walk in. The elevator dings on the thirty-ninth floor. I gasp as the doors open, revealing our suite. The room is filled with neutral tones and floral silk wallpaper. Grayson leads us in, and my eyes are immediately drawn to the London skyline. I can't help but admire the Tower Bridge. I walk past the cream couch, scattered with an array of brown pillows. A little Chinese tea set sits on the coffee table.

Our luggage has been neatly placed next to the bed. Excitement zips through me as I launch myself over and jump onto the mattress, sinking in the luxurious covers. I sprawl out on my back and starfish. "Grayson, get over here. This is the comfiest bed I've ever been on."

The mattress dips as his massive frame joins me. Resting my chin on my hand, I turn to face him. His sandy hair is ruffled, his chiseled jaw not as tight as it usually is. Damn, does he look good in all black.

"We have to be somewhere in an hour."

"What are we doing?"

"That would ruin the surprise element."

He runs the pad of his thumb along my cheek. "You are so beautiful, Maddie."

I lower my gaze. I guess when you've been brought up by a mother who never fails to pick out your flaws, it's all you become used to.

He tips my chin back up with his index finger. "You are the most beautiful woman on this whole damn planet. Don't hide from me, sunshine. Embrace it."

"I'll try."

"Good. I'd never lie to you."

Our kiss is slow and sensual. His hand cups my jaw as he deepens it. I hook my leg over his thigh.

I bite down on his lower lip, and he groans into my mouth. "Mine," he rasps, bringing his forehead to mine.

"Yours," I say through a smile.

He catches my wrist and brings the palm of my hand to rest over his heart, which beats strongly through his ribs beneath my fingers. "And this is yours."

"Thank you for trusting me with it," I whisper. I don't want to push him too far; I know his scars run deep. This is just enough confirmation to know he feels the same way.

"Come on, let's get showered and to our appointment." As he sits up, I snatch his wrist, catching his Rolex. He turns his head back to me, cocking his brow. I grab his hand and lead it along my thigh, opening my legs for him.

"Shower. Now."

Reluctantly, I jump off the bed and shuffle out of my dress, leaving it in a pile on the floor. A naked Grayson watches my every move. I stand before him, biting my lower lip, and say, "I'll go get started."

He chases me.

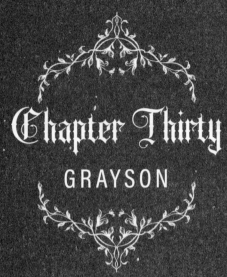

Chapter Thirty

GRAYSON

"What shall I wear?" she calls out as she walks out of the bathroom, drying her hair with a towel, another wrapped around her body. The water shimmers against her porcelain skin. My dick twitches, despite being inside her only a few minutes ago.

A knock sounds. "I'll get it," I say, rushing over to the door. My first little surprise for her.

I swing open the door in only a towel wrapped around my waist. I'm greeted by a smiling older man, who gives me a bottle of champagne and two little black boxes.

"Who is it?" Maddie shouts.

The man nods and closes the door for me before I can even give him a tip. I pick up the boxes, stuffing one slyly back in my luggage. The other remains in my hands. I can't wait to see her face when she opens this. I walk back into the bedroom.

I close the distance between us and stand behind her, looking at her in the mirror. She smiles as I approach, shutting off the hair dryer. My hands are behind my back. She spins around in her seat, tipping her head up to me. Fuck, she's perfect.

"Hold your hands out and close your eyes," I tell her.

She raises a brow before doing as I asked. "You better not stick your dick into my mouth."

"And why not?"

"I'm joking." She opens her mouth wide so I can see her tonsils, and I have to stop myself from actually taking her up on the offer. "Well, go on then."

I place the box in her mouth and her teeth bite down. Her eyes shoot open in surprise. She snatches it out of her mouth and rips the lid off. Her eyes settle on the handmade, diamond-encrusted sunshine necklace.

Her eyes well up, and with shaky hands, she brushes the necklace with her index finger.

"Grayson, oh my God. It's beautiful." She sniffles. "It's too nice to actually wear. I'm so clumsy I might lose it."

"Then I'll buy you another one. Seeing that smile light up your face is priceless." Tears stream down her cheeks as she takes the necklace out the box and hands it to me. Pulling back her hair to the side, she turns back around so her back faces me.

I secure the jewelry. The gold chain looks stunning against her skin. I bend and plant a kiss on the back of her neck and crouch beside her.

She spins in her seat.

"You know, none of this is about the money. I just need you to know that. I don't need gifts to keep me around. Just you." She pauses. "And your huge dick."

"Fucking hell, I don't know which one of us is worse."

"Match made in heaven," she teases, opening her legs and then spinning back around. I run my hand over my face and let out a ragged breath. There isn't a minute of the day I don't think about sinking into her. I know in my heart, it's way beyond fucking. I love cuddling her, kissing her, laughing with her, winding her up. I want it all with her. Fuck, I love her.

"Be a good girl for me and get dressed. We need to leave. I think this might even be better than sex."

She gasps in horror. "Don't call me a good girl if you don't want to fuck me, Grayson. You know that gets me drenched."

Holy shit.

The hair dryer buzzes back to life.

Looks like I'm getting dressed in the other room, as it's the only way I can resist this temptress. And we aren't missing this surprise.

Chapter Thirty-One

MADDIE

The Bentley pulls up outside a little pub on the corner of the street. The London Eye illuminates the sky in red to my right.

Grayson exits the vehicle, walking around and opening up my door, looking sexy as ever, more so tonight in a black suit, a fresh white shirt, and a black tie. The black skintight dress stops just above my knee, which restricts my movements. Grayson, the gentleman he is, holds his arm out for me to steady myself as I stand.

There's a bitter chill in the air. I thought it would have been a little warmer being nearly April. I'm glad he packed me my leather jacket. We make our way past the little pub and across the street over to the lawns just in front of the big wheel. "Wow, look at it."

"Stunning," he replies, his eyes only on me, which makes me blush.

"No fucking way, it's closed, isn't it?"

"Not for us, sunshine."

He leads us over to the metal railings, and a young guy awaits us. He opens the red rope to let us through to the platform. The Thames flickers with lights as the skyline twinkles. It's truly enchanting.

An open glass pod is waiting for us at the podium. Tears prickle in my eyes as I take in the sight before me. The pod is lit up with the flickering of candles in lanterns. Red rose petals are scattered on the wooden floor.

"Grayson," I sob, covering my face with my hands.

He embraces me tightly. "Baby, what is it?"

"I-I just can't believe you'd do all this for me," I manage to choke out.

"Hey, look at me." He takes a step back, holding firmly on to my shoulders. "You deserve nothing less than the world. I promised you I would try my hardest to give you that. I always will. So get used to it; I don't plan on stopping."

I launch myself into his arms, wrapping my hands around his neck, his hands cupping my ass to hold me up against him.

Everything twinkles behind me, but all I can focus on is this man. A man of darkness is the only one to bring me light. It might be wrong; he might not be perfect. But he's mine and I love him.

"I love you, Grayson," I whisper against his cheek.

"You stole my line."

"What do you mean?"

My heart rate accelerates, my clammy hands almost throbbing.

"That's what I wanted to tell you up there," he says, pointing to the top of the Eye.

"It's okay. You can do it now."

"I love you."

My heart skips a beat. *Thank fucking God.*

"I love you more than anything. You are my sassy bundle of sunshine. I knew the moment I laid eyes on you, I was fucked. I don't know why we tried to fight it so hard. But I'm glad we gave in."

"Sooooo, does that make me your girlfriend?"

"You can be whatever you want. You are my everything. I mean it, I will do anything for you."

My heart can't handle so much love. It's on the verge of combustion. A sense of completeness washes over me. Like the universe has given me the other half of my soul. My missing piece.

"Although I'm not sure how your mom's going to take this." He chuckles. "I'm not quite the prince fit for her princess."

"Well, it's a good thing I don't want a boring prince. I want the villain to fuck me like a whore while telling me he loves me. I'm done living my life for everyone else. I just want you. Only you."

"Villains know how to fuck far better anyway."

Fuck, how long does this pod take to go around?

"You can remind me later," I tease.

"Why do you think I booked the whole damn London Eye?"

"How did you know I was going to say I love you back?" I ask, biting my lower lip.

"Because there's no way in hell you could deny this."

He grabs my hand before I can reply and walks us into the pod.

"See, there is a little romantic in you somewhere." I turn to him and poke him in the chest. He wraps his fingers around mine and brings my hand to his lips. The doors close behind us, and the floor jolts as we start to move.

He takes my index finger into his mouth. I drag my gaze away from the twinkling skyline as he sucks on my finger. I pull it out and drag it down his chin, following down his throat. I loosen his tie and start undoing his shirt, one button at a time, all the way down until I reach his belt. I almost salivate as those tribal tattoos peek through the gap.

I sink to the ground on my knees and unbuckle him, freeing his massive cock. I've never seen anything like it. I swirl my tongue around the tip, sucking up the salty liquid.

As I take him in my mouth, all the way to the back of my throat, I close my eyes as they start to water. "If you're not choking on it, you're not doing it right," he says in a husky tone, and I push my head further down, doing everything I can not to gag.

"Eyes up here, sunshine. I want to see you as you choke on my cock. Maybe later, I'll choke you with my hands."

I clench my legs together as I start to slide up and down his cock, all the way to the tip and back down as far as I can go.

"Deeper, baby. I'll make it worth your while. I promise," he grits out.

He brings his hand to cup my face, his thumb chasing a tear away on my cheek.

"Good girl."

I bring my hands to hold his hips as he thrusts into my

mouth a few times before sliding out. Using the back of my hand, I wipe my mouth.

Every inch of me is on fire. Ready to explode around him.

"Stand. Take that dress off. Palms on the window. Heels stay on for me."

I nod, peeling off the dress and letting it drop to the floor before making my way over to the window, my palms flat on the cold glass. Now that we're nearly at the top of the Eye, the city of London is beneath us, glittering in the night. It's magnificent.

Grayson's warm breath hits the back of my shoulder. He licks all the way down my spine, making me arch my back, my tits now squashed up against the window, my ass pressing against him.

"Every single inch of you is delicious."

The ground beneath me shakes as he takes his turn to get down on his knees. He taps the inside of my calf, and I open my legs further apart. I shiver in anticipation as his strong hands go between my thighs and he pushes against the front of them, bending me from the hips, my hands still on the glass.

"Mine," he growls just before his mouth covers my pussy. He licks all the way from my entrance up to my clit and back in slow movements.

"Holy shit, Grayson."

"We can get you louder than that, baby." He returns to where I need it. I squeeze my eyes shut, as he starts to thrust his tongue in and out of me, squeezing his hands around my thighs, literally fucking me with his tongue.

"Open your eyes, baby. I want you to watch the city below us as I claim you as mine."

I open my eyes, only to be greeted with our reflection. Grayson moves behind me, and his eyes catch mine in the reflection. Full of pure hunger, he doesn't take his eyes off mine, his hands caressing my cheeks. He bites down on my ass cheek, hard. It sends pain shooting right through me. Then he presses an open-mouthed kiss there. If I wasn't drenched before, I certainly am now.

He cups my breast and bites on the flesh. "Are you ready to be filled up now?"

"By you, always."

He slides his cock along my seam, before slamming straight into me, causing my body to thrust forward. "Fuck." I grit my teeth as I adjust to him stretching me.

"Mmm, such a good fucking girl."

I scream out as his hand slaps my left ass cheek. "Do you like that, sunshine?"

"Yes, again!"

"My dirty whore," he says, before his palm connects with the same spot.

"I want your lips," he rasps and grabs me by the hips and lifts me in the air, walking us backward toward the round wooden bench in the center of the room. He sits, and I spin around on his lap to face him.

I sink back on his dick, throwing my head back in pure pleasure.

"Ride me, sunshine."

I bite my swollen lips. "Yes, sir." I wink before slamming my lips down over his, rolling my hips to get some friction on my clit as I ride him.

With one hand on my ass, he cups my cheek in the other as he deepens the kiss, moaning into my mouth. Everything in this moment is perfect. Breaking the kiss, with a feral look in his eye, he brings two fingers up to my mouth. "Suck," he commands.

I close my eyes, still bouncing up and down on his dick, and suck. He pulls them out, his other hand now spreading my ass cheeks apart.

His fingers tease around the entrance. "Relax, sunshine," he says before kissing me while sliding his fingers in. I hold still as they enter, concentrating on his mouth owning mine, rather than on the burning sensation. It's been a while since I've had anything more than one finger in there.

"God, Maddie. You are so fucking sexy." He peppers kisses down my neck. I start to move up and down, wanting more, needing everything. With his fingers now thrusting in and out, I need to be fucked.

"I need more, Grayson. Fuck me harder."

Before I even know what's happening, I gasp as he lifts me off of him and spins me round. My hands slap against the wooden bench. One hand guides his dick along my cheeks, stopping right at the entrance of my puckered hole.

"Every hole is mine to fuck." He guides himself in.

"Good girl, stay still for me."

Bringing his chest to my back, he plants kisses along my spine, sending tingles across my body. His fingers find their way back to my pussy. "Open your legs wider for me," he whispers against my back. And I do.

"God, so fucking beautiful, spread for me." His warm breath tickles against my back. His fingers push into me at the same time he moves in and out from behind. Filling both of my holes. The pressure, the pleasure, all morph into one, sending my body spiraling on the edge of release. Grayson's hands tighten on me.

"I've dreamed of fucking you in the ass for so long," he pants, quickening the pace.

His fingers lace around my throat, squeezing around my windpipe.

Holy fuck.

Stars fill my vision as he hisses, "Come for me, baby." And that's all it takes to set my body on fire, my release consuming me, and him reaching his own too.

"Holy fucking shit."

I sag against the bench, fighting for air now that his grip has loosened around my throat. He pulls himself out of me, and I rest my head against the wood.

"I love you, Maddie. So fucking much." He picks me up off the ground, turning me to face him and pressing me into his chest.

I snap my head up to his. His eyes are full of admiration, glistening like the skyline behind us.

"You promise?" I ask, lacing my arms around his neck.

"With my whole heart. I'm not going anywhere, and not even you could make me."

"I love you, Grayson. Just for being you. Don't ever forget that."

"You know I'll always protect you, right? I will do everything to ensure I don't bring any danger back to our door. I can't make promises about that; but know that I'd lay down my life for you. This is my dark and dangerous world. You have to know that. But every time, you over me. Okay?"

I'm not going to stop him. I just want him to be safe and I want to feel safe. He hasn't given me a reason not to yet.

So, I nod cautiously. "The thought of that makes me feel sick, Grayson. I'd never ask you to change your world for me;

just keep us both safe. That's all I want. You're just as important as me. I need you here with me."

He pushes my face toward his and claims my lips. "I'm glad you broke my no-kissing rule, but fuck, I don't think I can stop."

"That was actually true?"

"Yep, I didn't want any form of intimacy. After what Amelia did, yeah, I wanted to fuck but I didn't want anyone to stick around. That seemed to keep the lines from blurring. It worked. Well, until you came along."

I'd love to slap that bitch of a woman, but equally, I'm glad she fucked it up because now he's mine.

"Well, I'm glad my lips can be of service to you." He raises his eyebrow, unamused.

"Is it bad it makes me feel all warm and fuzzy on the inside knowing it's only me you've kissed in so long?"

He lets out a deep, husky laugh.

"No, I love that you're possessive of me. Because that's exactly how I feel about you. I'm jealous of every man that's ever kissed you."

"Well, you'll be the only man kissing me from now on, and no man has ever fucked me like that," I say in my most seductive tone, giving him a quick peck. Cuddling into him, I rest my head on his shoulder.

"We best get dressed before that guy opens up the pod and is greeted with my bare ass."

He slaps my ass.

"For fuck's sake, Grayson. You can't be doing that and expect me to just get dressed."

"That ass is mine now," he rasps against my ear, biting on my earlobe.

Shortly after I throw my clothes on, the wheel comes to a

stop at the platform and the doors open. Hand in hand, we walk out. Grayson thanks the guy who let us in and we walk toward the stone wall encasing the Thames.

"Ready for dinner?" Grayson asks, tucking me neatly into his side, instantly warming me up.

"I'm famished, so yes, please."

Happy and in love, we walk off into the night.

Chapter Thirty-Two

MADDIE

After a whirlwind weekend in London, my exhaustion is bone-deep. We slept a solid ten hours last night. I don't even know what the time is. Grayson scrolls through his phone, naked. I cuddle up into his side, my fingers tracing along the outline of his abs.

We managed to fit in Buckingham Palace, a walk across the Tower Bridge. We had ice cream sitting on a bench in Hyde Park, while the swans ate bread out of little kids' hands. Kinda strange, but I guess it's very British. I won't be sticking my hand near a swan anytime soon.

We even snapped a selfie in front of the Palace and sent it to Sienna. Of course she lost her shit that we looked so happy. I'm not sure who's happier at this point.

Grayson chuckles, bringing me back to reality. My brain goes into overdrive. He mentioned on our trip he was a Taurus, which means his birthday is next month.

"Wait, how old are you?" I ask, still tracing along his stomach.

"Thirty-five. Problem?" He arches a brow at me.

"Okay, nine years, we're good. Should I start calling you *daddy*, then?" I try my hardest to keep a straight face.

He rolls on top of me, spreading my legs with his body. His dick twitches against my panties. His glare is so intense, it burns with desire. "You can call me whatever the fuck you want. As long as you're screaming it for me while bouncing up and down my dick, I don't care."

"I think I'll stick with sir for now," I mutter, giving him a sheepish grin.

His phone rings from the bedside table. Huffing at the interruption, he hauls his weight onto one arm, and I almost drool as the veins protrude from his tattooed forearms. A male voice chats away on the other end. Grayson's brow cocks up, and he glances to me.

"Okay, I wasn't expecting her, but send her up. Tell her to wait in the kitchen," he says, cutting the call and throwing the phone back on the side.

My shoulders bunch.

"Looks like you get to meet my mom today, sunshine." He beams, and the color drains from my face.

Shit.

I try to wriggle out of his hold, but he simply grabs my wrists in one hand and places them above my head.

"She's going to love you. I promise. She also knows me better than to come waltzing into my bedroom."

"Okay," I squeak, and he smiles, leaning forward and claiming my lips with his. I can't help the moan that escapes.

"Grayson, we need to get dressed," I say, trying to pull my hands from his grip, but he only tightens his hold.

"She won't come in here." He presses his hard cock against my pussy. "Plus, I can't go out there with a raging hard-on." My cheeks heat as he slides his cock up and down, making my whole body buzz.

"Can you be quiet?" he whispers, nipping at my neck.

"I can try."

"Good girl." He slams his lips over mine, and as his cock slides into my wet heat I clench my teeth, letting out a hiss as I stretch around him. I hook my legs around his waist, giving him better access.

"Fuck, sunshine," he grits out.

Just then the bedroom door flies open and a woman stands there, shell-shocked, while Grayson's face is buried in my neck.

There is no way this is his mom.

"Grayson," I hiss, biting my bottom lip as he slams into me, my eyes still on this woman in our doorway.

"There's a woman in our fucking bedroom."

He falters immediately and cranes his neck toward the door. She scowls at us, a blush spreading up her chest.

"Care to explain why you're fucking my husband?" Her high-pitched voice makes me roll my eyes.

A giggle escapes me. Who does this bitch think she is?

With a heavy fake gasp, I say, "Grayson, how could you!"

A confused-looking Grayson turns his attention back to me. I give him a wink before death glaring at who I assume is his ex-wife.

"Are you just going to stand there and gawk or did you want to join?" My tone is patronizing. Her mouth parts, cheeks red, and her eyes flit between me and Grayson. Thank fuck we're under the covers.

A moment of silence passes. Grayson bursts out into a

full-bellied laughter, collapsing on top of me and pressing his face into my neck. His body vibrates against me, his cock still safely inside me.

Once he catches his breath, his eyes bore into mine. Those icy blues are filled with adoration. "I fucking love you, sunshine," he says, loud enough for that bitch over there to hear. I don't want to look at her, I can't. I'm captivated by my man. Right now, he's all I see.

"I love you, too, so much."

His perfectly white teeth emerge as he gives me a wide smile, enough to show those creases by his eyes.

An irritating cough breaks the moment. He swings his head around to her—gone is the happy Grayson, back is the raging monster. I swear his eyes darken the second he looks at her.

"Get the fuck out of my house, Amelia. I thought I made it clear. I never want to see your disgusting face again." Anger drips from his tone, and his hands still squeeze my wrists so I can't even calm him down. Instead, I clench my legs around his waist tighter, pushing his cock further into me.

She still stands there, glaring at us.

"Do not make me repeat myself, Amelia," he warns.

"I need to speak with you . . . privately," she whispers.

"Yeah, well, I have more important things to be doing right this second. And I sure as shit am not leaving my *girlfriend* unsatisfied for you. So, if you could close your door on the way out." He dismisses her, turning his attention back to me. The door clicks closed, and he visibly relaxes, closing his eyes.

"Grayson, look at me."

"I'm sorry about her. Fuck, she's the last person I wanted to see today. I promise you she's not my wife, nor does she ever come here."

He releases his grip on my wrists, my fingers now completely numb.

"It's okay. You know you can show your emotions, right? Especially with me. She hurt you, Grayson. I know you. I trust you. Now go and get rid of that bitch from our lives and come back in here and fuck me. Don't think I'm letting you get away with leaving me naked and dripping for you. It will only ever be for you."

He lets out a groan. "Fuck!"

Bringing my palms to his chest, I push him back. "Come on, big boy, I want to scream your name. I can't until she's gone. I'll get stage fright." I smirk. Reluctantly, he pulls himself out of me. I snatch the cover and pull it up around my neck as he throws on a pair of gray sweatpants.

"Seriously? You're going out there, showing her your fine-ass body in a pair of gray fucking sweatpants. Do you want her to jump on your dick?"

He cocks a brow at me and stalks back toward the bed.

"Let's get one thing very clear. The only woman I ever want jumping on my cock is you. Every inch of me belongs entirely to you."

My breath hitches at his intense words. He bends and presses the softest kiss to my lips. I wrap my hands around the back of his skull and push him further into me.

Breaking the kiss, he grabs a black T-shirt from the floor and pulls it over his head. His sandy hair is all scruffy on top. He gives me a wink and walks toward the door.

"You have five minutes before I finish myself off," I warn him as he walks through the door.

"The only way you're coming is with my cock in your pussy and my finger up your ass. So, I suggest you wait," he shouts back.

Great. I don't know what's worse, meeting his mom or his ex-wife while being fucked.

I pull the duvet all the way over my head and close my eyes, trying to concentrate on anything else other than my throbbing pussy.

He better hurry the fuck up.

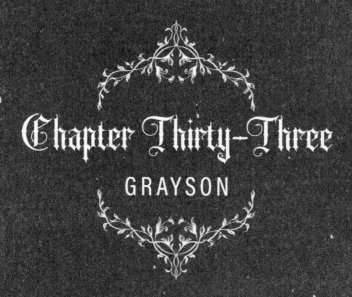

Chapter Thirty-Three

GRAYSON

The playfulness is all gone, replaced by anger as I round the corner and see my ex-wife making herself at home in my fucking penthouse. She's sifting through the cupboards, looking for a cup. The kettle boils away in the background.

"You aren't staying, so I wouldn't bother making a coffee."

The only thing stopping me wanting to wring her neck is Maddie.

"Oh, don't be silly, Grayson. Just go and get rid of your little slut and talk to me properly." She bites her lip, her eyes roaming up and down my body.

Is she fucking high?

My jaw ticks as I stride toward her. "I don't think so. And don't you ever call my girlfriend a slut. Don't forget who was fucking my best friend behind my back. There's only one whore in this house, and it's you."

"You don't mean that, you loved me."

"Did I, really?" I snap, my patience wearing thin. I know for a fact I've only felt love for one woman in my life, and she's in my bed.

"Yes, we had four amazing years together. Can you really just let that go? I miss you." Her long red nails shoot toward my chest. I flinch and take a step back.

"Why are you here?"

She shuffles her feet, her gaze dropping to the floor.

"I bumped into your mom the other day, in a café down the road from our place. She told me about your exciting new life here in New York. I saw the fight last year with Keller. I thought, maybe, enough time has passed for you to finally forgive me. We can make a home again, build a life."

My nostrils flare. What the fuck does my mom think she's playing at? I barely speak to her anyway; why would she decide to interfere now?

"It's his birthday tomorrow." A tear slips down her cheek, and it makes me sick.

"You need to leave before I strangle you." I pin her with a glare to show her I'm not joking. I'm not the man she was married to anymore.

"We could help each other. Maybe you need to let it all out with me, fuck me like you used to," she says, and I squeeze my fists tight, every muscle popping out of my body.

Rage, pure fucking rage, blinds my vision. As she looks around my home, her eyes almost light up with dollar signs.

"What do you say, a fuck for old time's sake? To help us grieve?" She sashays, licking her lips, and I cringe, taking a step back.

Delusional.

Something brushes past me from behind, and I flick my

head around. All I see is a bundle of bright blonde hair whirl past me.

"I've fucking heard enough. Take the fucking hint, woman. He doesn't want to fuck you. He hates your guts. Now get the fuck out before I kill you first."

Maddie storms over with anger, grabbing Amelia by the hair and dragging her to the front door.

"Grayson, get this lunatic off me!" Amelia screams in agony, clawing at Maddie's arms.

I try to contain my laugh as I open the front door, and Maddie shoots me a look. "Thanks."

Amelia crumples to the floor with a thud as my woman shoves her out.

"You fucking bitch!" She stands and launches herself at Maddie, but I swiftly jump in front of her, and Amelia crashes into me.

"Out!" I roar.

"Never come anywhere near me again, Amelia. Nothing on this planet could ever bring me back to you." I pull Maddie tight against my side. "This woman is my life. Now get the fuck out of my property."

Teary-eyed, she leaves.

Jesus fucking Christ.

"Thank you." I sigh.

Her face lights up. "Your walls are quite thin. I was a bit worried you might actually kill her. Then when I heard her proposition you, I wanted to murder her myself. Plus, you can't fuck me if your ass is hauled up in jail."

My sunshine has a little dark side.

"You're perfect, you know that, right?"

She bites her lip, looking at me through her lashes.

"Perfect to you, maybe."

"Perfect for me, yes."

This woman can bring out just about every emotion in me. But this one is the one I crave. Her ability to see me, to accept me. It's something I never shared with Amelia. I spent our whole relationship hiding behind a mask, pretending that a normal life was enough. She never wanted to hear about any of my kills on duty. She didn't realize that was my only way of calming the monster within me.

Yet Maddie . . . she gets me. She doesn't want me to change; she just wants me to be safe. She just wants to be loved.

Now that's the person I want to spend the rest of my days with.

"I meant what I said earlier. I love you." I trail my finger down to that gold sunshine necklace I bought her in London.

"I love you, Grayson. It was perfect when you called me your girlfriend. Do it again."

No matter how dark my life is, I'll need her light with me every day.

"You'll be more than my girlfriend one day."

The little smile that creeps up the corner of her mouth just proves to me I am right. She will be my wife.

Chapter Thirty-Four

MADDIE

We've fallen into a pretty normal routine. After the excitement of throwing his bitch ex-wife out the door last month, we've been inseparable. Cooking together, cuddling up on the couch watching films. Most nights, he slips out of bed to go to *work*. He thinks I'm still asleep when he brushes his lips against my cheek and tells me he loves me. I'm restless the whole night until he's home safely.

For some reason, tonight, it's worse than any other night. No matter how much I toss and turn, my mind won't switch off, imagining the worst. The last couple of nights, he hasn't come home until sunrise. He showers and slips straight into bed.

I'm worried.

With a huff, I kick the blanket off and stomp into the living room, picking up the first dirty book on the pile next to the couch.

Getting myself comfy on the couch, I pull out my book-mark and open up the latest smut book Sienna has lent me.

The penthouse elevator pings. I stand and pad over toward the elevator after putting the book down.

Since our trip to London, Grayson and I haven't spent a day apart. He meets me for lunch every day. We stay at his penthouse, but on a few occasions in the last month, he has stayed at mine.

I gasp as Grayson stumbles out of the elevator. My eyes are glued to the crimson dripping from his neck. "Shit, Grayson, oh my God!" I wrap my arm around him and assist him over to the couch.

"Fuck," he hisses.

"What do you need me to do?" I ask, avoiding the blood.

His eyes flicker to mine, and his features soften.

"There's a first-aid kit under the sink. Can you grab it for me, baby?"

I dart over, throw open the cupboard door, and snatch the red first-aid kit.

"Oh, and a cloth!" he shouts, hissing in a breath after.

Spinning on my heel, I grab the black cloth on the drain-ing board and run over to him. I hold the cloth up and press it against the wound.

"Okay, what next?"

He rummages through, lining up a variety of random white items on the seat, then rips open one of the packets with his teeth.

"Use this wipe, clean the wound, and tell me how big the cut is."

I gently wipe around the wound, as delicately as I can, with shaky fingers.

Once the area is clean, there's a clean horizontal slice on the left-hand side of his neck, around two inches or so.

"It's not that big, I don't know what you were bitching about."

"Oh, I'll remember to be less of a pussy next time I'm stabbed."

Next time.

Shit, next time could be worse.

He hands me some funny-looking tape. "Stick that across the cut, then dress it up, and I'll be good as new."

I chew on the inside of my mouth as I put the tape over the cut. I hold my palm out for the dressing. Holding the padded dressing, I tape around the edges.

"All done, my wounded soldier," I say, rubbing my hands together.

"There is one last thing you can do for me that would really heal me."

"Hmmm?"

He holds his hand out in front of him and flicks his wrist, motioning for me to come to him. He catches my wrist and yanks me down onto his lap. My butt lands on his hard thigh. I hoist my legs up to rest over his.

"And how can your nurse assist you?"

He taps his index finger to his lips. I roll my eyes. He chuckles, and before I know it, his hand grips the back of my head, and he pushes his face toward me, claiming my mouth. I smile and bite down on his lower lip.

"Thank you." Sincerity drips from his tone.

"Try not to make this a habit. I thought you were good at your job," I tease.

"What can I say, I was too eager to get home to you. I

didn't spot the guy waiting for me by my car. Although, I'm the one still breathing, so give me some credit."

His words hit me like a ton of bricks.

I'm the reason he got hurt. His obsession with me could kill him.

"Hey." He tips my chin up.

"This is a me problem. It's not your fault. You can't help the fact I'm completely, utterly obsessed with you, woman. I always will be. I just need to work on somehow keeping you out of my brain while I'm at work."

I give him a tight smile and pull myself out of his hold.

"Come on, we need to get to bed. I have to be up early for work," I say, giving him a quick peck. I dart to the bedroom, straight to the en suite, locking the door behind me.

Shit.

Tears roll down my face as I slide my back down the door.

I love this man more than anything in the world. What the hell am I going to do if something happens to him?

"Baby, can you let me in?" His deep voice echoes through the room.

With a sniffle, I wipe my nose and stand, opening the door. I don't want him to see me like this. It's pathetic.

Warmth encases me as he pulls me into his hold, squeezing my frame against him.

"Baby, you need to tell me what's going on. Shit, I'm sorry you had to patch me up. It won't happen again. Okay?"

I nod.

"Look at me." My face lifts to his, and I blink through my tears. His expression is so woeful.

"Maddie, I never, ever want to leave you. I want a life with you, to grow old with you. It won't be long before all this dies down. We are so close to solidifying our place and eliminating the Falcones. It will be easier after that. Just don't hide your feelings from me. I can't bear to see you this unhappy, knowing I'm the one doing it to you."

I cut him off. "I'm not unhappy; I'm worried about you. The thought of anything happening to you makes me feel physically sick to my stomach."

"I don't know what I did in a previous life to deserve you, Maddie." He sighs, dropping his forehead to mine. "Just trust me, I will always come back to you. No matter what."

"It won't always be this bad?"

"No. Once we take out Marco, the Falcones will fall. Then it's up to Luca to lead the way and take over the city. Be the leader he truly is. Then we're home free."

"Okay. Maybe it would help if you told me what you were doing. That way, my imagination won't run wild."

I sense his hesitation.

"I don't need all the graphic details." I run my hand along his chiseled jaw.

"I bet you never saw your life being like this. Hardly the fairy tale, is it?"

"It's better. I am in love with the man of my dreams. He's a bit rough around the edges, but he makes up for it in lots of other ways."

"As long as you're happy, baby. That's all that matters. Now, let's go back to bed. I can't sleep without some Maddie cuddles."

Chapter Thirty-Five

GRAYSON

shoot Maddie a text to tell her I'll be home late. After the stabbing incident last week, I can see the pain on her face when I leave late at night. The fact she tries to hide it from me hurts. I don't ever want to cause her pain. But she knew the monster she was jumping into bed with.

It's different now, though.

She's not just in my bed. She consumes my entire life, my heart, and my head. I just need to work out a way to stop upsetting her.

Which is why Frankie and I have advised Luca we need to ramp up our efforts in taking out the Falcones. The quicker they're gone, the less I have to be out at night. I have hundreds of fighters signed up at King's, all fired up and ready for blood. I could train them up in no time to work with me and Frankie. Luca has shot the idea down, but we can't deny the

Frankie can hold this down essentially on our own. We might be good, but we're not invincible.

For the past week, we have scoped out the Falcones' new meet spots on the outskirts of the city. Their preference is still old, abandoned warehouses. I kill the engine and open the glove compartment. Frankie grumbles as he has to move his knee out of the way. My eyes widen as a pair of Maddie's little red thongs come into view, wrapped around my gun.

Frankie bursts out into laughter.

"Fuck, Grayson. Where do you find a woman like that?"

"I got lucky," I answer honestly, grabbing the gun and pocketing her thongs.

"How we doing this today?" He smirks, spotting the grenades in the glovebox.

"We haven't blown shit up for a couple of weeks. I was in the mood for an explosion. How many guys are in there?" I ask.

"At least seven. They're waiting for a shipment to arrive, according to Carlo."

He wiggles his eyebrows, snatching the two grenades out and handing me one.

"Let's go blow shit up," I say, and he chuckles.

I slam the car door and stride toward the building, grenade in one hand, the other gripping my gun.

As I approach the building, one of the men, dressed in black, points his gun at me. Without hesitation, I pull the trigger, hitting him straight in the chest. He collapses to the floor in a heap, clutching at his chest. Blood pours out of his mouth as he chokes.

I kick him out the way without so much as a second glance.

"Nice shot," Frankie calls out behind me.

"Thanks. You head to the back exit." I check my Rolex. "In exactly sixty seconds, we blow this place up."

"Got it, boss."

The seconds tick by, and excitement flows through me. I fucking love watching shit burn to the ground.

Ten seconds . . .

I throw open the metal door, depressing the striker lever and pulling the pin. All the heads in the room spin around. I give them a smile before chucking the grenade in and slamming the door shut. And fucking leg it as fast as I can.

The building erupts into flames. Stopping in the middle of the parking lot, I turn and admire the view.

"Fuck being blown to pieces. Although, I think I'd prefer that to being burned alive," Frankie says, his face completely serious.

"I'll keep note of that, just in case I have to kill you one day."

"Thanks, bud."

"Well, isn't this a good birthday present." He turns to me with a wicked grin.

It is.

But I'm looking forward to Maddie's birthday present for me.

"Let's go. I gotta go spank my girl for leaving her panties for the likes of you to see. Talk to Luca again, tell him we need to move forward with our plan with the new recruits. I'll speak to Keller and get him on board."

"You got it, boss."

THE SCENT OF freshly baked cake hits me as I walk through the front door. I rummage through my pockets, pulling out her red thong, lacing them around my fingers. As I approach the kitchen, I spy Maddie's blonde bun bobbing above the counter. She's on her knees on the floor, staring intently into the oven, watching the cakes rise. The counters are smothered in white powder. My kitchen resembles a drug den.

This is what it's like being with Maddie. She's exciting. I never know what I am going to return home to. The other day she was in some strange yoga pose, ass up in the air with see-through leggings on. Some days, I turn up to her apartment and she's half asleep reading a book. Other days, she's sipping wine from the bottle, rapping to Eminem.

I've never smiled so much in my life. The moment I return back to her, no matter how dark my day may get working with Luca, she brightens it. Every single time. I think that's why I am so obsessed with being with her at every opportunity I can.

"Hey, gorgeous," I call out, putting her panties between my teeth.

She spins her head around.

"Hey, birthday boy." She jumps up from the floor and launches herself at me, jumping into my arms and wrapping her arms around my neck. "I see you got present number one."

"Who told you?" I say, cocking an eyebrow at her as she plucks it out. I don't do birthdays, not since Casper died. Our birthdays fell close enough that we celebrated them together. Always.

"I may or may not have forced Keller to tell me. I mean you told me you were a Taurus. Which, may I add, you are a typical Taurus—stubborn as hell, a great lover. The fact we couldn't stand each other for a year." She giggles. "*Aquarius* doesn't have the best compatibility score with a Taurus."

"Sunshine, you've bagged yourself a man of the most loyal star sign. I, however, have the unpredictable, sometimes moody Aquarius."

"You mean, free-spirited and kinky."

"Oh, I know all about that. Aquarius enjoys praise"—I bring my mouth to her ear—"and anal."

It's true, that actually fucking came up when I searched. How the hell they come up with this is beyond me.

My hands find her ass, and I squeeze.

"Now that's a birthday present idea," she purrs, her eyes twinkling.

The oven dings, and she pushes herself out of my grasp, running over to the oven, flapping her hands as the steam pours out of the door. She carefully grabs the cakes out and drops them down on the counter.

"Fuck, that's hot."

Swiping up the wooden spoon, she starts beating the buttercream with ferocity, the white bowl resting under her arm. As she wipes her forearm across her forehead, it leaves a trail of white powder. I'm smiling so much my cheeks hurt. This is already the best birthday I've had for as long as I can remember.

I walk up behind her and wrap my arms around her

middle, pulling her against me. My dick twitches as her ass rubs up against it.

"Grayson . . ."

"Yes, baby."

I'm hoping the next two words to leave those pretty lips are "fuck me." It is my birthday after all.

"Would you rather sit on a cake and eat a cock, orrr, sit on a cock and eat cake?"

"Sit on a cock and eat cake. Why waste a perfectly good cake?" I chuckle. "But what I really want is you sitting on my cock while feeding me cake. Is that an option? It is my birthday, sunshine."

I can't see her face, but I know those emerald eyes will be full of desire, and her cheeks will be rosy pink. Dipping my palms under her vest top, I slide them up her smooth stomach and let her gorgeous round boobs fill my hands, rubbing my thumb across her perky nipples. She tips her head back against me, exposing her slender neck. I can't resist biting her neck, at the same time pinching her nipples. She moans against me, arching her back.

"You are fucking perfect, sunshine." I lick up her throat, and the remnants of her sweet perfume lace my tongue. Removing one of my hands, I dip my index finger in the bowl of buttercream she's still cradling, scooping up a big dollop. "Open up, sunshine." Her warm tongue licks the length of my finger until she takes the whole thing in her mouth, sucking hard.

"Grayson!" she shrieks, jumping out of my hold. "I may or may not have organized a night out to celebrate. Which is happening quite soon."

Shit.

I can't. I have a hit at the casino to deal with tonight. Two of Marco's top advisors are scheduled to attend a charity night at the casino. Luca managed to persuade the manager of our plan to remove these two Falcone men. In exchange, we funnel our money through their casinos.

"Baby, I have to work tonight."

"But it's your birthday. No one should work on their birthday, Grayson!" she whines, pouting at me.

"You know I don't work a job where I can request a day off, right?" I laugh, but it guts me that I've ruined her plans.

Unless maybe I can have both tonight. It's a quick and clean job. Luca and Frankie will be with us. In a public space.

"What about if you came with me tonight?"

"I don't think you need a ride along. I'm a bit squeamish."

"It's at the casino. I don't even need to do the hit. Frankie will be there. I just need to make sure nothing goes to shit. I'll stay with you, and we can bet on the tables. Once the hit's done, we're in the clear anyway. What do you say?"

This could be one of the stupidest ideas of my life. I would never risk her like that. Never. Losing her would kill me.

"Then can we meet Sienna and Keller at the club after? I don't want Keller anywhere near your and Luca's shit. It's not fair. He's out of that life."

God, she amazes me.

"Okay, baby, thank you." I wrap my arms around her and lift her off the floor.

"I need to go get ready then. You can't walk into a casino with a woman with greasy hair covered in powdered sugar. Plus, I gotta finish this cake so I can sit on your cock and feed it to you. Happy birthday." She presses a kiss to my lips before I can even open my mouth to respond.

With that, she pushes herself out of my arms, bowl still in hand, with a mischievous look in her eyes. I walk over to the barstool and take a seat, watching this firecracker decorate my birthday cake in my kitchen.

I know what I really want for my birthday.

Let's just hope I can get her to agree.

Chapter Thirty-Six

MADDIE

My breath hitches at the sight of him. A walking sex god in a perfectly tailored black tux and bow tie. His sandy hair has a slight spike on the top. His stubble is styled immaculately, showing off that killer jawline. Just looking at him makes me hot. I already have a blush creeping up my chest. He looks every part the powerful, rich mafia hitman.

With my strappy silver stilettos in one hand, I pad over to him. His eyes are on me the entire time. He bites his lower lip as he drags his gaze up my body, the heat from his stare making my pussy clench. It's on the tip of my tongue to ask him if we can stay here.

"You are simply stunning." A smile forms on my lips.

"And you, sir, look like a walking sex god." I wink, and he sucks in a breath as I brush past him and plop onto the couch. My dress is so tight, resting just over my knees, that I literally can't move. I'm basically a penguin for the night. But it's worth it; this sweetheart neckline makes my tits look incredible, and the tight bodice sucks in my period bloat. I attempt to put my shoes on, bringing up my leg to meet my hands. I let out a huff and edge myself forward, but it's no use. With a sigh, I throw myself back on the couch in annoyance.

Without saying a word, he drops to his knees.

He lifts my right foot and places it on his thigh. He does the buckle up, and the tingles shoot up my leg from his touch.

"I like seeing you on your knees for me," I tease.

"You'll be the only person to ever say that to me." He plants a delicate kiss on my ankle before picking up the other foot. My heart swells at his kindness.

He lifts himself back up, holding out his large hand to me. I place my hand in his and he pulls me to my feet. Tipping my head up to his face, his knuckles brush my cheek and I melt into his touch. I slide my arms around his neck as he cups my ass.

"Seven years, Maddie. That's how long it had been before my last kiss. Before you barreled into my life and smashed those perfect lips over mine." He chuckles. "But fuck, am I glad you did. I promise that you will be last person I'll ever kiss, no matter what."

Tears sting in my eyes; I've dreamed my whole life of finding a man who loves me with this much passion. I love him with my whole heart. But I know I've given my heart to a man who can only love me so much, who can't give me a forever. I lower my gaze to the floor. His index finger rests under my chin, tipping my face back up to his.

"Where did you go, sunshine?"

He searches my face, concern etched across his features, his brow furrowed. I knew who he was and what he could offer me before I got involved with him. Stupid me, always believing in fairy tales, letting my heart get carried away. Secretly wishing the villain would become the prince.

"Nowhere." My voice wobbles as I speak. He grabs my shoulders and leans back.

"Don't lie to me. I know you better than that. You're upset, why?"

"I don't want this to end," I say truthfully.

He winces at my words.

"Sunshine, you hold the power here. I will be yours until the day I die. Completely and utterly yours," he says, and a sob catches in my throat. He brushes the tear away with the pad of his finger, giving me a sad smile. "I love you. I think I've loved you from the moment I first laid eyes on you. This might not be the fairy tale you imagined in your head your whole life. But know this: Every day I will treat you like a princess. I will love you how you deserve to be loved. You just have to accept you've fallen for the monster, not the prince. I'm not him, I can never be him, I don't even want to try to pretend to be him. But I promise, the love and the life I will give you will make up for that tenfold."

I believe every word.

I'm in love with the monster. The last thing on my mind since I started dating Grayson was weddings and fairy tales. *He* just consumes my life.

I want everything he can give me. And I'm going to take it. Being loved by this man for the rest of my life. What else could I possibly need?

"You promise?"

"Cross my heart."

"I love you, Grayson. As long as I have you, I don't need anything else."

"You promise I'm enough for you?" he asks nervously.

This powerful man doubts if he's enough.

"Oh, trust me, you are more than enough."

WE WALK ALONG the red carpet into the casino arm in arm. The bright flashing lights of the slot machines steal my attention first.

Grayson leads us over to the bar, his eyes focusing across the room. He's completely in military mode right now. I might be on his arm, but his head is not with me at all. I follow his gaze and spot Luca, dressed up in his black suit. The guy beside him is huge, with dark hair and olive skin. His intense stare puts me on edge. He's kind of scary. I tighten my grip around Grayson's arm.

"Would you like a drink, baby?" he mutters, shaking me out of my thoughts.

"Champagne, please."

Grayson leans over the bar and orders with the bartender.

"Here you go." Grayson hands me the flute, and I take a sip.

He's busy scanning the room, his eyes darting from one place to another, his jaw tight. With a sigh, I tip the rest of the champagne back in one. There's no point pretending to be someone I'm not. So, I'll just get drunk instead.

Leaning back over the bar, leaving Grayson to his duties, I give the bartender a smile to grab his attention and mouth, *Could I have another?* tapping the flute in my hand. He chuckles and removes the glass from my hand, refilling it to the brim. "Thank you."

As I turn back around, I notice Luca and his companion aren't standing where they were a minute ago. I guess shit's about to go down. Grayson laces his fingers through mine. "I'm sorry about this. It should all be over soon, then we can leave."

His features soften for a split second when he looks at me, before he slips that mask back on, walking us over to the first roulette table in front of us.

He pulls the red velvet stool out for me, holding my waist as I prop myself up. I lean back into his hard stomach. I have no clue what I'm doing. He bends over me, placing a stack of yellow poker chips that must be three inches tall.

"What do you want me to do with those?" I ask, picking up one of the chips and rolling it between my fingers.

"Whatever you want, it's yours." He shrugs.

Holy fuck. A thousand dollars a chip. There must be at least twenty here.

"Grayson," I hiss.

"I'm not throwing away your money like this."

"Why not? It's just money."

"Too much money. I don't know what I'm doing."

"That's the beauty of it."

I stack the chip back onto the rest and push it toward me, but he grabs my arm to stop me.

"Fine, how about we make our own bet?"

"I'm listening . . ."

"We split it. You put your half on red, I'll go black. If you win, you keep the money. If I win, you move in with me?"

"Excuse me?" I splutter, my cheeks now on fire.

"You heard me. Hell, if you don't like my penthouse, I'll buy us somewhere else. I just know that that would be the best birthday present I could ask for." He bends further, bringing his mouth to my ear.

"Well, second to you riding me while feeding me cake. Now *that* I can't wait for."

"You know I am perfectly happy with our relationship as it is, right?"

"Baby, I never do anything I don't *want* to do. I want you. You are everything I didn't know I needed. My glimmer of sunshine, always."

His intense gaze hits me straight in the heart.

"But I have to win first." He winks, leaning over me and picking the stack of chips up, splitting them in half and handing me my collection. I take them with shaky hands.

The croupier calls for all bets to be placed.

I hook my stilettos over the bar at the bottom of the stool and stand, reaching forward and sliding all my chips onto the red box. Grayson's palm rests against the bottom of my back as he coolly slides his chips into the black box. The croupier drops the shiny ball onto the roulette wheel. I suck in a breath, closing my eyes.

Please be black, please be black.

Time seems to slow as the table spins and spins, gradually coming to a stop.

"Sixteen. Red."

My shoulders sag as he calls out the number. I should be ecstatic; I've just won a shit ton of money.

"You win this time, baby."

"Yep," I nervously squeal, faking a tight smile to hide my disappointment. Grayson lets out a huff next to me, collecting my winnings and sliding them over to me. He's just as disappointed as me.

"I call for a new deal," I say, scooping up my chips and passing them to him.

He gives me a questioning look.

"You take the money back, in exchange for me moving in."

"Deal."

He rummages in his pocket, pulling out something small and silver. He puts it between his teeth, grabbing the host of chips in my hands and dropping them onto the table. I can't take my eyes off the key in his mouth. With a grin, he retrieves the key and places it in his palm.

My hand brushes his as I pick it up and stuff it down my bra.

Resting my fingers on Grayson's forearm, I lean over and whisper in his ear, "I'm just going to pop to the ladies'. I'll grab us another drink on my way back." He stacks his chips up into a neat line. I jump off the stool and run my fingers along his stubbly jaw.

"Okay, baby," he says, straddling the stool. Just that action alone makes my pussy throb.

"If I'm not back in ten minutes, come and find me. I'll probably be stuck in this stupid dress." I giggle, the champagne starting to hit me.

I head toward the bathrooms. The flashing of the fruit machines catches my attention, and suddenly, my body comes to an abrupt halt, whacking into a solid structure. I hold out my arms and whip my head in front of me. *Oh shit!* I'm staring straight into a rather burly man's chest; thick, black hairs peek out from the top open button of his shirt. Ew.

"Oh my God. I am so sorry." I immediately take a step back.

"It's okay, miss," he drawls out in a thick Italian accent, taking a step toward me. I fake-smile and walk past him as fast as I can, barreling into the bathroom and slamming the door shut, locking myself in a cubicle. My heart pounds against my ribs. I take a couple of deep breaths.

That guy got right under my skin.

As I start unzipping the side of my ridiculously tight dress, the bathroom door squeaks open and slams shut. Heavy footsteps grow closer and closer. I stay deathly still, holding my breath.

I jump as the cubicle next to me clatters open, vibrating the walls around me.

Fuck.

Squeezing my eyes shut, I wait, blood thumping in my ears.

"Sunshine, I know you're in here." That same thick Italian accent pierces my ears.

The blood drains from my face.

The madman starts pounding against my cubicle door. On trembling legs, I walk backward until my back hits the tiled wall next to the toilet. I have nowhere to go, no way to escape.

I pull out my phone out of my purse and dial Grayson. Through watery eyes, I pull up our texts when he doesn't answer.

ME

Help me!!!

I can barely see what I'm frantically typing.

ME

Please.

A cold breeze hits me as the door crashes open, and my phone falls from my fingers and thuds to the floor.

"You could have just let me in, sunshine." The way he addresses me makes me nauseous. With a sadistic smile, he marches toward me, snatching my wrist and yanking me out of the cubicle behind him.

"You're hurting me!"

"Good."

Gripping me by the biceps, he pushes me in front of the mirrors above the sinks.

"Get the fuck off me!" I shout, but he only tightens his grip, his knuckles turning white. I stare into the mirror, watching in horror as he slicks back his jet-black hair with his hand. His hand moves to the back of my neck, and he pushes me with force so I'm bent over the sink. I try to resist with all the strength I have, but it's no use. He kicks my legs open with his foot. Pain sears from my ankle as it twists.

"Hmmm, you smell delicious," he says, moving my hair off my back and licking up my spine. Bile rises in my throat, and I close my eyes.

Too petrified to move or even breathe, I flinch as his hands run down the side of my boobs.

"Please don't do this," I beg.

The sound of him unzipping his pants fills the room. Muffled shouting outside the bathroom catches my attention. He turns around. Relief washes over me when he removes himself from me, the panic in his features evident as he struggles to pull his trousers back up. Before I can even stand, the bathroom door flies open, and a furious Grayson strides in, his gun aiming straight at the Italian guy. I let out a shaky breath and straighten my spine.

Grayson's eyes flick to mine, roaming over my body as if assessing the damage. I can almost feel his relief as he realizes I'm still fully dressed.

"Maddie, baby. I'm going to need you to go back in the cubicle and shut the door."

I nod and shuffle into the nearest stall. Once inside, I hover my fingers over the lock, but something screams at me to leave it. I want to make sure this man can never do this to any other woman. Slowly, I pull the door open, just enough to peer through the gap.

"On your knees," Grayson says with authority. The man sinks to the floor.

"You will die for laying a finger on her. You piece of shit," he spits out. I gasp as Grayson's gun connects with his head.

He squeezes the trigger and the man collapses on the floor, blood oozing from his head.

Oh fuck.

Opening the door, on unsteady legs, I launch myself at Grayson, being careful to miss the body slumped on the floor. He opens his arms wide as I throw myself into him. He squeezes me tight, so tight it's as if he's scared to let go.

The tears cascade down my cheeks. "Is he dead?" I hiccup.

He nods. "Did he hurt you?" I shake my head. He lets out a ragged breath, tipping his head back. "Fuck," he sighs. "I'm so fucking sorry."

"You didn't do this to me. You saved me."

Now it's my turn to save him from his own demons. I cup his face in my palms and drag him down to me. He melts into my kiss, and his body relaxes around mine. His gun clatters to the floor as his arms wrap around my waist.

"I love you, Grayson."

"God, I love you so much, sunshine."

Chapter Thirty-Seven

GRAYSON

Her hand tightens around my bicep as I turn to face her. Her features pale. "Grayson, I don't feel too good." Her voice trembles. The rage that burns through me is morphing into panic. I fucking told Luca we needed new recruits, handed him a plan on a platter. This wouldn't have fucking happened if he'd listened to us.

She stumbles forward, crashing into my chest. I grab her shoulders to steady her. Shit. Her eyes flutter closed. Panic rises in my chest. I need to stay calm and concentrate. "Maddie, baby. Can you hear me?" I raise my voice enough to get through to her, but she doesn't respond. I hoist her up into my arms and cradle her limp body into me. "It's okay, sunshine. I've got you." The world moves in a blur as I rush us out of the fire exit door and jog to my car, rummaging through my pockets for my keys. As I open the passenger door, her face brushes against my chest. I almost sag in relief. She's awake.

Crouching, I gently place her in the passenger seat. Her eyes are still glazed over, and she's awake, but not entirely. I bring my palm to cup her cool cheek, and her face sinks into my touch. "I'm taking you to the hospital now, just stay awake for me. I won't leave you. I promise." She gives me a weak nod, and I press a kiss to her forehead before standing and rushing around the front of the car.

She drifts in and out of sleep on the journey to the hospital. I squeeze her hand in mine the entire time, needing the reassurance she's okay.

I carry her into the emergency room. The clinical smell burns my nostrils the second I walk in. I can barely hear the chatter in the waiting room above the ringing in my ears. I stalk over to the receptionist.

"I need a doctor. My girlfriend, Maddie Peters, collapsed, and is in and out of consciousness. She needs help. Now."

She looks up from her computer screen, her attention straight on Maddie's still form in my arms. A flicker of concern passes across her features as she glances at Maddie. "Now." I'm not fucking around.

"Come with me, sir." She pushes herself off her chair and walks out of the glass door. I follow behind her down the bright white corridors. She opens up a door on the right. A tiny room with one bed and one plastic chair greets me. "I'll send a doctor in right away."

I give her a nod and walk over to the bed, laying Maddie down softly. "Hey, baby, the doctors are just coming."

Her eyes open and a frown creases her forehead. "W-where am I?"

"The hospital."

"What happened?" she asks.

"You passed out on me. Do you need anything?" I ask, and she shakes her head.

The sparkle in her eyes returns, which brings a smile to my face. "Maybe a kiss?" she says sweetly, biting on that plump bottom lip.

"Always, sunshine. I never want to stop kissing those sweet lips," I whisper. I lean forward. The door clicking stops me in my tracks. Someone clears their throat from the doorway, and Maddie giggles, her warm breath hitting my lips. I give her a quick peck before pushing myself up to turn to the doorway. A young, lanky, dark-haired doctor stands there, unsure where to look.

"Miss Peters?" he almost squeaks, unable to look in my direction.

"That's me," Maddie says.

Taking that as my cue, I take a seat on the pathetic plastic chair.

The doctor walks over, shuffling the paperwork in his hands. Is he qualified to be looking after her?

"We'd like to take some blood tests if that's okay?" he asks, his back now to me as he approaches Maddie's bedside.

"Of course, thank you, doctor."

"How are you feeling now?"

"Better. I do have a pounding headache and feel a bit sick. But other than that, I'm fine."

After asking a few more questions, doctor takes her blood. Maddie turns her head in the opposite direction, squeezing her eyes shut. The doctor informs us we have to wait for the results before we can go home. So in the meantime, I scoot my chair up to her bed, enclosing her hand in mine. I don't want to let her go.

Her eyes flick to the blood on my shirt. A stark reminder

that I could have been the reason she passed out. She got to witness the devil.

As if sensing my inner turmoil, she slips her hand from under mine and places hers on the top. "I'm not bothered, Grayson." I cock my brow at her. "You know, about what happened earlier. You saved me. I won't ever forget that."

My body is rigid. I blew someone's brains up the wall, and she's thanking me. She doesn't need this bullshit. She deserves so much more. Way more than I could ever offer.

I stare at the white wall in front of me. "Grayson, listen to me. I know who you are, what you do. I'm not scared of you."

Now isn't the time or the place for this. I shouldn't feel the things I do for her. She's well and truly clawed herself into my black heart and spread her light through my entire life. I can't help the dread that settles in my stomach. She isn't mine to keep.

"Good," I reply with a smirk.

She shoots me a questioning look, ready to speak, but shuts her mouth before the words come out. Instead, she sighs and settles herself into the pillow, still gripping my hand.

We stay like this in silence.

The door flies open, and in walks the doctor, fumbling with the doorknob as if he didn't mean to make such an entrance. I can't help but roll my eyes.

"Miss Peters, we have the results back. Would you like some privacy?"

I straighten my spine, turning to face him.

His eyes focus only on Maddie. The tremble of his fingers gives his fear away. Maddie squeezes my hand, turning my attention back to her. I can see her heartbeat thudding against the skin on her throat.

"I can stay, or I can go. It's up to you, sunshine."

I put my other hand on top of hers, doing whatever I can to comfort her.

"Grayson stays." Her voice quivers as she speaks.

I hold my breath, waiting for the doctor's next words.

"Miss Peters, you are pregnant. Congratulations."

Maddie gasps, and my vision goes hazy. The room starts to spin.

Fuck.

Fuck. Fuck. Fuck.

Chapter Thirty-Eight

MADDIE

oly shit. Pregnant?

The doctor excuses himself and leaves the room.

"Grayson, talk to me. Please." Warm tears stream down my face. My breathing becomes labored. What have I done?

"I didn't do this on purpose, I promise you. I'm sorry," I sob, letting go of his hands.

I bring my knees up to my chest and wrap my arms around them, smothering my head on my thighs. The bed squeaks. I peer above my knees. Grayson is sitting on the edge of the bed, his hand reaching out to mine.

"What are we going to do, Grayson?"

His hand squeezes mine. Tears well in his eyes, which only makes mine fall harder.

"We deal with this together. I will support you with whatever you want to do, Maddie." His voice almost breaks as he speaks, but he pulls himself together.

"No wonder my dress is so tight!" I hiccup, and he gives me a sad smile, his eyes briefly settling on my stomach, lighting up as he does.

"Lie down," he demands, and as always, when he uses that authoritative tone, my body responds instantly. My head hits the pillow. The mattress dips as he pushes himself off the bed. He bends over, his head resting on my lower stomach. I push myself up onto my elbows.

He presses kisses around my stomach.

"Ours," he chokes out. He rests his head on me, and I put my weight into my right arm and reach out to him with my other, running my fingers through his hair. To the rest of the world, this would be the perfect moment.

For us, I'm not sure what this means.

I've always dreamed of being a mom. I know I'd be a damn good one. But can I really bring a baby into our life?

"I can hear your thoughts from here, sunshine."

I can't even bring myself to answer him. I can't.

"I will protect you and this child with everything. Never doubt that. No one touches what's mine and gets to live to tell the tale." The violence in his tone makes the hairs on my back stand to attention.

I don't doubt him.

That man would risk it all for us.

I take a deep inhale, mustering the courage to ask.

"Do you want to be a father? This was never in your plan. I can't force you to be something you aren't. You told me you wouldn't change. This"—I gesture at my stomach—"is a pretty big life change, Grayson."

I can't do this on my own.

I can't be without him either.

"That was all before I fell in love with you, Maddie. I want to give you everything. Fuck, you changed everything for me, sunshine. Just like I knew you would."

His eyes pin mine, welling with tears, just like my own.

"I want this." He cups my jaw. "What do you say, sunshine?"

"I want this too."

He kisses the top of my head. "I love you."

I nuzzle into his chest and close my eyes, his fresh smell of aftershave lulling me to sleep.

We're having a baby.

Chapter Thirty-Nine

GRAYSON

G loved up and ready to go.

I've been living on the edge of a knife for the last forty-eight hours. I've barely slept. My mind is reeling. I couldn't protect her. Another man had his filthy hands on her.

I'm ready to end every single one of those cocksuckers today.

But I can't.

Not when my head is like this. I'm going to be a dad. What child deserves *this* as a father?

All I can say with certainty is I want this. More than fucking anything. That's why it is fucking killing me that I couldn't protect them.

No matter how many times Maddie promises me she's okay, the baby is okay, that I *saved* her, I can't tame this urge for blood. This anger bubbling inside of me ready to burst out at any second. I've sat there at night, watching her toss and turn, dripping with sweat in her sleep. No doubt reliving that moment.

When Keller texted this morning demanding I help train our new boxers, I flew out the door. Boxing was once my outlet for my anger; maybe it will work again today. Something fucking has to.

Ducking under the ropes, I join one of our more promising recruits in the ring.

"You alright, Gray?" Keller shouts.

"Fine."

"Let's fucking do this. Show me what you've got. You want to be the next Keller, fucking prove to me you've got it in you," I goad the man as he jogs to the center of the ring, gloves up and ready to attack. I mirror his stance, anticipating his first move. He comes at me with a left hook. "Fucking sloppy," I mock.

He grunts in response, and this time, his right arm shoots out, connecting with the underside of my jaw. My head snaps back at the contact, pain shooting through my face.

Recovering fast, I come at him with an onslaught of punches. He ducks away, but I don't let up. He bounces back as I smash my gloves into him.

"Grayson, what the fuck are you doing!" Keller shouts from beside the ring.

Right now, all I see is that fucking sleazy prick who tried to rape Maddie.

Rage burns through me. I grab his weak body and hurl him onto the canvas, blood thumping in my ears.

"Enough," Keller screams, ripping me away and shoving me hard in the chest. I blink at him, before he cracks me right in the side of the head so hard I almost see stars.

"Go get some fucking air, then meet me in the fucking

office. Now!" he shouts. Blood trickles from his eyebrow.
Fuck.

The room is deadly still. Silent.

What the fuck am I doing?

Keller drops to his knees next to the other man and tends
to him.

"Fucking go!"

I toss my gloves on the floor and storm into the office,
slamming the door shut.

———•————————————•———

"SIT THE FUCK down." Keller points to the couch in our office.

"Fuck, I'm sorry."

"I don't need an apology. I need you to tell me what the
fuck is going on. You could have killed that guy. With everyone fucking watching. They are looking up to us. We are there
to train them and you pull this shit. So enlighten me."

He pulls out an unopened bottle of scotch, slamming it on
the desk in front of him. Two crystal tumblers appear next.
Filling them almost halfway, he slides mine over to me.

"Drink that first, you look like shit."

Swiping up my glass, I take a long sip.

"Maddie was attacked at the casino last weekend." It hurts
me to even say it out loud.

"What do you mean, attacked?"

"One of the Falcones tried to rape her."

Bile rises up my throat as the images flash in my head again.

"Fuck. Is she okay?" he asks.

I crack my knuckles and take a breath.

"She's holding up okay. I think more putting on a brave
face for me. I'm keeping a close eye on her."

Keller nods, deep in thought.

"And you? Are you okay?" he asks, studying me.

"No," I answer truthfully, and fuck, it feels good to say out loud. "Not even close. Maddie's pregnant. I've let them both down. How am I supposed to be a dad? I don't think I can do this, Keller."

Tears burn in my eyes. I bow my head, resting it in my hands.

I've fucked up. I couldn't even stop my wife from fucking my best friend, so what makes me think I could ever be a decent husband? A decent dad? I'm not cut out for this.

The chair scrapes against the hardwood flooring as he rounds the desk toward me.

"Look at me, Grayson. You need to get a fucking grip. All that doubt, it's in your head. No one can protect Maddie and your baby better than you. Not a single person on this planet. She's fine now, right? I assume the guy is dead?"

I nod.

"Remember what you always tell me. You can never win a fight if your head's not in it. Number one fucking rule, Grayson. *Your* rule. Now live by it. You don't need me to tell you you'll be an epic father. You can't be, if you run away from your problems. Or let your anger take over. You're better than that. We both know it."

There's no excuse for what I did back there. I'm letting my anger rule me.

"Now go home to your woman and show her how much you want this. Be the man she needs right now, 'cause you're not doing it being here trying to kill our rising boxers."

He's right.

My head's a dangerous place. It always has been. But I'm in control. I can do anything with Maddie by my side.

"Thanks, Keller. I think I needed that."

"Congratulations. It's the best fucking job in the world. I promise you."

Such a big softie, this one.

His grip tightens on me. "But if you lose your head like that in there again, I will knock you the fuck out without hesitating. You get me?" He cocks his brow, and I chuckle.

"I'd like to see you try."

Chapter Forty

MADDIE

After the night at the casino last Saturday, we spent the rest of the evenings this week moving all my crap into his penthouse. I mean, it could do with a touch of color. I don't want to spend my life staring at black and gray walls if I can help it. I'm not too sure how amused Grayson is with the addition of the nude cushions and the pictures now hanging on the wall of us in London and at Sienna's wedding.

It's gradually starting to look like a home someone actually lives in.

It's been keeping my mind busy. The shock of the pregnancy masked the fact someone tried to rape me and the fact I watched my boyfriend blow his brains out. Both of which are giving me sleepless nights. I'm trying my hardest to be strong and put on a brave face. Grayson is already a pent-up ball of anger, waiting to explode. He told me about what happened at the gym earlier this week with Keller: It broke my heart, knowing he was hurting so bad and couldn't tell me.

I meant when I told him it wasn't his fault. That he saved me. Not many men on this planet would literally kill someone for touching their woman. Grayson didn't even so much as hesitate.

I'm only a few weeks pregnant—six at most. So we've decided to keep it to ourselves for another month or so. I'm petrified of something going wrong. We want this so bad. I can't help the gut feeling that life isn't going to let me have that perfect ending I was always looking for.

I smile as Grayson carries a brown box of my clothes into the spare room. Or, as he now calls it, my walk-in wardrobe.

"How many fucking dresses do you own?" he shouts, throwing the box on the floor. I lean against the kitchen counter.

He hasn't come across my collection of toys yet. It's definitely in one of these boxes. I can't wait to see his face.

My phone starts vibrating on the side.

I click the accept button and hold my breath, walking over to the lounge and sitting on the couch.

"Hi, sweetie, are you still okay for our dinner tonight?"

Grayson watches me intently from the hallway. He walks toward me and sits next to me.

"Yep. I actually have someone I'd like you to meet," I say to my mom nervously.

"Oh, finally. I can't wait to meet him. Did you hear that, Robert? Maddie has a boyfriend!"

I roll my eyes. "Okay, see you later," I say before hanging up.

God, I'm already dreading this.

"So I get to be formally introduced to their lordships tonight. How special."

I turn to face him.

"What if they don't approve of your murderous boyfriend? What are you going to do then?" He keeps his voice light, but there's a hint of seriousness there.

"Ooh, I don't know. I'll probably have to dump you," I say, biting my bottom lip.

"Hmm. Is that right." His mouth hovers over mine.

"Well, you could try. But you won't get rid of me that easily." He nips my bottom lip as he lifts one of his arms and drags his finger along my thigh, leaving tingles in its wake.

"Come on, sunshine. We need to get ready. And I need at least half an hour in that shower with you."

Reluctantly, he breaks the kiss, leaving me horny. God, he's frustrating, but he's right. Can't be late for Mommy Dearest.

He holds out his hand, and I lace my fingers through his as he lifts me off the couch.

HALF AN HOUR turned into an hour. I've never been cleaner. It's as if he could sense my nerves on the drive over here, because he hasn't let my hand go since we got in the car.

My leg bounces under the table as we wait for my parents to arrive.

His strong hand grips my thigh, forcing it to stop jumping up and down. I let out a breath and turn to him.

"It's going to be okay, sunshine. It's just dinner with your parents. I'll be on my best behavior tonight, I promise," he whispers, tucking my hair behind my ear. "Well, unless someone comes in flinging a gun around again. Then we might have a problem."

I can't help but laugh.

"Although, I wouldn't mind a do-over of what happened

after that." His deep voice is full of desire. I squeeze my legs together.

He laughs quietly against my cheek and plants a soft kiss.

The sound of my mom's voice declaring they've arrived to the hostess makes me straighten my back.

Dad ruffles my hair.

"Hey!" I shout, and he chuckles.

Mom breezes straight past me.

They take their seats opposite us. Grayson stands and sticks his hand out to my dad, who accepts his firm handshake.

"Nice to see you again, Mr. Peters."

"Ahh, yes, Grayson, isn't it?" Dad says, giving him a smile.

Okay. *One down, one to go.*

Grayson extends his hand to her, but she eyes it skeptically. And then ping-pongs her gaze between us in disgust.

"Mom, this is Grayson. My boyfriend," I say.

"Yes, we've met." She scoffs.

"Carol," my dad chastises, giving me an apologetic smile.

The waiter breaks the silence.

I grab Grayson's hand on my thigh and squeeze, trying to calm myself down. *This fucking woman.*

"Could I get you some drinks?" the waiter asks.

"I'll have a water, please," I say.

Once the waiter leaves, my mom's attention turns back to me.

"So, how long have you been together?"

"Four months now, but we've known each other for over a year," Grayson replies.

She rolls her eyes.

"Well, spit it out, Mom. Tell us what you really think. I've just about had it already with these looks and comments."

Grayson's fingers tap against my leg, and I weave my fingers through his as I brace myself for her response.

"I don't know what you mean. If this is the type of man you want to settle for, then that's your poor decision. I didn't realize you were into thugs. I mean, come on, he's hardly going to offer you long-term; he's probably just using you. For *you know what*," she says, looking me up and down as if I'm some cheap whore.

Grayson stiffens next to me, and it's my turn to squeeze his hand to calm him. If I've learned anything, it's that Grayson will never shy away from defending me.

"Don't let her words get to you. I love you, sunshine," he whispers.

Years of her putting me down, of making me feel like a disappointment. Her pushing me to want this fairy-tale fantasy, when actually, I have everything I need sitting right next to me.

Mom picks up her menu, covering her face. I rip it out of her hands.

"I'm pregnant," I blurt out.

"Congratulations, honey," my dad says, a smile lighting his face.

My mom cackles like an evil witch.

"Don't tell me you're keeping it," my mom spits.

Sadness consumes me, but anger quickly takes over.

"How fucking dare you!"

Grayson scoots his chair closer and wraps an arm around my shoulders.

"No. I've had enough. You disgust me. Is this really how you're going to speak about your first grandchild? How dare you continue to treat me like this. I am done. I've put up with your shitty behavior, your snide comments and downright disrespect for years. I'm not going to continue to live my life trying to please you anymore, Mom. This is me; this is the man I choose to love. I don't want your dream of a perfect life. I want my own, and if that's not good enough for you, you know where the door is. I will make sure I never treat my child like this. I will aim to be everything you aren't. So, thank you for teaching me how not to be a mother."

"Don't you dare talk to me like that, Maddison."

I slam my trembling hands on the table and stand. Grayson joins me, wrapping his arm around my waist, almost holding me upright.

"Grayson, take me home, please." The tears I tried so hard to hold on to trickle.

"Of course, baby."

He pulls out his wallet from his pocket and throws a wad of cash on the table. My mom's eyes widen as she stares at the money.

"This should more than cover whatever you want. I suggest you stay the fuck away from my family. No one gets to treat Maddie like this. I will stop at nothing to protect her and our baby. You've seen what I'm capable of."

He renders her speechless.

His hand returns to my lower back as he guides us out of the restaurant onto the sidewalk. I feel like the chains that have been holding me back my whole life have been broken. For the first time in my life, I feel free. My arms cradle my stomach as I let the tears take over. He pulls me into his muscular frame, and I nuzzle my face into his chest, his musky aftershave soothing me. His heart hammers against my ear.

"Shhh, sunshine. I'm so fucking proud of you. For sticking up for yourself, for finally fighting to be the person you truly are. I might not deserve you, deserve this life you're blessing me with. But thank you." His voice hitches as he speaks.

"I love you, sunshine. So fucking much."

I tear my face away from his chest and look up at him. His eyes are brimming with tears as he stares at me.

"I love you more. Now take me home."

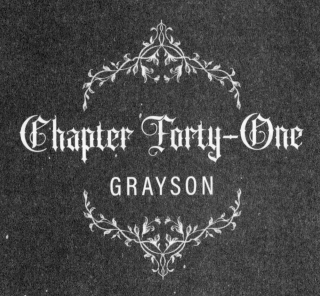

Chapter Forty-One

GRAYSON

On the drive over to La Brasserie, Maddie stares out of the passenger window. She's been unusually quiet the last couple of weeks since the predicament with her mom. I know it hurts her. She deserves better.

So what better way to bring it back, to give her something to keep her busy.

Something to get that bright smile back on her face.

A wedding.

Our wedding.

Before Maddie, I would have bet my life I would never have gotten married again. I think that's why I tried to keep such a barrier up with her. Deep down, my gut told me she was my person. I never wanted to open my heart up again after Amelia and Casper stomped all over it.

Maddie is my heart now. It beats only for her.

I knew that from the moment our lips touched. That's why I had her engagement ring made in London. I want this more than anything. To spend the rest of my life with her by my side is the only way I want to live.

Cutting the engine, I turn to her.

"You know you can talk to me about anything going on in that pretty little head of yours," I say, bringing my thumb to cup her jaw.

"I know," she sighs, giving me a sad smile. "According to the internet, I'm probably just hormonal. I'm pissed off at my mom. I'm more pissed off at myself, for not realizing how much she has manipulated my whole life. I just wish I didn't spend all these years trying to live her warped idea of a life."

"Are you happy? Do I make you happy?"

"Oh my God, Grayson. Happy? I've never been happier. I've never been so in love. I can't even tell you how grateful I am for you. I would never have had the strength to do any of this without you."

She unbuckles her belt and jumps over the console into my lap. "I'm sorry I've been a moody bitch. It is kind of half your fault I am though." She looks at her flat stomach.

I can't wait to see her with a bump. That primal urge, knowing I did that to her, that she's carrying *my* child, it's the sexiest thing in the world.

"I don't care about you being moody. You're giving me a whole new life. I just want you to be happy, baby. I'll always do everything in my power to scare your demons away. Always. Okay?"

She shuffles against me, gently brushing my cock, which instantly sends my blood rushing there.

"Let's go eat, I'm starving. And you know I'll end up eating you if you touch my cock again."

She grins, wiggling her eyebrows.

"Fine, as long as you promise I get your tongue after." She leans across me and opens the door.

As soon as I pull open the wooden door to the cozy little Italian restaurant, the one she decided to trip me in, I know something's off. I feel it in my gut.

The room goes eerily quiet as Maddie brushes past me while I hold the door open for her. Her stilettos click against the wooden floors. Instinctively, I follow behind her and pull her into my side.

"Welcome to La Brasserie. May I take the reservation name?" the waitress asks, pushing her glasses back up on her nose.

"Mr. Ward."

Her eyes light up and she gives me a knowing smile.

"Ahh, Mr. Ward. Please follow me. I'll take you to your table."

Maddie eyes me suspiciously. Maybe everything's feeling off because I'm nervous. I chuckle and shake my head.

She leads us over to a table for two tucked in the far corner of the restaurant. I clock a table of four Italian men, all watching me closely since the moment I arrived. Our table is covered in deep red rose petals on top of the white cloth. A pillar candle flickers in the center. I pull out the wooden chair for Maddie. She pulls on the hem of her short black dress and wiggles it before taking a seat.

I walk around the table and take my seat in the corner of the room.

A young blonde waitress rushes over with a smile and places down two glasses of champagne.

"But we didn't order these—" Maddie says, picking up the flute and handing it back to the waitress.

"It's on the house, madam," she replies in a hushed voice.

"Thank you."

Maddie slides her glass toward me. "I can't."

"Does this mean I get double drinks for the next seven months?"

"I think the fuck not." She squints her eyes, but I catch a glimpse of a smirk.

Taking another sip, I stare into her eyes, but she shakes her head and that infectious bright smile crosses her glossy lips. She lights up a room just with her presence.

She spins her head round, watching the room. I can't remember the last time I was this nervous. Since she isn't paying attention, I search for the box in my suit jacket.

I clear my throat and her head spins back to me. She hasn't noticed the box in my hands. Her eyes glimmer as she looks at me.

Fuck, I'm sweating here.

I stand, and the chair screeches against the wooden floor. Maddie watches me with confusion as I walk around the table to her and drop to one knee.

I open up the box to her, revealing a huge black diamond, encased by smaller natural diamonds, which then span all the way around the gold band. I had it made for her, the perfect reflection of our relationship. She owns my black heart.

She gasps, bringing her hand to cover her mouth. Tears form in her eyes.

"Sunshine, I may have said I couldn't give you everything. But I want to. I want to give you the life you deserve. It might not be quite how you imagined it. I don't think you could find anyone on this planet who loves you quite as fiercely and wholeheartedly as I do. I want to make you mine in every way possible. Do things the right way for our child. I want more than anything for you to be my wife."

My voice falters, so I suck in a breath to steady myself.

"Maddie, will you do the honor of becoming my wife? Marry me?"

A few moments pass where she just stares at me in shock. It feels like a fucking lifetime.

"Sunshine, say something."

She reaches out to me and closes the box in my hand.

"Grayson, you know I love you more than anything, right? I don't need this. As long as I have you and this little one, I have everything I could possibly need. I know you don't want to get married again. Hell, after that conversation with my mom, I've realized I don't need the wedding. I just need you."

I don't know how to explain how much I fucking want this.

"Grayson, look at me."

As I do, I clock movement happening from the table across the room.

Time blurs as the first three men walk past the table toward the bathrooms. My right hand instinctively grips the gun holstered in the back of my pants. The last man stops halfway between his table and the bathroom, about five meters from me, then turns to face me with a sadistic smile and pulls out his gun, aiming it at the back of Maddie's head.

Fuck no.

Still on one knee, I unholster my gun, at the same time shielding Maddie's chair.

I will protect her with my life if I have to.

The bathroom door swings open to my right. I adjust my body but still aim my gun at the man in front of me. But before he can pull the trigger, I aim and shoot. The bullet hits him in the side of the head. Maddie gasps from behind me. He thuds to the ground in a heap.

I don't hear the other gun go off as my body vibrates from the impact. I stumble backward, hitting into the back of Maddie's chair. Pain radiates through my chest, so intense my vision goes blurry.

Fuck.

I try to aim for him. The fucker isn't there. As I turn my head toward the bathrooms, I see a figure running through the door, but before I can get a shot, the room erupts around me into chaos, high-pitched screams, bodies frantically rushing.

"Grayson!"

I can't fucking die here; I can't leave her exposed.

Using my free hand, I clutch at my shirt. Warm liquid seeps through my fingertips. Fuck. The room spins, the pain taking over my every thought.

No. I need to get her out of here.

With all the strength I have, I grip her chair to hold myself up. I know this isn't good. I can feel the warmth pouring out of my body. But I'm still standing, just about. I have time to get her out of here.

"Maddie, we need to leave," I choke out.

She shoves a cotton cloth into my hand, and I press it over the bullet wound.

She wraps her arms around my waist. The sound of her sobs rips me apart. Gritting my teeth, I hobble along, trying with everything I have not to put all of my weight on her. As we walk into the street, the blue lights flash in my vision.

"Down the alleyway," I force out.

We take a sharp left, and I wince. This is the longest walk of my life. Every step just feels like one step closer to hell. Maddie keeps telling me I'm going to be okay, yet the panic in her voice doesn't really provide me much comfort.

By the time we reach the car, I heave out a breath, slamming my hand on the roof of my Audi. Maddie rummages through my suit jacket until I can hear the jangling of my keys. She opens up the passenger door and helps me in. As soon as I'm in, I recline the seat back and rip open my blood-soaked shirt. I try to feel for the bullet. It hasn't come out the other side; it's fucking wedged in there somewhere.

"Grayson, it's going to be okay."

I suppose if I'm going to die, at least I have my sunshine with me.

"Just stay with me, Grayson."

"I fucking love you, sunshine."

Chapter Forty-Two

MADDIE

I race us to the hospital. Warm tears cascade down my face. This is the longest journey of my life. How I haven't crashed his precious baby, I don't know.

My heart has been in my throat the entire time.

Grayson's holding the napkin I ripped off the table over his wound, but blood still seeps out across his abs.

"Grayson, baby, stay with me."

He hums in response.

"Don't you dare fucking die on me. You just offered me forever. Don't take that away from us."

"I fucking love you, sunshine," he croaks out, and I barely recognize his voice.

"No, don't do this. Please."

I sob, squeezing his thigh.

"Stay with me, please. I'm begging you."

"Grayson!" The panic in my voice is evident.

His breathing is heavy, but he doesn't respond.

"Grayson!"

Nothing.

I pull up outside the hospital, slamming the brakes and flying out of the car.

"Somebody help me, my boyfriend's been shot!"

Three men run over to me, one stubbing out a cigarette.

"He's in the car."

I let out a shaky breath as another brings over a stretcher. They drag his still form onto the stretcher and rush him toward the entrance.

I run over and shut the car door behind them, but not before reaching over to the center console and grabbing his phone and that black ring box I picked up off the restaurant floor. I follow behind through the glass doors.

"Miss, we are going to need you to wait here. They are taking him straight to the ICU."

I spot a bathroom just at the end of the waiting room. I run to it, slamming the door shut behind me. I put the phone and box on the tiled floor and lift the toilet lid up and empty the contents of my stomach. Once I finish, I flush and sit on the floor.

He's going to be okay.

His phone starts ringing on the floor next to me, and Luca's name flashes on the screen.

"Did you do it?" Luca's voice booms down the phone.

Perhaps he's talking about the engagement.

"L-Luca, he's been shot."

There's a crash, then he asks, "Where are you, Maddie?"

"St. Luke's-Roosevelt Hospital."

"I'll be there in fifteen. Don't let him out of your sight."

"He's in surgery, Luca. I've locked myself in the bathroom."

"Fuck! Okay, Maddie. I'm on my way now. Just stay where you are. We have to keep you safe. Keep the door locked and I will knock for you when I'm there."

"Luca, what if he dies?"

I try to suck in a breath, but it's no use.

"Maddie, it's going to be okay. Grayson won't go down without a fight. He will do anything to make his way back to you both. I'll see you soon."

I hang up and put the phone back on the floor next to me. And wait.

A KNOCK ON the bathroom door startles me.

"Maddie, it's me." For some reason, it calms me. Knowing Luca's here to look out for us both.

I bring myself to my feet, not forgetting the box and the phone, and unlock the door, peering through to see his blood-shot green eyes staring back at me.

I push open the door and throw myself into his chest, wrapping my arms around him. His body goes stiff, then I feel him relax, returning the hug. Grayson isn't here to kick his ass for touching me right now. And I need a fucking hug. I tighten my grip around his muscular frame and squeeze my eyes shut.

"Shhh, it's going to be okay, Mads," he murmurs.

His heart is racing, despite his calm tone.

"They are taking us to his room. He's not going to be out of surgery for a while but we can wait there for him."

I nod against his chest, not wanting to let go.

"Frankie, go grab us a couple of coffees, please." Luca whispers, "Frankie won't hurt you. He's one of us."

I nod against his chest, but something inside me is screaming not to trust him.

"Come on, let's go."

He grabs me by the shoulders, taking a step back.

"You ready?" he asks.

I nod, and he takes my hand and kicks open the double doors.

He leads us down the gray corridor, and that horrid clinical smell burns my nostrils. In room 14, there are two leather chairs, a white table, and some monitors. The only noise is the clock ticking.

I take a seat and Luca sits beside me. Frankie arrives shortly with two steaming cups of coffee. He barely looks at me as he hands one to me. Weird.

"I'm so sorry, Maddie," Luca blurts out the second Frankie leaves the room, positioning himself outside the door. I completely forgot we're now basically in the middle of a mafia warzone.

"It's not your fault, Luca. You didn't shoot him."

I know Grayson loves working for Luca. It might be wrong, but it's him.

"I should have known they were going to retaliate." He sighs and sips his coffee.

"Retaliate?"

"We kidnapped Marco's older daughter. The brat is currently living in my house, causing me all kinds of shit."

I don't know what to say.

"But they killed Nico, right?"

A sadness washes over his face. He runs his hand through his dark hair and leans back in his chair.

"I need to get a fucking grip on this organization. I'm a fucking failure."

"Hey, stop it." I reach over and grab his hand.

"Grayson respects you; he wouldn't work for you if he didn't. Not everything can go perfectly as per plan all the time. Tonight was bad luck. Maybe, if Grayson wasn't so wrapped up in me, this never would have happened."

Luca's eyes flick down to my hand.

"Where's the ring?"

Tears well in my eyes, and I shake my head.

"I said no, Luca. That could be his last memory of me." I tear my hand away from his and cover my face.

"Maddie, listen to me. Grayson loves you; he's loved you from the moment he laid eyes on you. Never fucking forget that. Why did you say no? I thought you always dreamed of marriage?" He crosses his leg, staring at me intently.

"I did. I mean, I do. I just didn't want Grayson to feel forced into marrying me because of, you know . . ." I dart my eyes down to my stomach.

"He wanted nothing more than to marry you, Maddie. He wasn't doing it because he thought you wanted it. He was doing it because he did too."

My heart breaks at his words. How did I get this so wrong?

"I fucked up."

Luca stands and picks the black box up from the side table and places it in my hands.

"Do you want to marry him?"

"Y-yes."

"Then put the ring on. When he wakes up and sees you wearing that, he might forget about all the pain."

I open the box and stare at the gorgeous ring glistening in the box.

It's perfect. I mean, it's a statement and a half, but that's Grayson.

I slide it over my ring finger. I hold my hand up to the lights and admire how it shimmers.

"You never know, he might have forgotten you said no." Luca chuckles, giving me a wink.

Time ticks by as I sip my coffee, not being able to take my eyes off my ring. Luca is busy tapping away on his phone next to me. I glance at the clock—1 a.m. He's been in surgery for two hours already now.

"Hey, Maddie. I just need to pop out. I have a shipment coming in, and I need to make sure it goes smoothly. I'll leave Frankie here with you. If you need anything, you just ask him. I'll be back in the morning. Let me know if there are any updates."

I nod, and he walks over, slipping his phone in his pocket. He drops a kiss to the top of my head.

"Call me if you need anything."

"Thank you, Luca."

Chapter Forty-Three

MADDIE

It's been three hours and still no Grayson. No anyone.
Frankie brought in another coffee, again not making
any eye contact. I phoned Sienna just after Luca left.
She was adamant she wanted to come here for me. It's the
middle of the night and she is going to have to deal with
Keller. He isn't going to take this well at all since he loves
Grayson like a brother.

The engagement ring weighs heavy on my finger. Sadness
washes over me as I realize he might never see this on my
finger. I thought I was out of tears, but the ones now rolling
down my cheek tell me different.

The sudden urge to go to the toilet distracts me. As I stand
up, a shooting pain radiates from my lower stomach, just like
a period pain. But worse, radiating down both of my legs
and into my lower back. I suck in a breath and rest my palm
against the wall.

Shit, this hurts.

270 - LUNA MASON

After a moment to get over whatever the hell that was, I push off the wall and drag myself over to the door. I stumble forward, crashing against the door as the pain returns, this time far worse. Enough for stars to form in my vision. I fumble around, trying to find the doorknob. I need help. Something isn't right.

Panic sets in. I open the door, only to be hit with another wave of pain. I double over. Frankie crouches before me.

"Are you okay?" he asks.

"N-no. It fucking hurts," I shout, squeezing my arms around my stomach and trying to quell the pain.

"Go and get someone!" I shout, wincing in agony. Frankie looks horrified.

I close my eyes as he runs off down the corridor. I'm losing them both. Everything I've ever loved is leaving me. *Please be okay, little one. Mommy needs you right now more than anything.*

Frankie returns with a doctor following behind him, her hair pulled up into a tight bun.

"Miss Peters, if you'd please come with me."

Frankie nods, so I push myself off the wall and stand. The pain subsides for a moment. He holds his arm out for me. I grab onto it, and he leads me down the corridor to a room up on the right.

He walks us over to the bed, and I pull myself up onto it. It's already in an upright position, so I lie back. I'm scared the room might start spinning.

The doctor shuts the door behind us and walks over to the bed, clipboard in hand. She has a warm smile, which provides me a tiny bit of comfort. Unlike Mr. Clenched Jaw over there.

"How many weeks are you?"

"Ummm, around ten now. I have my twelve-week appointment in a couple of weeks."

"Would you mind pulling your dress up so I can get to your stomach? I would like to do an ultrasound. Is this the father?"

"No," we both say in unison.

Frankie senses the awkwardness in the air, perhaps, because he barges out the room.

"Have you had any bleeding?" the doctor asks.

"I had a little bit earlier before I went out. I looked it up online and it said it could be spotting. It was only a little bit."

I know I'm rambling. What if I missed something? I didn't want to tell Grayson.

"Let me get the ultrasound and we can take a look. Okay?"

I nod, and she shuffles out the door.

"Time to go, Maddie." Frankie rushes in.

"What, I can't leave."

He pins me with a glare. I scoot back on the bed away from him.

He reaches behind him, straightening his arm out, and points a gun straight at my head.

"W-what are you doing?"

He runs a hand over his dark stubble. "Either come with me now and you live. If you don't, you die."

My mind goes into overdrive.

"But you work for Luca," I say vehemently.

"I work *for* no one."

Oh shit.

"Luca and Grayson will kill you."

Grayson will hunt him down and send him straight to hell if he touches me.

But Grayson can't help you now, Maddie.

"Right now, Grayson can't do shit. I need you out of the way for my plan to work."

This makes no sense to me.

"What plan, what the fuck is this?"

He takes a step toward me, and I flinch away from him.

"Get the fuck away from me," I scream.

He shoots across the room, his hand muffled over my mouth. Gasping for breath, I hit against his muscular arms, trying to wriggle out of his hold.

"Shhh, Maddie. Grayson said you were fiery. Goddamn, he was right. You couldn't just make this easy for me, could you? I'm doing this to save you both," he adds when I refuse to relent my struggle.

"Maddie, calm the fuck down. I'm not going to hurt you. I just need you to come with me. If you stay, Marco will come after you in exchange for his daughter. I need Grayson. I need him furious and ready to burn down the city."

No, this can't be happening. I can't leave Grayson.

"Will you be quiet if I let you talk?"

I nod against his hand. He releases it, and I gasp for air, my hands holding my throat.

"I can't leave him," I sob.

"It's temporary. It's the *only* way to keep you both safe. Grayson can't protect you right now. I can. Now, you need to write him a letter, break up with him. I need to be able to keep him reined in. I can't do that if he's distracted thinking something's happened to you."

"Wh-what, no, I can't do that to him. Please don't make me do this. What about my baby?"

Pulling out a folded-up piece of paper and a black pen, he hands them to me. Through trembling hands, I snatch them out of his tattooed fingers.

I want to stab him in the eye and run. But I know how dangerous it is out there. I don't have Grayson here to protect me anymore. Plus, this lunatic has a gun pointed at me.

"Make it believable, Maddie. I need his full attention for this."

How am I supposed to find the words to break his heart?

Dear Grayson,
I want you to know, I will always love you.
You are the man of my dreams. To be treated like a princess by you is every woman's dream.
But I can't be with you anymore.
I can't live a life where you risk your own for me.
I can't live in the dark anymore. Not with our child.
Please don't try to find me.
I don't want to break your heart. This is already ripping my own out too. But it's for the best.
We were never meant to be together. But I'm glad we had these last few months together.
I will cherish every single moment we shared.
I'm sorry.
Maddie. Xoxo

I fold the letter in half, and Frankie holds his hand out to take it.

"I would like to put it in his room."

"Fine," he grunts. "We have to be quick, Maddie."

I slide off the bed and follow him. As we reach Grayson's door, I turn the knob. My heart is in my throat as he lies there, tubes coming out of his mouth, monitors beeping erratically. But he's alive.

"I need to say goodbye properly."

"Five minutes. Luca will be back in ten."

Sucking in a breath, I walk in, pulling up a chair next to his bed.

He's so still, so peaceful. I take a seat and put my hand over his.

"Grayson, I don't know if you can hear me. I will marry you. I have the ring on and everything, so there is no getting out of it now. Please don't stop looking for me. I'm begging you."

Tears spill onto his arm. I place the letter on the side table with his phone atop it.

"I'll see you again one day. Soon, I hope."

I have to be strong right now—for the baby, for Grayson.

With my head held high, I have one more shot to get away.

I peek into the window as Frankie is checking his watch and looking down the corridor to the entrance.

I open the door as quietly as I can, my eyes glued on the red exit sign to the left. I thought hospitals were busy, so where the hell is everyone? Where the hell is my doctor anyway?

Taking a deep breath and flinging the door open, I run as fast as I can toward the fire exit.

"Maddie," he growls.

His heavy footsteps get louder and louder behind me. I push the barrier and fall through the door, turning around and pushing it shut, straight on a furious Frankie.

"Someone help," I scream.

The door flies open, crashing into me and sending me hurtling toward the rubble, and I land straight on my ass. My hands sting as they slide across the floor. "Fuck," I hiss, scooting back as Frankie towers over me.

"Fine, have it your way," he mutters, bending and lifting me into his arms, throwing me over his shoulder.

I pound my bruised hands as hard as I can against his back and kick my legs frantically.

"Let me fucking go, you asshole!"

"Shut the fuck up."

He marches us into complete darkness across the parking garage, the lights flashing on his black Mercedes.

"Please don't do this, Frankie."

"This is the only way to keep you and Grayson alive. Now get in the car and no more fucking running. If you do, it will only take me one call to have Grayson killed in his hospital bed. Do you understand?"

I nod, holding back the tears.

Chapter Forty-Four

GRAYSON

Luca's face crowds my blurry vision. The persistent beeping is the only thing I can hear. I blink a few times to clear my vision; the fucking white and bright lights aren't helping. God, my mouth is so dry. As I cough, a sharp pain sears into my left side.

"Fuck!" I hiss.

"Grayson, let me get the doctor."

Doctor?

It takes me a while to come round.

Maddie.

Where is Maddie?

Panic rushes through me, and I bolt upright in the bed. Which is probably the worst thing I could have done, as the pain is almost unbearable.

"Lie the fuck down, Grayson. You nearly died, for fuck's sake!"

"Where's Maddie? Luca, where the fuck is Maddie?" I roar and immediately break out into a coughing fit.

He shoves a plastic cup of water into my hands. My arms are so heavy as I bring it to my lips and take a sip. Even the effort to swallow is exhausting.

"Just hang on. Let the doctors do their thing, then we talk."

I shoot him a look. The doctor comes over. The cold air makes me grind my teeth together as he opens up my gown, pulling back the dressing just under my ribs.

"All healing nicely. No signs of infection. You are lucky. Just a few millimeters either side and you'd probably be in a lot worse condition, if not dead. You need rest. You've been in and out of consciousness for two days now."

Well, fantastic.

"We need to keep you here under observation for a few more days. Mr. Russo has covered your stay."

"Great, thanks."

The door clicks as the doctor leaves.

"Spit it out, Luca."

He shifts uncomfortably in his seat. He leans over to my bedside table and hands me a white letter, folded neatly in half.

What the fuck.

I unfold the paper, my eyes scanning over her words. My hands shake with rage.

"This is bullshit, Luca."

"I know."

I re-read the letter over and over again. Her tears stain and smudge the black ink. I don't believe this, not for one second. Scrunching the paper in my hands, I launch it across the room.

"Fuck!"

Suddenly the machines next to me go ballistic, and I faintly hear Luca calling my name as I slip back into the darkness. There's no sunshine to bring me back this time.

Chapter Forty-Five

GRAYSON

Three fucking days have passed since I read Maddie's letter and basically passed out. Three days of staring at these same dull white walls, listening to Luca and Keller chat utter shit.

I read Maddie's piece of shit letter again. I scrunched it up and hurled it across the room.

I know my sunshine better than this, and apparently, she knows me well too.

The dried tearstains that smudged the black ink tell me something isn't right. Maddie would dump me to my face. She'd never take the coward's way out. Also, she's not stupid enough to run away with my child and expect me to sit tight.

"Why are you two fuckers here and not out looking for Maddie?" I hiss as pain shoots into my lungs.

The fuckers got me good. The bullet missed. But fuck does it hurt.

"Grayson, we've got Enzo and his team doing everything they can. My guys are keeping tabs on the Falcones. Shooting you wasn't their endgame. It's just the start."

"And what if she's not in the fucking country?" I seethe.

"I've reached out to my connections in Europe. There may be a few ties to an agreement. I'm working on it. Trust me."

Keller eyes him suspiciously, and the last thing I need is him talking Luca out of that.

A war is brewing and we need an army.

Keller turns to me. "Grayson, what if she has just left you? What if she needs space? She turned your proposal down."

Luca whisper-yells at Keller to shut the fuck up.

"No, Grayson, she's wearing that ring. Look." Luca shoves the ring box at me. The ring is gone. "She was devastated. I asked her, if you were to propose to her again, what would she say? She said yes. So I gave her the ring and she put it on. She loves you. There is no doubt."

"What did Frankie say?" I ask.

"He alerted me that she was missing. He said she was taken into another room, something about having stomach pains. He hasn't seen her since."

Our baby.

I run my hands through my hair and close my eyes. This is too much.

"Has Enzo pulled up the medical records?"

"Yep, nothing has been recorded from that day."

"I swear to fucking God, I am going to rip their heads from their necks once I get hold of them."

Luca chuckles. "I have no doubt about that."

"Get me the fuck out of this hellhole. I'm building us that army whether you like it or not. They've declared a war and I intend to finish it. I have at least fifty guys at King's Gym—the best fighters around. Give me a couple of weeks and I'll have them trained into ruthless killing machines. You in?" I ask Keller.

Before he can respond, a tearstained, tired Sienna walks through the door, sniffling. He pulls her in close.

"I spoke to her mom, her brother, our college friends. No one has seen her." She throws her head into his chest and cries.

"Princess, it's going to be okay," he whispers.

"I need you out there looking for her, Keller. You're too skilled to be sitting at home with me, waiting for everyone else to find her. Please, champ."

Keller's eyes flick between me and Luca. We know he's been itching to be involved. Sienna has finally given him a green light now.

Luca warns, "One job, Keller."

"Brother, the only person who tells me what to do now is Sienna."

She stands and whispers in Keller's ear. His eyebrows shoot up as she speaks.

"Please find my best friend," she sniffles, walking over to my bedside. She clasps her hand over mine, giving me a smile. "She loves you, Grayson."

"I know, I love her too. I will find her, I promise you."

"See you at home, baby. Give Darcy a kiss from Daddy," Keller shouts after her as she leaves.

It stabs me straight through the heart. This could have been my life, but now, that feels like a lifetime away for me. The pain of being shot is nothing compared to this.

Keller rises from his seat with a new determination.

"Fuck it, let's build a goddamn army."

Chapter Forty-Six

GRAYSON

Two Weeks Later

Darkness surrounds me as I knock back the scotch, letting it burn its way down my insides. The gym is finally empty and now it's time for my brain to run wild.

Two fucking weeks.

I slam the glass on the wooden desk of my office.

Sunshine, where are you?

Every single minute that passes by that I can't find her, the further I plunge into the darkness.

Nothing.

Not one single trace of her.

It's like she vanished into thin air.

Tears well in my eyes as I stare up at the white ceiling.

Never in my life have I felt so hopeless. So lost. I don't think I've left this boxing gym since Luca not-so-subtly forced the doctors to discharge me. I might not be back to my full physical strength, but that doesn't stop me from molding my fighters into bloodthirsty warriors. Keller's been here every day without fail. Between us, we're building Luca a force to be reckoned with. We have Enzo tapping into every security system he can. There are no records of her passport being used, no medical records popping up. Her cards haven't been used.

Frankie has been busy hunting down the Falcones for me. He swings by the gym every day to give me an update and check that I'm healing properly, as per Luca's orders. I'm itching to get back into the chaos, to burn this fucking city to the ground. But Frankie and Luca are right; I can't go out there and risk myself yet. I need to be at full strength to take them all down. I can't find Maddie if I'm dead. I can't protect her.

The CCTV from the hospital has been completely wiped. Even with Enzo and his team, we have nothing to work with.

Losing her has been like losing the ability to breathe. I'm suffocating. Right now, I would give anything, even my own life, to make sure she's safe.

I can't even think about our baby. If I do, I might truly lose my head and do something stupid. I've kept myself busy, trailing through the footage from Enzo and plotting attacks with Frankie. Something in my gut just doesn't sit right.

People don't simply vanish; the Falcones aren't clever enough for that. I just can't quite put my finger on what isn't adding up. Running a hand through my hair, I pick the crystal up and hurl it against the wall.

My phone pings on the desk. Swiping it up, I scan the latest text from Luca.

LUCA

No deal with the Capris yet. I am arranging alternate operations to search in London. I'll be flying back tomorrow. Don't do anything stupid before I get back.

I get the same warnings most days. Hence, Frankie the babysitter. The Capris are well-known. The largest mafia organization in Europe, they're a slick unit, almost indestructible. Having them on our side would have been a game changer.

The door flies open, revealing a disheveled Frankie. His white shirt's unbuttoned, splattered in crimson. He glances down at the glass crunching under his feet.

"Fuck taking your anger out on the crystal. Let's go kill some Falcone fuckers." He cocks his brow at me, unholstering a Glock, flipping it around so the grip faces me.

Hell fucking yes.

"Where are we off to first?"

"Marco's got a new pizzeria opening up next week. It would be a shame if a fire started in the kitchen."

"As long as we get some of his men in there cooking too, count me in."

I wrap my hand around the gun.

"It's good to have you back." He slaps me on the shoulder, and I shoot him a glare. Fuck, why does my body still feel like I've been hit by a bus?

"Good to be back. Now slap me like that again and I'll knock you out. We clear?"

"Sorry, boss, forgot you're an injured soldier."

Fucker.

Adrenaline buzzes through my veins as we storm toward the glass doors of the gym.

It's time to get my life back.

My sunshine back.

Chapter Forty-Seven

MADDIE

I whip my head up from the cushion as the door creaks open. "Wakey wakey, lazy bones," Frankie announces as he walks through with a brown shopping bag in each hand.

After one month of living in this tiny flat in the middle of God knows where, I can actually say I don't *mind* Frankie's company. After my initial rage, he's proven me wrong about him so far.

"Hardly lazy. Just bored out of my head and pregnant and tired."

"Well, I come with more smut." He chuckles, dropping a bag full of books next to me before heading off to the kitchenette.

"I threw in a mother and baby book as well. In case your brain fancied a break from dicks."

"Hey! They have a plot too."

I follow him into the kitchen. He's busy refilling the

refrigerator full of goodies. I even spot a massive carton of strawberry ice cream that I demanded, blaming it on cravings.

"I'm making us carbonara tonight, my mother's recipe."

"Do you need a hand?" I ask.

"No. It won't take me long. I'm a pro."

He doesn't need to tell me twice. His cooking is delicious, after all.

By the time I've stacked my new books in the shelf in my bedroom, organizing them in the order I want to read them, Frankie calls out to me.

"Smells good." I smile as I take a seat at the little two-seater table.

I can't help but notice Frankie's frown every time I start chopping the spaghetti up with my knife. I guess that's not how it's meant to be eaten.

"How's Grayson?" I ask.

"He's fine."

He never gives much away. He told me about Grayson's recovery from the shooting and how he's been put on bed rest. Other than that, I get the same two-word responses. But I have to ask, I have to know he's okay.

"How long in days?"

"I don't know. I've been working on this for over a year now. I can't fuck it up now."

"Right . . . What is this grand plan anyway?"

"Eliminate all the enemies, take back what's rightfully mine." He shrugs, biting into the garlic bread.

"What about Grayson and Luca? Where do they fit in this *take over the world* operation?" I ask nervously, hoping they aren't his means to an end. Although he's shown only respect when he speaks of them so far.

"Think of it as more of a joint enterprise. Me and Luca could dominate the world."

"If they don't kill you first." I smirk.

"I mean, if you could put in a good word with them for me, I might survive."

I snigger.

"Depends how much longer I'm here. Every day, there's less chance of me saying anything nice about you."

"I see why Grayson likes you. You're full of spirit."

"Gee, thanks."

"Come on, you need to eat. It's not just for you anymore, think of the little one," he says.

Since the episode in the hospital, Frankie's had private doctors around every week to check up on me and the baby. I've had no more bleeding and apparently everything's going as it should.

"I've got a new TV coming tomorrow. Thought I'd replace the one you smashed up." He smirks.

Oops.

"Yeah, sorry about that."

"No, you're not. Does it get me back in the good books though?"

"Fine. Just hurry up and finish whatever it is you're doing and let me go back to my life."

"I'm trying. You have my word. The second it's safe for you to leave, I'll let you."

"Anyway, how come you have so much time to come and have dinner with me most nights? Don't you have a wife or someone to go home to?"

I've been dying to ask. I bet he's not short of options, plus, he must be in his late thirties. I find it hard to believe he hasn't forced his way into someone's life yet.

"Nope. Too busy for that."

"Don't you want a family?"

"Watch it."

"Just an innocent question," I say, then stuff my mouth with pasta.

"I'm more than happy being Uncle Frankie."

"You might regret saying that. Uncles have to do lots of babysitting, you know," I tease.

"No problem, how hard can it be? I was brought up in a big family. I have lots of nieces."

"I guess we'll see." I shrug, pushing away my plate. Every now and then, this overwhelming sadness consumes me. I miss Grayson so much.

No matter what, I will make sure Frankie makes this right.

For now, I'm grateful we're alive and healthy.

Chapter Forty-Eight

GRAYSON

I enter the code to the gates to Luca's gothic mansion on the outskirts of New York and make my way down the gravel drive.

I'm working with Enzo and coordinating the operations in Europe. At night, well, the devil comes out to play. Frankie has been busy scoping out the Falcones' operations so we know where to hit them at night. I hate to say it, but he's pretty damn good. He hasn't been wrong once.

I've left Keller finishing up training our new recruits. In the past six weeks, they've come a long way. I'd say they're ready to join the chaos.

Last night, we raided one of Falcones' main industrial units. We cleared their drug supply out and burned the lot to the ground. It warmed my cold soul as I watched the flames tearing the building apart.

I've taken out all four of Marco's advisors. One by one in their own homes. I sit and wait for them to come back from their nightly poker games. The shock on their faces when they unlock their doors and see me sprawled out on their couch is priceless.

Not one of the fuckers has given me any information about Maddie. In fact, they don't even know who I'm talking about. I squeeze my grip tighter around the steering wheel.

Something about this isn't sitting right with me.

I get out of the car and slam the door behind me. A panicked Luca swings open the door.

"What's going on?"

"Just come inside."

Frankie is standing next to the grand staircase, dressed perfectly in a navy suit and tie.

I give Frankie a nod and turn back to face Luca.

"Well?" I ask, not even hiding my irritation at this point.

Since Maddie left, I have no tolerance for anyone or anything.

"Rosa is fucking dead."

Well, shit.

Frankie stiffens next to me, and I cock my head at him. His jaw tics, but he doesn't look at me.

Strange.

"And?"

"Well, she was our bargaining chip over the Falcones for Maddie."

Frankie shifts uncomfortably next to me. What the fuck is up with him today?

"Do you have a fucking problem?" I grit out.

Frankie rubs his hands along his stubble.

"No problem. Want me to take the body out, boss?"

"Yeah, fine. Go and get the supplies from the warehouse and come back. Grayson, with me."

Luca storms past me, heading up the stairs. I follow him, all the while thinking about Frankie's suspicious behavior.

I close the door behind me as we enter his office. Luca sits in his black leather chair in front of his dark oak desk. Paper is scattered all over the desk. CCTV pictures of Maddie the night she left the hospital.

"Should I send a condolence card out to Marco?" I smirk, and Luca shoots me a warning glare.

I take a seat.

"What do we do now, boss?"

My head flies around as the office door flies open, crashing against the wall behind.

"Luca, I can't get the coffee machine working!" a woman shouts, and I have to blink a few times.

Rosa Falcone. Alive, in the flesh.

I cock my brow as she waltzes over, her silky black robe open, displaying her lacy underwear. I tear my eyes away, taking in Luca's irritation. He doesn't take his eyes off her; he either wants to avoid me, or he's too busy eye-fucking her to even remember I'm in the room.

When I clear my throat, he whips his head to me. Rosa wraps her arms around his neck. Oh, now this is interesting. She whispers something in his ear.

He shoots me one of those looks to say *don't fucking say anything*, before leaning down and saying something in her ear that makes her cheeks flush crimson.

Of course he has to fuck his enemy's daughter.

She gives me a sheepish grin before tiptoeing out of the room, closing the door behind her. Luca lets out a huff, rubbing his hands through his black hair.

"So, railing your captive. That's a new one for you." I bite the inside of my mouth to stop myself laughing.

"Fuck off. It's not like that."

"Whatever, boss. I don't care. What I do care about is why you lied to Frankie."

He sighs, pulling his phone out of his pocket. "I was able to make a deal with Romano Capri after all. I think Frankie is working for the Falcones. You were right; something isn't adding up. He appears out of nowhere wanting to work for me. Frankie wasn't just Romano's damn bodyguard. He was his right-hand man. He left because he had family business to attend to in New York. Every damn time, he knows exactly where the Falcones' new hideouts are. He was the last one to see Maddie."

Fuck.

He's right.

How didn't I see this? And what price did Luca pay for this information?

"He's smart. He all but ran the Capris in Europe. His reaction to Rosa's death was exactly as I suspected. He's refused to go anywhere near her. Always found an excuse for not checking in on her."

"Because she'd recognize him?" I answer.

"Exactly."

"Can I do the honors when he's back?"

"Why do you think you're here?"

The fucking asshole is going to die a slow and painful death.

"I swear to God, I will rip him limb from limb if he's touched her."

"I'm banking on that. How I didn't shoot him on the spot back there, I don't know. We need to get Maddie first before we kill him. I'm waiting on Enzo's call. He's digging into him for us now. If I've learned anything from you, it's that we need intel before we act."

Hope blossoms in my heart at the prospect of getting closer to finding Maddie.

Luca sets his phone down. "We are going to find Maddie. We are so close."

I drop onto the sofa and cover my face with my arm.

"I need to go and check in on Rosa. Give me five minutes." Luca heads to the door.

"Only five? I would have put you down for lasting longer than that," I mutter into my sleeve.

Luca chuckles. "Around her, five is probably about right."

<hr />

SOON AFTER LUCA returns, his phone starts to buzz on the table.

The fury that passes across his features cannot be mistaken when he answers.

"Where is he now?" he asks, violence dripping from his tone.

Oh, I'm so fucking ready for this.

"Keep tabs on him. Marco is already at the restaurant?"

At the mention of Marco, I get to my feet.

"Frankie's a dead man. He's on his way to meet Marco at his family restaurant. You ready for this?" Luca asks me, hanging up.

He opens up the deep gray container in the corner of the room, and an array of guns and knives greets me. I stare at it with a big fat grin on my face.

"Fuck yes, let's do this."

We grab our guns of choice.

"Call Keller now. He can bring some of our new recruits and see who can hack it." He smirks.

"On it," I say, sliding out my phone and dialing his cell.

Luca storms past me with determination in his step. I've never seen him this enraged. I can't fucking wait. Holstering my gun and sliding a knife in my pocket, I follow his lead.

Chapter Forty-Nine

MADDIE

The door slams open, making me jump out of my skin. I scoot back on the bed until my back hits the metal railings.

A red-faced Frankie barrels in. He's almost out of breath.

"Pack your shit, you need to get the fuck out of here."

"What, why?"

He stalks over toward the end of the bed. Fuck, he looks so exhausted. His usual pristine black stubble is starting to grow out. The top of his black shirt is open, buttons missing.

He just throws a suitcase on the bed and unzips it. He races around the room like someone possessed, hurling in all of my minimal belongings.

"It's not safe. If something happens to you, Grayson will definitely kill me, and I need him on my side for now."

"Why are you speaking in riddles?"

"It's not what you think, okay? I'm sure Grayson will fill you in eventually. Just know I am doing this to look out for you. That's all I've been doing this whole time." There's a sadness in his tone beneath that hard exterior.

But he's lying to me, and worse, he's lying to Grayson and Luca.

Once everything is packed, he zips the bag up and walks it toward that cracked front door with hundreds of locks on. My prison door.

"Come on, Maddie!"

"Where are you taking me now?"

"You'll be going with an old friend of mine, Theo, to London."

"I'm not leaving the fucking country, Frankie." I wrap my hands around my chest. The only thing getting me through this is the fact that I was close to Grayson.

"It wasn't a question. Please don't make me drag you. I really don't want to." His features soften. "It's just a few more days. Then you will be back where you belong and you will be safe. I promise you."

With a sigh, I swing my legs off the bed and slip on my biker boots.

He shoves a black beanie into my hands and says, "Put this on." Once I'm ready, he jogs down the stairs and opens up the fire escape door. The sunlight beams through.

God, I've missed the fresh air.

Just a few more days of this hell.

A few more days until I am complete again.

With my chin held high, I make my way to the black Mercedes. Frankie opens up the back door for me and I slide into the cream leather seat. Theo, the driver, I assume, stares at me through the rearview mirror.

"I'm sorry for all of this, Maddie. I hope maybe one day,

you'll understand, and you never know, maybe we could actually be friends." He almost sounds sincere.

I hold in a laugh.

Like hell would Grayson ever let that happen. So, instead, I give him a smile.

He holds out a black card to me. "Take this. Once it's safe, I will let Theo know. Do what you want, stay in London for a bit, go sightseeing, spend what you want, I don't care."

"Is that your way of apologizing for kidnapping me?"

He rests his hand on the roof of the car. "I like you, Maddie. I see why Grayson is obsessed with you. You're a good one."

"Bye, Frankie. Don't you dare hurt my Grayson."

He grins and slams the door, and we pull away.

I fiddle with the black Amex in my hand, but the name written in gold catches my attention.

Francis Falcone.

That sneaky asshole.

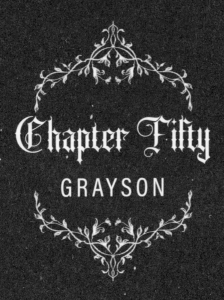

Chapter Fifty

GRAYSON

We park across the street from the dingy-looking Italian restaurant that is Rico's—Marco's family restaurant. The *I* in the sign just about hangs on. The formerly grass-green canopy over the window is now a faded brown.

Keller kills the engine, and Enzo is watching a live feed of the restaurant's CCTV. My fingers are just itching to wrap around his neck. In fact, I'm getting a little impatient.

"I can't wait to kill that fucker," Luca grits out, his eyes not moving from the restaurant door.

"You and me both. But remember, we need to find out where Maddie is before he dies. Okay?"

Luca is pretty close to losing his head. If it came down to it, I'd even pass up killing both of them to go and get her. I'm holding on to this last shred of hope.

Luca's phone lights up on his lap. "Frankie's just entered the back exit. It's fucking go time." He flashes me a grin. As he gets out of the car, slamming the door behind him, I let out a breath. This is it. I need to keep my head calm to get what I need.

Keller spins around to face me from the driver's seat, still gripping the wheel. "Keep him safe, Grayson. He's on the fucking edge right now. I'll be watching from Enzo's feed. We've got our guys surrounding the building, waiting on my instruction."

In just a few short weeks, the numbers in Luca's organization have doubled, and we're fighting back hard.

"I'll do what I can." I nod and catch up with Luca, who's already storming across the road toward Rico's. For fuck's sake, the last thing I need is him going in there and shooting them both before we get a chance for answers.

"Luca, fucking wait," I hiss, quickening my steps behind him.

I reach him and grab him by the shoulder before he can open the door.

"Do not fuck this up, Luca. This is for Maddie, remember that." My fingers dig into him, holding him in place. I can see in his eyes the pure hatred. I can't risk this.

"I'll go in first," I tell him and grab the metal door handle on the battered red door. It squeaks as I push it open. I aim my gun straight ahead and take a step in.

Marco and Frankie are sitting in the center of the room. I point my gun straight at a relaxed-looking Frankie, who simply smiles at me, with both hands flat on the table in front of him.

"Welcome, come, take a seat." He gestures at the two free seats opposite him. Marco scowls at me, but doesn't move. His hands are tied behind the chair. He shoots Frankie a look, but keeps quiet.

"I don't think so, Frankie. How about I just shoot you instead?" Luca announces as he breezes past me straight in his direction and presses his gun to the side of Frankie's head.

Frankie laughs and looks at me. Fucking Luca.

"I wouldn't do that if you want to see your precious Maddie again."

My heart rate spikes, and it takes every ounce of willpower not to shoot this prick between the eyes.

"Where the fuck is she?" I shout.

"Where would be the fun in simply telling you? Come and sit." He gestures to the perfectly laid table.

I raise my eyebrows at Luca and nod toward the chair, making my way over and pulling it out and sitting in front of him. He's so calm, considering he's in a room with two rival mob bosses and a raging monster whose girlfriend he's kidnapped.

"Frankie, just shoot the asshole," Marco grits out, and Frankie shoots him a look.

Luca whips his gun from the side of Frankie's head and aims it straight at Marco.

"If anyone's killing my brother, it's me."

Luca's mouth falls open. Frankie pulls out a handgun from inside his navy suit, presses it between Marco's eyes, and pulls the trigger without so much as flinching.

Fuck.

Marco's head falls backward, blood splattering all over the white table cloth. The gun is still smoking in Frankie's hands. Luca attacks him. "You motherfucker!" he shouts at Frankie, before punching him straight in the jaw.

A fucking good punch, if I do say so myself.

Frankie rubs his jaw and looks at Luca in amusement. "I'll

accept that one. Good shot," he says, looking at me and nodding. "I might need to get some sessions in with you."

"I don't fucking think so."

Frankie says, "Please, just sit. I will explain everything first."

Luca reluctantly pulls out the chair next to me and sits, lighting up a cigarette. His gun's still in his other hand. "Spit it out then," Luca says, letting out a puff of smoke.

"Maybe I'll start by formally introducing myself." He places his hand to his chest. "I'm Frankie Falcone. And this, next to me"—he nods to Marco's slumped dead body next to me—"was my older brother."

We knew he was working with the Falcones, but his fucking brother. My grip tightens around my gun. If it wasn't for Maddie, they'd both be dead by now. The beast inside me is raging to come out.

"You fucking lying prick." Luca abruptly stands up next to me, but I grab his arm and pull him back, so his ass is back on that seat.

"Is that really any way to speak to the new head of the Falcone family?" Frankie cocks a brow, like he's fucking proud of himself.

My blood is boiling at this stage.

"I do have a peace offering." Frankie grins and opens up his suit jacket, sliding out his phone.

"How about a fresh start for both of our organizations. Luca, I believe we can work together and we can rule over this city."

"What makes you think I need you? I can't fucking trust you," Luca snaps back.

"Day by day, you are losing control. Half of your men are snakes, trust me. How do you think I managed to pull all of this off and stay off both of your radars? Now, my plan was to take control of my family and then obliterate your organization. But, over the past few months, I've come to like you two."

"Enough to kidnap Maddie," I grit out.

"I did that to protect you both. You might not understand it now, but you will. I've made sure she's been looked after and is out of harm's way. I'm sorry, I had to use you to get what I wanted. I needed you, Grayson, to be angry enough to take out most of the Falcones for me. I couldn't risk Maddie getting in the way, not after seeing the state she was in at the hospital."

He looks me straight in the eyes, dropping his gun onto the table.

"I swear, I would never do anything to harm her. No matter how feisty she may have been. She did not make this easy on me, that's for fucking sure."

"Where the fuck is she!" I roar, standing up from my seat and slamming my fists on the table.

"Somewhere safe. We need to come to a deal before she gets released, so now sit."

I resist the urge to kill him with my bare hands, clenching my fists.

He leans back in his chair, lacing his fingers together.

He turns his attention to Luca. "I want our organizations tied up, Luca. I want to make this city our empire. And expand to Europe."

"Release Maddie and then we can talk," Luca deadpans.

Frankie rolls his eyes. "I'm not releasing her until we reach a deal. I'm not stupid. As soon as she's free, one of you will more than likely try to kill me. Maddie has already warned me of my impending death."

Hell, he's not wrong there.

Luca flicks his eyes to me. If Frankie *is* telling the truth, those two could rule the city. They have the brains and the power to do so. If anything, these past few months, Frankie has proven himself to be useful. Can we trust him? Absolutely fucking not. He just blew his own brother's brains out.

"We will discuss the deal in private. Grayson needs to get to Maddie. It will just be me and you once she's released. I'm interested in what you have to say. But don't forget, I hold the upper hand here. So I suggest you start making amends for your errors if we ever consider trusting you again," Luca says, pinning him with a stare, and Frankie nods, chuckling.

"Grayson, take both of our guns," Luca orders, so I stride over as they both slide their guns toward me on the table.

Holstering one of the guns in my waistband, I aim the other toward Frankie. He immediately raises his hands in surrender.

"Fucking let her go."

He nods to his phone on the table. "May I?"

He slowly inches forward to pick his phone and bring it to his ear.

"Loudspeaker."

The phone connects after two rings.

An Italian voice rumbles through the speaker. "Boss."

"She can go, Theo," Frankie orders and cuts the call.

My heart pounds in my chest. Maddie is free. I let out a ragged breath, doing everything I can to keep my emotions in check.

"Grayson. Go and get your woman. I've got this from here," Luca says with a tight smile.

I lower my shaking arm. I'm so fucking close to getting her back now.

"I swear to God, if there is a single hair out of place, I will skin you alive, Frankie."

"I expect no less, Grayson."

"You might want to fire up the private jet to go get her though; London is quite the flight. I thought it was best after Rosa's death to move her out of the war zone while I was killing my brother. You know, in case anything went wrong." He flicks his gaze to his brother's dead body still slumped in the chair.

London. She's thousands of miles away.

Luca turns to face me and gives me a knowing smile.

"Go." He points to the door. "Tell Keller I'll be out in twenty minutes."

My phone vibrating in my pocket distracts me from wanting to wring his neck for a split second. When I pull the phone out of my pocket, a +44 number lights up the screen.

I answer.

"Grayson?" Maddie's beautiful soft voice fills my ears.

I choke on a sob.

"Sunshine."

I pinch the bridge of my nose. She's alive, she's okay.

My heart is whole again.

Chapter Fifty-One

MADDIE

The big burly Theo grunts as he shuts the phone off and clicks the lock on the front door. It's a nice little Airbnb in central London. Very swanky with a view of the London Eye.

I've been drinking tea at the dining table, watching the pods go around. Reminiscing about my experience with Grayson there. I swear at one point my cheeks were so red, Theo was asking if I wanted a window open. The day's sunny. That summer sun is just the best.

Theo breaks my moment. "You are free to go now."

A smile beams across my face.

"For real?" I exclaim.

He nods, holding the door open.

I've only been here a few hours, and I haven't unpacked. Everything is still in that brown suitcase next to the front door. I rush over and grab the handle.

"Boss says spend whatever you want, stay in London for however long, and then you are free to return to New York."

Grayson. I need Grayson.

I bolt out of the door without so much as looking back. I can't risk him changing his mind.

I'm free.

I can finally get my life back.

I can get my man back.

I step into the lift and press the button to the ground floor, tears streaming down my cheeks. Happy tears. *Damn hormones.*

The sun beats against my pale skin. I guess that's what being on house arrest for six weeks does to one's complexion. I close my eyes and let it burn against my face. The scent of fresh doughnuts makes my stomach rumble. Placing my palm over my rumbling belly, I can't help but grin.

I walk over, the wheels of my luggage whirling against the pavement. This part of the embankment is heaving with people. Kids are running around, laughing at the men painted in silver pretending to be statutes. Someone here will surely let me borrow their phone.

I spot a woman in front of me who's busy texting. Her blonde hair is pulled up into a high ponytail, big black sunglasses covering half her face.

"Excuse me, miss," I shout, making my way over to her. She looks up from her phone and frowns at me before she rushes over.

"Hey!" she says. "Are you okay?"

"Would you mind if I used your phone to make a quick call? I don't have mine on me."

"Of course, here." She hands over the phone.

"It's to the States. I can give you some cash?"

She waves her hand and shakes her head.

The phone makes a weird connecting noise in my ear.

Please pick up, please pick up.

I hold my breath the entire time, stepping from side to side as I wait.

The call connects, finally.

"Grayson?" I whisper.

Nothing.

My heart sinks. What if he thinks I broke up with him? What if he hates me right now?

"Sunshine?" His voice fills the speaker, and my heart almost leaps out of my chest.

"Oh my God, Grayson," I choke out, tears spilling down my cheeks.

"Oh fuck, Maddie. I've missed you so fucking much. Tell me you're okay."

"I'm fine, I promise. Frankie looked after me. If you haven't already, please don't kill him. He's not a bad guy deep down."

"We can talk about that later, baby. Where are you exactly? I'm coming to get you."

Thank God.

"London. Well, near the London Eye."

"I'll be there in a few hours. Hang tight. I'll book us a room at the Shard on my way, you can go check in. Then meet me by the London Eye in say, eight hours?"

I hear a car roar to life; he really isn't messing around.

"I've got Frankie's card. I'm sure I can entertain myself for a few hours."

"I'd be disappointed if you didn't."

"I love you, Grayson. I never stopped. I didn't mean anything in that letter, please believe me."

"Baby, I never believed you would leave me. I've been painting the city red searching for you. Every second of every day. I am never letting you go again, sunshine. I love you too much. Without you, I barely survived."

I twiddle with my engagement ring.

"I'll see you soon."

"Damn right, be ready for me. I'm a starving man, ready to devour you."

I let out a laugh and shake my head. I fucking love this man.

"I'm banking on it."

"I love you more than life itself, Maddie. I hope I can prove that to you every day for the rest of our lives."

"I'd like that."

We say our goodbyes, and I cut the call.

Eight more hours.

Easy.

Chapter Fifty-Two

GRAYSON

The city lights pass by in a blur as we approach the embankment in Waterloo. My driver was waiting for me outside Gatwick Airport. My knee bounces up and down, all the stress of the last few weeks almost evaporating. Every kill, every tear, forgotten.

The only thing that truly matters in life is her.

I swear, as soon as she's back in my arms again, she's never leaving.

I can't live through this pain again.

I couldn't bring myself to ask about the baby. I am just hoping and praying, for everyone's sake, they are both okay. I could barely survive thinking Maddie was hurt, let alone my own fucking child.

I never wanted kids, until her.

Now I want everything.

I want to get her pregnant as many times as she will let me. I once told her I couldn't give her the family life she so desperately craved. But I was so wrong. I can, and will, give her everything she dreamed of.

The car pulls to a stop. The red lights of the London Eye fill my vision. This is the last time I'll ever be without her. I slip out of the car, and the cold air wraps around me. Goosebumps spread across my skin as I approach the walkway. My eyes are focused on picking her out in the crowd.

My world stands still as her blonde hair comes into my vision, swishing in the breeze. She's wrapped up in a black fur coat. I swear to God, my heart stops beating for a second. She has her back to me, her hands resting on the wall overlooking the Thames.

Fuck it, I can't wait another second.

I jog in her direction, my heart in my throat the entire time. I slow up my pace as I near her, wrapping my arms around her. Her sweet peachy scent calms me. I'd almost forgotten how delicious she smells.

"Did you miss me?" I whisper, nuzzling my nose into her hair.

She sucks in a breath. I slowly move my hands from her ribs, down to that little, perfect round bump. Her cold hands cover mine.

Our baby.

I've got them both back.

She turns around in my arms and loops hers around my neck. The second our eyes meet, it's like I've been put back together. All the broken pieces are back into place.

My heart beats again.

My hands settle on her ass, and I kiss her with everything I possibly have. Weeks of pain, heartache, poured into a kiss. I reluctantly break the kiss, pressing my forehead against hers.

I grab her face between my hands, assessing her face, her

body for any injuries. She laughs, a sound that warms me from the inside. My gaze stops as I reach her left hand. The engagement ring glistens in the city lights. I grab her hand and bring it to my mouth, pressing a soft kiss over the ring.

"Yes," she whispers. "If you'll still have me."

Using my thumb, I tip her chin so her eyes meet mine.

"There is nothing I want more, Maddie. I'd marry you right this second. I want you as mine in every way possible."

She smiles against my lips. I brush my hand across her jaw and trace down her body, settling on her stomach. I place my palm just under her belly button. You wouldn't be able to tell there was a bump there from looking, but I can feel it.

"Thank you," I choke out, closing my eyes.

"We have a strong little one in there. I can't lie; we had a couple of scary moments. But Frankie has had a private doctor out to check up on me every week."

My jaw ticks at her too-friendly mention of Frankie.

"Frankie looked after me. Well, both of us," she adds.

I nod, taking in a deep breath. I don't need my anger to rear its ugly head right now. I just want to focus on the love of my life.

"I want to know everything later."

She nods. "Can you take me home?"

"That's what I've been waiting to do from the second I woke up in that hospital bed. Are you ready to go home and spend the rest of your life with me? A life being fucked by the devil?"

"I just need to be fucked, Grayson. I can't tell you how fucking horny I am right now. These hormones are crazy, and your aftershave is making me want to jump you right here and now. So yes, I am more than ready."

This woman was made for me.

There is no doubt we were put on this planet for each other. Nothing could ever come close.

"Let's go." I plant one more kiss onto her lips.

I lace my fingers through hers and we walk back to the Bentley waiting for us. I open the car door for her. As she bends to get in, I groan as her ass brushes against my thigh. She whips her head around as I slap her ass lightly. I raise my eyebrows and shut the door, then climb into the seat next to her.

"Shall we use that room at the Shard and fly back in the morning?" I whisper in her ear. Her cheeks heat against mine.

I'll take that as a yes then.

Chapter Fifty-Three

MADDIE

As soon as the elevator doors slide closed, his muscular frame cages me in.

I squeeze my legs together. I can't remember the last time I went this long without sex. He takes a step toward me, so our bodies are flush. His erection rubs against my hip. I bite my lip and look at him. I stroke along his jeans, all the way around until I cup his cock. He groans and tips his head back.

"Fuck, my dick might explode."

I go still as I realize how long it's been since we were last together. Shit, he thought I'd broken up with him. *What if he—*

"I would never let anyone else touch me. I'm yours and will only ever be yours."

"But I left you. I wouldn't blame you."

"Baby, look at me." I lift my head back up to his.

"I never believed you left me. I never thought we had

broken up. The only thing I have been focused on for the last six weeks was finding you."

The elevator pings and opens up onto the same suite we stayed in the last time we were here. My luggage is still next to the bed where I left it earlier when I checked us in. I spent most of the afternoon in that freestanding bath that overlooks the skyline. God, it was perfect.

He pushes off the wall behind me, grabbing my hand and leading me into the suite. He chuckles as he walks us through the living room and spots the mountain of shopping bags. "You really did have a shopping spree on his card!"

"I mean, I think he owes me one."

He stalks toward me like a lion hunting his prey. He unbuttons my coat, and I shrug it off so it drops to the ground.

His fingers trail down my knitted black dress all the way to the hem.

"What did I tell you about wearing tights?" he mutters, shaking his head.

He pulls the dress up and over my head. I lift my arms to help him. I look down at my body. My boobs are a little bigger than they once were. My stomach kind of looks like a bit of period bloat. It definitely doesn't look like a proper bump, that's for sure. I just look like I've eaten a little too much takeout.

I also don't particularly feel sexy right now either.

A thud steals my attention. Grayson is on his knees, pulling my tights down over my stomach.

"Beautiful," he says, pressing a soft kiss to the center of my stomach.

I smile down at him. With just one word, my insecurities don't feel anywhere near as bad. When he looks up at me, those icy blues meeting mine, I feel sexy.

"God, woman. You are so fucking perfect."

He starts to pepper kisses along the inside of my thigh as he rolls the tights down my legs. Each kiss sends tingles throughout my body. I lift one leg up and then the other. He slides my boot off and then the tights are gone. He throws them behind his shoulder, kissing his way back up my legs.

Until he reaches right where I need him.

"On the bed, those sexy legs spread as wide as you can get 'em. I want to own every single inch of you tonight, sunshine. And that starts with you coming apart on my tongue. I'm a starving man, Maddie. And the only thing I want to eat is you."

"Mmmm, yes please," I moan, staring into his eyes. "*Sir.*"

He growls, launching himself at me, lifting me up by the waist and throwing us down onto the bed. I wrap my legs around his body and pull him closer to me. His breath hits my cheek. His suit rubs against my naked skin. As soon as his fingers swipe up my dripping seam, I can't hold in the moan. "Jesus, you really did miss me. I love how you soak my fingers," he says as he slips them inside me.

I tip my head against the mattress, arching my back to give him better access. He licks along my jaw and down my neck, fucking me with his fingers. My hands find the buttons of his white shirt. He goes still and grabs my hand. "No touching." He leans back on his heels and undoes his tie. I sigh in frustration as he removes his fingers, my pussy now throbbing with need. I cock my eyebrow at him.

"You can't be trusted not to touch." He grins, pulling his black tie off.

"Hands above your head," he commands, and my arms move before my brain even catches up.

He leans over me, wrapping the tie tightly around my wrists.

The bed dips as he gets off. His hands grab my thighs as he pulls me down the bed toward him.

My legs rest over his shoulders as he kneels on the ground.

"Oh my God," I scream as he licks me all the way from my entrance to my clit.

He slides his fingers back in, sucking on my clit, as he picks up the pace. I writhe on the bed, my whole body on the edge of an explosion. He pulls them out and trails them backward toward my ass.

Oh, fuck yes.

He continues to lap me up, using his other hand to spread my cheeks. One finger slowly rubs around my back entrance, and I thrust my hips down so he finally enters me. It stings just for a second as I adjust, since it's been a while. That is completely counteracted by the pure pleasure as he lifts my butt up and pushes his tongue inside my pussy, all the while fucking my ass with his finger.

"Grayson!" I shout, gritting my teeth. My legs shake like leaves around him. I try to pull my hands apart to touch him. Every cell in my body is screaming at me.

"Come for me, gorgeous. I want you all over my face."

And that's all it takes. An orgasm rips through me like never before. I scream out his name, my body convulsing, as he sucks on my clit, literally sucking the orgasm from me.

"That was so fucking hot," he says as he stands, his face glistening with my wetness. He doesn't even wipe it. He unbuttons his shirt and shrugs it off, along with his black suit jacket. His tattooed, ripped body makes me lick my lips. I squeeze my eyes shut as I spot his scar just below his ribs. My mind flashes back to that day. The day that ripped us apart.

"It's okay, baby. It's just a scar now. It's a reminder that I would literally die for you, Maddie. For you and our children. I will take all the pain to keep you safe. I promise you."

I wince as it comes flooding back to me like a living nightmare. The way my heart was ripped from my chest when they pulled his unconscious body out of the car.

"I can't lose you, Grayson. I can't live without you. I don't want to bring this baby up without a dad either. I'm not asking you to give up your job. All I ask is you be safe. And come back to us."

"I promise. Now, do I get to make love to my fiancée? I've got six weeks' worth to catch up on."

"I don't want you to make love. I want you to fuck me."

"The princess likes to be fucked rough and hard by her villain. I remember." His dick presses against my entrance.

"You aren't my *villain*. You are my everything. I love your darkness. But I also love your light. I love every single part of you."

With one swift move, he slides into me and groans.

I'm finally home, back where I belong.

"Now fuck me like the pretty whore I am, Grayson," I whisper, biting down on my lip.

A darkness flashes across his eyes. Then he leans down, taking my lips with his and hooking my leg around his back, pushing all the way in.

"Oh fuck, Maddie. I almost forgot how good it feels to sink inside you."

His lips slam back over mine before I can respond. Sweat beads on my forehead as he thrusts in and out of me, his finger circling my clit at the same time. He grabs my hips and flips me over, my face squashed into the mattress, my arms still tied above my head, with my ass in the air.

He lets out a hiss as he shoves his cock back inside me, his fingers digging into my thighs. I bite down on the mattress to muffle my screams.

"I want to hear you scream for me, baby." His deep voice sends pleasure straight to my core. His finger circles my clit, smothering himself in my juices. He then guides two fingers into my back entrance, at the same time fucking me with such ferocity my entire body slams forward.

I scream out his name as stars fill my vision. He swears over the heartbeat thumping in my ears.

I shoot forward as his palm connects to my left ass cheek, the pain only intensifying the pleasure rolling through me right now. Hot liquid spills into me and runs down the insides of my thighs.

He stays in me for a while. It's like I've just run a marathon. When he eventually pulls out, he drops a kiss to the middle of my spine. Then leans over to untie me, rubbing my wrists after.

He flops on the bed beside me, and I cuddle up into his chest, lightly tracing around the red scar.

"I can't wait to marry you," he says, fiddling with the engagement ring on my finger.

"I can't wait to be Mrs. Ward."

"You know, I had that ring made here in London. The same time I had your necklace made."

"You wanted to marry me even before the baby?" I can't hide the shock from my tone. I'd just assumed that was why he proposed.

"Maddie, I knew from the moment you kissed me, if I was going to ever marry anyone again in this lifetime, it would be you. That's why I stayed away, why I let you keep pushing me away. I knew once I had a taste, I'd never want to stop. So yeah, I was always going to try to make you mine in every way possible. Baby or not. That's just a bonus."

"I was so worried that would be the last thing I ever said to you. I'm so sorry, Grayson. I thought, after all, I didn't need the big fancy wedding, because I didn't have that stupid fairy-tale dream being forced on me anymore. But actually, I do need it." I take in a deep breath. "I need it with you, and only you."

"I'll give you everything you've always dreamed of, including the wedding, the kids, and the house. I can't ever lose you again."

"You won't."

"Now, how long do I have to wait for you to marry me?"

"Well, we either do it soon before I get massive, or we wait until the baby has arrived—"

"Nope, too long. How about three weeks? We've got an unlimited budget. I want you to have everything you want down to the very last detail. I imagine you have a mood board or some shit ready to go, right?"

I smack him on the chest. "Hey! Doesn't every girl have a wedding pinboard?"

"Fuck knows. You're the one obsessed with weddings. I'm just obsessed with you."

"Aww, that's cute. Now when you say unlimited, how unlimited do you mean?" I ask, biting down on my finger, batting my lashes at him.

"I'll give you five million, but my only request is I want an exotic honeymoon on the beach. Somewhere with a private villa so I can fuck you wherever I want, whenever I want."

"Five million is ridiculous!"

"There isn't a price on that smile, baby. You spend whatever the fuck you need to, to make sure we can get married in three weeks. Okay?"

"You are going to look so fucking hot with a wedding ring on."

"Actually, I was thinking I might get the ring tattooed on. I've been married before. Rings can come off. Tattoos are more permanent. I'll wear the ring on a chain around my neck instead."

"That's so sweet."

I swing my leg over his body to straddle him, his eyes roaming up my body.

"Three more weeks," I whisper.

"I can't fucking wait, sunshine."

"Now, we need to sleep. And then tomorrow, you'll finally be back home where you belong." He rolls me off him by my waist. I turn my back to him so he can spoon me. His dick settles by my ass. His arms wrap tightly around me.

"Sweet dreams. I love you, baby." His hand strokes my lower belly.

Our family.

"Can we get a dog?"

His laugh vibrates against my back. "Not a small fluffy one. I need one that is manly enough to take to work with me. And yes, we can look for a big family house as soon as we get home. The dog needs a garden, anyway."

I shake my head, biting back a smile. Right in this moment, life is perfect. It turns out, I had it all wrong. I was never a princess in need of a prince to whisk me away. I've been reading the wrong books. It wasn't a fairy tale I was after; a dark romance is where it's at.

I craved to be worshipped by the villain for the rest of eternity.

Would a prince burn down the world to keep me safe? Or take a bullet for me? No.

I needed the darkness to set fire to my soul.

That's why we fought this for so long. Our love was never going to be easy. It's intense. All-consuming. It's everything.

That's our happily ever after.

Epilogue

GRAYSON

Three Weeks Later

Sweat beads on my forehead as I stare at the entrance of the barn.

In just three weeks, Maddie managed to pull off this masterpiece. She booked a barn that is now filled to the brim with every shade of pink flower you could imagine, even across the beams on the ceiling. Fairy lights twinkle through the flowers. My best men—Keller and Luca—are next to me.

It might be cold outside, but I am on fire. I don't know why I'm nervous. I know my sunshine will be walking through those barn doors in a few minutes. I'd bet my life on that.

We wanted to keep it small and intimate, but I was clear I still wanted her to have the lavish, princess-style wedding she always dreamed of. That was never up for negotiation. Mrs. Russo is busy cradling Darcy, and Keller hasn't taken his eyes off those two. I just fucking hope I can even be half the father he is, to our little one.

Hell, even my mom and dad made it. They were pretty shocked when I phoned them to tell them the news. I've never been particularly close to them, not since they sent me away as a teenager. But I don't think that relationship will ever be the same. I do want to give them a chance to get to know their only grandchild though. So who knows.

Maddie's mom scowls from across the room. Perfectly seated right at the back so I can't fucking see her when I'm saying my vows. If it was up to me, the bitch wouldn't be here. She might have apologized to Maddie. She's just lucky her husband, Robert, is a good guy. I can tolerate him. He loves Maddie unconditionally. I swear to God, if her mom makes my wife cry one more time, she's gone.

The barn doors open, and I suck in a shaky breath. Heads turn to the entrance in anticipation. Frankie walks in, looking slick as anything. "Sorry, had a few things to take care of on the way," he says, slipping into the first available seat. I shoot him a look, and Luca chuckles behind me.

Yep, the guy who held my soon-to-be wife hostage is here. Turns out he and Maddie struck up quite the friendship, and technically, I guess he is my boss now that he and Luca have joined forces, planning world domination together. So I can't kill him. He knows where he stands with me. I'm not entirely convinced about his new arrangement with Luca. I'll just be there to pick up the pieces if it goes to shit. I have other things to concentrate on now, anyway. Things that are far more important to me.

The room goes silent as "If I Ain't Got You" by Alicia Keys fills the air. Tears well up in my eyes. A smiling Sienna, wearing a full-length deep pink dress, holding a matching

bouquet, starts to walk down the aisle. I can hear Keller mut-
tering behind me. A smile creeps across my lips. Her eyes
never leave her husband.

The second Maddie walks through the door, it's like I've
been sucker-punched in the gut. I couldn't take my eyes off
her if I wanted to. Her long blonde hair is curled and flowing
over her shoulders.

She is simply the most beautiful woman I have ever come
across.

Her white floor-length gown fits snug against her changing
figure. It shows off that tiny little bump she has, with a plunging neckline that has me licking my lips at her now-fuller
breasts. A pregnant Maddie just knocks me out of the park.
Fucking perfect.

Her sparkling sunshine necklace sits on her collarbone. It
matches the little sunshine tattoo just behind my ear. I had
it done the same time as getting my wedding ring tattooed
on. A thick band with an *M* above it now permanently
brands my ring finger. I want the world to know I'm hers
forever.

She flashes me a bright smile. Warm tears slip down my
cheek. I wipe them away with the front of my hand. She
makes her way down the aisle, smiling to our friends and family. She nods to Frankie, and he gives her a grin back. Once
she reaches the third aisle, she flashes me a mischievous grin
before hoisting up the bottom of her dress and running down
the aisle toward me. She launches herself into my arms. I wrap
my arms around her waist as she loops her arms around my
neck.

The room bursts into laughter.

"You couldn't wait just thirty seconds," I tease.

She brings her nose to mine, her eyes full of love.

"I don't want to wait another second."

"I love you," I whisper.

"Now let's make you my wife," I growl.

She slides down my front. I steady her on her feet and press a soft kiss to her cheek.

The officiant clears his throat, pushing back his glasses. Sienna rushes over, taking Maddie's humongous bouquet out of her hands.

I've never been more ready for anything in my life.

I can finally be the person I was meant to be.

No more hiding.

THE WEDDING PARTY is in full swing. Maddie set up a marquee outside, decorated to the brim with fresh flowers, fairy lights, and lanterns on the ceiling. And let's not forget the glittery dance floor in the center of the room.

Everyone is seated at their tables.

I turn to Maddie, who's busy staring out at the room, smiling to herself. Her engagement ring is now complete with a matching black-and-silver diamond-encrusted wedding band.

My fucking wife.

"How long do we have to stay here for? I really want to rip that dress off and fuck my wife. I've been a good boy to wait this long."

"One more hour."

I can do that.

Her hand trails up my thigh under the table. "But there are some pretty secluded places out in the field. I could think of a few ways to see you through the hour." She bites her lip, her eyes twinkling.

I grab her hand and stand. She giggles and joins me. I'm a man on a mission.

"Hey, Grayson, Maddie, over here!" Luca shouts.

"Eurgh! For fuck's sake," I mutter. Maddie laughs.

Reluctantly, I walk us over to their table. Sienna, Keller, Luca, Frankie, and Enzo are all silent, watching us approach. Keller is particularly frosty-looking. I cock my brow at him, and he shakes his head.

Luca stands as we reach the table. I rest my hand against the back of Sienna's chair.

Keller pipes up first. "Here, have your ten grand and shut up." He throws a large wad of dollars at Luca. The little shits.

"Thanks, brother, and congratulations. Beautiful wedding, beautiful bride—" He smiles at Maddie.

He opens his suit jacket and pulls out some white cards, throwing them into the center of the table.

My eyes go wide as I read:

Save the Date:
You are officially invited to the wedding of
Luca Russo and Maria Capri.

It's written in black script, with two wedding rings pictured beneath.

"You fucking idiot," Keller seethes, tossing the card on the table.

Maddie snatches the invite out of my hand and gasps, looking at Sienna. I shoot Luca a questioning look. I can't help the guilt that rips through me. This must have been the deal he made with the Capris in return for them searching for

Maddie in Europe. I glance over at Frankie, who's smirking, taking in our reactions.

"You don't have to do this, Luca. We can find another way. What about Rosa?"

I know how much it hurt him to set her free.

Luca shakes his head. "I need a fucking drink," he announces, before storming off in the direction of the bar.

Fuck.

This is a dangerous game to play.

It's a good thing we're ready.

Bonus Epilogue

MADDIE

Five Years Later

Grayson's massive hand clamps down on my thigh as I reach for the blindfold.

"It's not a surprise if you peek, sunshine."

I lay my hand on top of his and guide it between my legs, slightly parting them for him.

The sound of his chuckle, a low rumble in his chest, makes my heart pound.

"You think you can distract me with your pussy?" I can hear the amusement in his tone, and I nod.

"Works most of the time?" I say, biting my lip.

"You are distracting entirely, baby. But the blindfold stays on. We've got ten minutes left on the road. Now be a good girl for me and do as you're told."

I try to remove his hand, but his grip only tightens, his fingers digging into my skin.

"What about a clue?" I press.

I can feel him rolling his eyes at me.

"Nope. Have I ever let you down?" he asks.

"Never," I respond quickly.

He's the love of my life. I am the center of his world. There is nothing this man won't do for me.

Even after being married for five years, our love is just as intense as it was at the start.

Nothing's changed. Even after having Hope and Kai.

I still wind him up relentlessly, and he fucks it straight out of me. It's how we work. And I wouldn't change it for the world.

The sound of gravel hitting the underside of the car has my heart racing.

"Can I see yet?"

"Maddie, I have never met someone as persistent as you. One more minute, then the first thing you'll be doing is getting on your knees to make up for all this bratty behavior."

I hear his seatbelt click and the door open; the breeze hits me as Grayson opens my door next.

I let out a squeal as I'm hoisted over his shoulder. His firm hand slides up the back of my thigh and dips under my dress.

"You better be soaking those panties for me, wife."

His hand smacks down on my ass as I wriggle in his hold.

"Put me down!"

The next thing I know, my back hits a surprisingly soft mattress, and with a grunt, his weight is on me. Smothering me. Squeezing one eye shut, I wait, anticipating the sudden burst of light as he slides the blindfold away.

"There are those beautiful eyes," he whispers.

I grab his cheeks and drag him down to me, kissing him

as hard as I can, at the same time wrapping my legs around his waist.

He takes charge of the kiss, stealing my breath, his hard cock pressing against my core.

"Fuck, Grayson. Please." I roll my hips, desperate for him.

Pushing my panties to the side, he slides in two fingers and my back arches.

It's been two whole days since he's been inside of me.

His damn work is busy, plus the kids and packing for this trip.

"Oh, you're ready for me, sunshine."

I nod, batting my lashes as he smirks. Those blue eyes of his, full of raw hunger for me.

"I'm always ready for you, sir."

My mouth falls open as he inserts another finger.

"Oh my god." I'm already trembling around him.

Hooking my arms around his neck, I press him tight against me.

"Fuck me, please. I need more than your fingers. Please."

He nuzzles his face against my neck and sucks, upping the pace of his fingers. "You'll take what I give you. And right now, I need your sweet pussy on my tongue."

Letting out a squeal as he flips me over, I let him pull my ass into the air by my hips.

I spread my legs for him, my face pressed into the pillow, and suck in a breath as he blows against my throbbing pussy.

"Stop teasing me," I whine. I can't take much more.

He chuckles, and I grip the bedsheet tighter. I'm about to explode with frustration.

Relief washes over me as he grabs my ass, his warm tongue making slow licks from my clit to my entrance.

"That better, sunshine?" he asks, and I hum in a satisfied response.

"Fuck, that's good, Grayson. Keep going." I roll my hips against his face while he expertly eats me out.

He's got that tongue and finger combo down to perfection.

"I could spend a whole day with your pussy on my face, Maddie. All fucking day."

"Well, we have three. Feel free," I tell him as my eyes flutter closed.

He sucks on my clit as he thrusts his fingers inside. I instinctively open my legs even wider for him.

"So good, baby. Such a good girl," he almost growls, and it sends me feral.

As I get closer and closer to the edge, my climax burning, he slows the pace and presses soft kisses against my thigh.

"Grayson, what the hell?" He slides himself out from beneath me and I fall onto my back.

"Do not make me finish myself, I swear to god." I let out an annoyed huff.

He gives me one of his boyish smirks and adjusts his cock tenting his pants.

I raise an eyebrow and grin.

"I can solve that for you."

"That's the plan, baby. But I wanna show you something first. That was just to get you ready, the next part is the real excitement."

He licks his lips and groans, holding out his hand to me.

"This better be good." I bite back my grin.

With him, it always is.

He smacks my ass and I jump forward, ignoring the stinging that's just turning me on more.

"Quicker you see this, the quicker you'll get your relief."

GRAYSON

WITH HER DAINTY hand in mine, I lead her through the cabin, watching the joy appear in her eyes, with that smile that knocks me off my feet every damn time.

And that flush on her cheeks makes me feral.

"This is gorgeous, Grayson."

I spin her round and wrap my arms around her, holding her close.

This was the most luxurious cabin I could find. Hot tub, wood fire, blankets, and the best part—silence. There is no one around for miles. Just us, in the woods.

Serenity.

"Only the best for you, baby." I press a kiss to the top of her head. "You know I'll give you anything, right?" I whisper against her silky blonde hair.

Her fingers trail down my abs, and I grin.

"Sunshine," I drawl out.

"Anything I want?" She looks up at me with a glimmer in her eyes.

Running my thumb along her jawline, I dip my head and kiss her, letting my tongue explore her mouth while her fingers fumble with my belt.

"Anything, everything. I just want you to be happy, Maddie."

She smiles against my lips, and my body is on fire for her.

"I want another baby, Grayson," she whispers.

I knew this was coming. And my girl knows I'll give her anything she wants.

But this one, I'll make her work hard for.

"You're asking me to fuck another baby into you? We've already got Hope and Kai. You really want to go again?"

She twists her wedding band on her finger, her green eyes dazzling me.

"Yes. I love being a mom. You don't want more kids?"

As she frowns, I cup her cheeks.

"Our family is everything to me. I'll have as many kids as you want to. But . . ." I trail off, pulling her lip back with my thumb.

"But what?" Her eyebrows rise.

"This one, you gotta earn, sunshine. You want me to put a baby in you, you gotta put in the work."

I bite back my grin as I watch her pretty face process this.

"How? Like this?"

She steps back, and as she goes to drop to her knees, I grab her throat and hold her upright.

"A blowjob isn't going to get you pregnant. Come on, sunshine, you've done this twice before."

She giggles, and I squeeze her neck tighter.

"So no anal either?" she pouts.

Fuck, I love this woman.

"No, baby." I chuckle, leaning in closer and brushing my lips over her ear.

"I think we should play a game," I whisper, feeling her skin heat under my touch.

"What kind of game?" She drags her nails along my abs, and no matter how many years have passed, her touch sets me on fire.

"I'm thinking a game of chase. You run, I hunt. Then, when I catch you"—I pause, pressing a kiss to her cheek—"I'll fuck that baby into you, after you beg me for it."

Stepping back, I watch in amusement as she looks down at her designer sneakers.

"I get a head start?"

Her gaze shoots to the ornate double doors, the faint scent of woodsmoke hinting at the yard beyond, and the deep, silent woodlands past it.

I tap my finger against my chin.

"Hmm. Ten seconds."

She shakes her head. "No way. You're trained to hunt. Twenty at least," she huffs, crossing her arms over her chest, pushing up those perfect breasts.

"Fifteen." I roll up my sleeve to look at my Rolex. "Starting now."

I stand still, watching the rush go through her as she darts to the doors, yanking them open, and then she's gone.

Slowly, I make my way over, the breeze beating against my face as I lean against the frame, watching the clock tick.

Ready or not, I'm coming for her, and I'll give her everything she wants.

MADDIE

JESUS. MY HEART is racing.

I breathe through my nose and out through my mouth. My fitness isn't too bad since Grayson has trained me at home to box.

I run as fast as my legs can take me towards the tree line, the leaves crunching under my sneakers.

I want him to catch me. But the thrill shooting through my veins right now is worth it.

His heavy steps pound the ground behind me, and I smile, a thrill of excitement running through me. Even with the cold air beating against my skin, I am hot with need.

I can't wait for him to get his hands on me.

Brushing my palm against the rough bark, I stop trying to work out my next move. The trees scale for miles.

"You want me to catch you? Run!" Grayson shouts behind me, and that kicks me into gear.

I hang a left, my legs feeling heavy with every step.

His scent, a mix of leather and wood smoke, precedes him. His hand brushes my hip, the contact sending a shiver down my spine, before I quickly evade his touch and run.

But it doesn't take long for him to catch up again. This time, when his hand wraps around me, we tumble to the dirt. I land on top of him, and he rolls me onto my back.

With a grunt, I shove as hard as I can against his chest, the force knocking me back onto the cool grass.

In spite of my frantic escape attempt, he crawls toward me, his rough hands scraping the ground as he snags my ankle and yanks me back.

"Gotcha, sunshine." He grabs my throat and pulls me to a sitting position.

As our lips connect, his fingers squeeze my neck, and he steals all of my breath.

I am burning for him.

The sound of his zipper opening echoes around us. He pulls the straps of my dress down in one swift move. As he trails his tongue along my scorching skin, I tip my head back.

Lifting me by my hips to straddle him, I roll my hips against his cock and he sinks his teeth into my neck, moving his hands to my breasts and squeezing.

"Fuck, this is hot." He groans, ripping my panties clean off of me.

I lift my hips and grab his cock, lining it up with my entrance.

"You're that soaking, I just slide right in. Perfect," he mutters.

I close my eyes as I sink down on him, letting him fill me up.

With one hand grabbing my ass, he sets the pace, thrusting up into me.

Hard. Deep. Feral.

Our teeth collide and his tongue dances in my mouth.

He claims me.

"This is what my bad girl needed, hmm?" he growls in my ear.

"Yes!"

I throw my head back, riding him to the peak of ecstasy.

"You can be as loud as you want, baby. Let me hear how much you love your husband's cock filling you up."

As if on cue, my moans grow louder as he pushes me onto my back on the ground. Pushing my thigh back to my chest, he grips my neck.

Every thrust consumes me. My body trembles, blood pounding in my ears.

"I'm so close, G. Please."

He nips at my jaw, the sound of his groans only intensifying my need to come.

"You want this baby? Beg harder. Tell me how much you want to be filled up."

I suck in a breath.

"Grayson, I need this. I need you to come inside me. Mark me as yours. Keep every last drop inside me. Please, please."

I lose my breath, and my back arches as he thrusts so deep inside me.

"Such a good girl, aren't you? Begging for my come."

"Y-yes. Come inside me. Give me everything."

"Fuck, sunshine," he grunts.

I scream out as he lifts my hips, hitting that sweet spot with every thrust.

"Scream for me, let me hear who owns your pretty pussy."

She nods slowly, tossing her bright blonde hair over one shoulder.

Damn, she's beautiful. The light of my goddamn life.

"Like a cowboy, we got a baby to make, so I want you inside of me at least 80 percent of this trip. Sleep with it in my pussy if you like."

My cock grows almost painfully inside her.

"Fuck, Mads. You know I love that."

She winks, a mischievous glint in her eyes, and offers a warm, dazzling smile.

"You give me everything, and I do the same for you." She leans down and steals a kiss. Before she can retreat, I grab the back of her head to hold her in place.

"Show me what you've got. And then I'm going to drag you back to that cabin."

With a slow roll of her hips, a soft moan escapes her, a sound both sensual and pained.

"And then what?" she pants out.

"Well, I'll throw you up against the tiles in the bathroom under the rainfall shower and make sure every single inch of you is clean."

"Deal. Now let me take what I want from my husband."

BY THE TIME we've showered each other off and unpacked, I'm ready to go again.

But we managed to slip into a nap. As I roll over, I'm met with an empty, yet still warm side of the bed.

Where did my beautiful wife go?

Throwing off the blanket, I stomp into the living room, watching in amusement as Maddie huffs in annoyance, poking the fire.

GRAYSON

IT'S LIKE A switch goes off. I slap her ass, and she comes apart, her body shaking and her pussy strangling me.

Her screams of pleasure rip through the air, and I erupt inside of her.

Every drop fills her up.

"So fucking good for me." I brush her hair away from her face.

Leaving my pulsating cock inside her, I lift her into my arms and smother her against my chest, letting her listen to my erratic heart.

I close my eyes as she leans up and presses a soft kiss against my neck, right on my sunshine tattoo for her.

"I love you, Grayson."

God, I love her husky post-sex voice.

"And I love you, sunshine. More than life itself."

As I stroke her back, she leans back and runs her hands over my stubble.

"I can feel your cock twitching. It's making me horny again," she whispers and bites her lip seductively.

"Baby, I'm hard for you always," I tell her, running my hands down her back to grip her ass.

She pushes on my chest, and I lay down, stretching my legs out so she can straddle me properly.

"You wanna ride me?"

God, I love it when she gets all worked up. Even over little things, her cheeks flush and her nose flares.

I scan the surroundings, my military training never allowing me to turn my brain off. Every window and door counted.

Every escape route plotted.

We're safe here, but Maddie being protected will always be my number one priority. Even this many years after I almost lost her. It's still in the forefront of my mind. That pain never leaves you.

She claps and jumps in the air when the fire finally takes, dropping the fire iron to the wooden floor.

"Oh, shit," she hisses, and I chuckle, gaining her attention.

"You could have swooped in and saved me." She turns to face me with her hand on her hip.

The space between us vanishes as I pull her close, feeling the warmth of her body against mine and hearing her breath hitch.

"I'm not a prince, remember," I whisper against her lips.

"Nope. You're my perfect villain. And you know what that means?"

Oh, I know.

"Tell me more, sunshine." I lower my voice, sliding my hands to grab her ass.

As she rises onto her toes, a whisper of her soft lips against my jaw leaves me breathless.

"A wise woman once said, 'Villains fuck better.'"

While I'm lifting her into my arms, she wraps her legs around me. I press her back against the wall.

"Well, here's to the rest of our lives proving that statement correct, baby." I capture her lips with mine.

She pulls back, a slow smile spreading across her face, crinkling the corners of her eyes.

344 ~ LUNA MASON

"I love you, Grayson. Now and forever. The man you were, the man you've become. Any version of you I adore."

I stroke her cheek, my heart racing.

"I'll love you until the day I die. I live for you and our little family. Everything I do is for you. And hopefully our next little addition. You are and always will be the light in my life, sunshine."

The End

NEED MORE OF THE BENEATH THE MASK SERIES?
WATCH FOR ROSA AND LUCA'S STORY IN *DEVOTED*.